SONIA ROWLEY

Fragmented Hearts

First published by Random Interpretations 2001

National Library of Australia
Cataloguing-in-Publication Data:

Rowley, Sonia, 1965- .
  Fragmented hearts.

  ISBN 1 876677 33 3.

  I. Title.

A823.4

Produced by: Publishing Solutions
                 38A Murphy Street
                 Richmond VIC, 3121
                 Tel: (03) 9427 7433
                 FAX: (03) 9428 4636
                 Email: solve@publishing-solutions.com.au
                 WWW: http://www.publishing-solutions.com.au

Printed in Australia

SONIA ROWLEY

Fragmented Hearts

Random Interpretations

RI

Dedication

For my daughters Stasia, Stephanie,
Sophia and Natasha, with love and admiration.

CHAPTER
ONE

In the small chapel of Georgetown University a modest group of friends await a bride to join her groom. The light from the sun flickers through the stained glass windows, dancing and darting around the room and upon the people. The groom stands, half turned, between his guests and the altar, watching as his best man checks for the third time that the ring is in his pocket, this time dropping it to the marble floor. Immediately they stoop to retrieve it, both pausing to stare at the shimmer from the ring as it is caught momentarily by the sun. The groom picks it up and slips it into his friend's pocket "it couldn't be more safe with you," he assures him with a smile.

The minister studies the gathering with interest, the congregation does not encompass the mothers, fathers, aunts, uncles, and grandparents as is usual at a wedding. He senses an exuberant spirit in the chapel that he has not felt before.

The sound of a solo flute is heard as the doors to the chapel open. The sunlight stretches down the aisle as if for the bride to walk on. She walks towards her groom, the room transposed by her grace and elegance. Now standing side by side, their eyes lock together as the room seemingly fades from their minds.

He is in his twenty-third year, though his demeanour is that of a man a great deal older. His dark eyes, enveloped in thick dark lashes, convey a sense of wisdom that one would not expect at such a youthful age. His manner is self-assured and gentle. At six feet, his height is imposing, it is his gentleness that confers a stature of serenity. Thick black hair is brushed smoothly from his forehead to the nape of his neck. With his olive complexion and broad shoulders, his handsome appearance presents a commanding vision.

She, a year younger, is enchantingly beautiful. Her pale face is delicate and astoundingly sculptured, with high cheek-bones giving way to soft blue eyes. Her tiny nose is dappled with freckles. Her lips are doll-like and her neck slender. Her fair hair is lacquered close to her head with a mass of tight curls at the back tied with a simple white ribbon under a silk flower. There is an engaging innocence about her demeanour and yet a resplendent strength showing in her eyes.

They had known each other since their early childhood. They met in the garden of 'The Manor', an orphanage in Washington. He was seven she was six. He had watched her stand in one of the many corners of the huge sandstone building that housed five hundred children. He knew why she stood there for so long, he had felt the loneliness, sadness and uncertainty that takes a child to a corner for comfort. Kindly, he left her there, knowing not to disturb her. In one hand she clutched a little doll, in the other a brown suitcase. Every so often she put the case down reluctantly, as if tired by its weight, but soon picked it up again. After a while he worried that he should not disturb her but at least help her hold her suitcase. He rose to his feet, put his two marbles in his pocket and slowly walked towards her. She, unaware of his approach seeing only the soothing darkness of the corner startled as he spoke. "Can I help you mind your suitcase?" he inquired nervously.

"No, leave me alone," she answered with her back to him.

"I won't talk to you, just mind your case, that's all."

Slowly turning around, she looked at him briefly and then to the ground, her eyes journeying between him and the dusty soil for several minutes, then finally she conceded. "You can sit on my case and keep me company if you want," she said in a quiet voice.

He smiled at her, feeling surprised with himself for having done so, as smiles were rare for him, as was being asked to keep somebody company. He gently eased the handle out of her tight clasp, positioned the case as close to her as he could and sat on it. There they stayed until a stern voice disturbed their peace. "You young scoundrels, don't you know that dinner is over, and you, what are you doing with missy's suitcase? You know the rules, we don't touch what isn't ours," she declared in a pious voice.

He could not look up, his body suddenly tense, his hands fidgeting with the case, his eyes unable to divert their gaze from the ground.

"He was helping me mind my case," the little girl told her shyly.

"Really, well here we help ourselves and we don't ask for help. You'll soon learn that! Now off to your dormitories, the both of you, at once."

SONIA ROWLEY

The children scurried off, the little girl not knowing where
her bed was but too afraid to ask. She had been moved that
day from another orphanage and nobody had thought to
show her her bed. Later that night the little boy could not
sleep. In the vast room, lined with beds and sleeping boys, he
wondered if she were asleep and more so, if he would see her
the next day. He had lived in the orphanage for as long as he
could remember, not having made any friends. Her friendship
was a novice to him, and something to look forward to.

In another part of the orphanage she too was awake, her
only blanket pulled over her face to muffle her sobs. This new
home seemed as cold and cruel as the last. A great weight lay
on her shoulders as it had always done. Without warning, her
body eventually succumbed to exhaustion and she dreamt of
the little boy minding her suitcase.

For three days neither child spoke to the other. It rained
incessantly and when it rained the garden was off limits. Girls
and boys were separated at all times in the orphanage, the
only exception being 'free time' in the garden. On the fourth
day the sun had its way and after completing their study in the
overcrowded classrooms and fulfilling their many chores, the
two found themselves looking for the other in the garden.
Again his eyes found her first. "I've been looking for you," he
said nervously, thinking she might not want his company a
second time.

"I've been looking for you too," she answered.

"Really!' he said, almost doubting her word.

"I'm glad we found each other," she giggled.

His face was exuberant, his mind racing with excitement.
"I've never had a friend before, could I be your friend?"

Her gentle smile answered his question. A warmth had
begun that neither child had known before.

"My name is Sarah and this is Beth, my doll. Should I guess your name?"

"Well I have two names," he said "people call me Ed, but you can guess my real name, if you want."

She studied him all over, wanting to guess correctly. "I think your name is Eden," she guessed "Eden is a beautiful name."

Eden was not his real name, but from that day, Eden became his real name to him.

That was to be their last meeting for many weeks. Every day he looked for her in the garden. When it rained he risked sneaking out in case she was there. Hundreds of children played in the garden but she was not amongst them. As the weeks lapsed by he became more and more despondent. He couldn't eat nor could he sleep. In the classroom he was apathetic, the print in his books a stark contrast to his pale face. There was but a solitary unfaltering capability that had not been stripped from him; the ability to feel the torture that clung to him like a shadow.

Two weeks later on his way to the showers he passed Tommy, a brutish boy, more aptly known as 'big ears', for he had a gift of knowing news before it became news. Tommy's leg went out and sent Eden smashing to the hard floor. "Get up you sissy," he jeered. "Only sissies are friends with girls! Girls are weak and stupid and it serves her right to be dead!"

With these words Eden scrambled to his feet, trembling with shock.

"Sarah's not dead, you're a liar!" Words then faltered him, and his fist made up for the loss of speech, hitting Tommy square in the eye. Within minutes the two boys found themselves sitting opposite each other in a darkened corridor, a corridor that Tommy was used to but Eden had not entered until now. All the other children at the orphanage either knew of this corridor or had been there. Once there, one was made to enter the room at the end, a room with a huge door with the words 'Head Mistress' inscribed on the front. Tommy was summoned first and returned with swollen eyes, staring at his beaten palms. For Eden, nothing mattered as he stood before the enormous oak desk that divided him and the severe looking woman on the other side. He could think only of Sarah and nothing else.

"Have you not been taught to close a door?" she asked in a hurry.

Promptly he pushed the enormous door shut and resumed his position in front of her desk. There he stood as she shuffled piles of paper around her desk, apparently forgetting his presence. As the piles were moved, clouds of dust wafted into the air. The room was musty and dark, lit only by a window of smoke yellow glass. Amidst her work she suddenly spoke. "Now, I have been told that you punched a boy in the face, is that correct?" He nodded in response. "Speak up," she snapped.

"I punched him in the eye, ma'am," he answered truthfully.

"Punching is neither an appropriate nor a useful form of expression. In future if you wish to convey a message then please convey it in English. I don't take kindly to repeat offenders," she said, as she commenced moving more paper. "However, knowing Tommy as I unfortunately do, I do concur that he is not a great responder to English," she said with a wry face. "Now be off with you and mind you tell the cook you won't be requiring dinner this evening, which should serve to remind you if you choose to use your fists again."

Thankful that she had finally finished her agenda, Eden took her gaze.

"Excuse me ma'am, but Tommy said that Sarah is dead?"

"Sarah who?" she replied in a bothered voice.

"She's a new girl here," he said anxiously.

With these words she began shuffling more paper. This time it struck Eden she was searching for something. "Yes here it is," she said surveying a small piece of paper. "Sarah is in a nearby hospital. She has been very ill but certainly is not dead. Sarah succumbed to pleurisy a matter of days after arriving here. She spent three days in our infirmary. It was discovered she has pneumonia, at which point we moved her to a hospital where she could be more adequately treated. She is apparently past the worst of her illness and by all accounts should return to the infirmary very soon," she concluded in an almost caring voice. "I can see now your reason for being upset," she continued. "Given the situation you are welcome to your dinner this evening. Now if that is all, I have a great deal of work to attend to."

"I am much obliged ma'am," Eden mumbled as he left her room.

All of Eden's worries had now left his mind as he skipped down the corridor. "Sarah's ok, Sarah's coming back," he quietly sang to himself.

Over the following days and weeks Eden spent his free time in the garden. It was the month of August and the days were hot and arduous. Eden had consigned himself to making another doll for Sarah and the days were passing almost too quickly for him. Though anxious for her return, he wanted the doll finished on time. Over the summer months the grass had become parched and brittle. Eden searched the uncut areas of the lawns for the longest strands of grass, then hid the bunches under his mattress. At night when he was sure all the boys were asleep, he worked on the doll. Soon it was complete. Her maker had been very exact. Her grass body was dressed with dried daisies and upon her head she wore a grass sun hat, again adorned with daisies.

With his work done, the days passed slowly. Eden endured this with ebbing patience. Then at last he heard a quiet whisper behind him as he drank from a tap in the garden "Eden, it's me, Sarah."

Eden spun around excitedly "Sarah, Sarah, Sarah," he said clapping his hands "I've waited and waited for you, I'm so happy you're…" all of a sudden his excitement gave way to worry as he stared at Sarah. Her slender body was gaunt, the whites of her eyes were yellow and her face was the color of the summer clouds.

"I'm sorry Eden. I've been sick, but I'm better now and I'm so glad to see you."

"I'm so glad to see you too, I'm sorry you got sick. From now on I will look after you, I won't let you get sick again."

"You didn't let me get sick, that just happens, but you did make me get better. Beth and I wanted to come back and play with you in the garden so I had to get better."

"Wait, I have something for you, sit down and rest, I will be straight back." Eden said, running off as he was talking. As swiftly as he had left he returned. "This is for you Sarah" he said as he bent over and put the grass doll in her lap. As Sarah stared at the doll tears filled her eyes and ran down her white face landing on the doll's feet.

"What's wrong Sarah?" he said brushing the coming tears off her face with his hand.

"I'm just so happy Eden, this doll is so beautiful and you are so kind. Beth is the only doll I've ever had. Now I have two dolls and I have you."

"Then, we will always be happy Sarah, you and me. We will look after each other and we'll be happy."

The minister opened his book, awakening them from their gaze. Their hands locked together as the ceremony commenced. "Eden will you take Sarah to be your lawful wedded wife? Will you love, honor and keep her, in sickness and in health, for better or for worse, richer or poorer, so long as you both shall live?"

"Yes, I do."

"Sarah will you take Eden to be your lawful wedded husband? Will you love, honor and keep him, in sickness and in health, for better or for worse, richer or poorer, so long as you both shall live?"

"I do."

His moment having come, the best man reached into his pocket and with an air of cherished honor handed the ring to the groom. Eden took his bride's slender hand "With this ring I thee wed, with my body I thee honor and all my worldly goods with thee I share." he said as he slipped the ring onto the third finger of her left hand that lay in his. Then Sarah adorned the second finger of Eden's right hand with a simple gold band, saying as she did, "With this ring I wed you and pledge my eternal love." The plain uninterrupted circle of the ring seemed an emblem of a perfect union. "Eden and Sarah, I now pronounce you husband and wife. You may kiss the bride."

As the congregation dabbed their eyes with hankies and smiled in delight, Eden took Sarah into his arms, her eyes meeting his, their lips touching, their bodies burning with passion, their breath and soul each existing for the other. They stood in a union belonging only to them; as the congregation clapped and cheered they separated, bestowing the joy in their eyes upon their friends.

After the registry had been signed by the couple, the best

man and bridesmaid emerged from the vestry. The chapel was empty, apart from the sound of echoing chatter from the congregation awaiting them outside and the sunlight still dancing inside. "Come on Mr. and Mrs. Parks, the snow will be falling without you." the best man said with a grin.

"We'll be there in a minute." Sarah said.

"Eden, do you remember the day you said we would always look after each other and we will always be happy."

"Yes."

"That was the day I fell in love with you."

"And on that day I wiped your tears away," Eden said as he pulled his handkerchief from his vest and mopped the single tear that ran down her beautiful face. "I love you Sarah."

"You can't stay in there forever you two, the world awaits."

"Calling Mr. and Mrs. Parks..."

"The snow's going to melt."

"Has anyone seen some newlyweds?" Came the jovial echoes from their friends.

"We'd better go before the snow melts." laughed Eden.

They walked out of the chapel and into showers of white confetti. Students stopped in the street, motorists pulled in alongside the pavement wanting to catch a few minutes of the marvellous scene. A beautiful bride in her white satin dress filled with euphoric laughter as she watched her handsome groom catching the confetti as it fell on his white tuxedo, only to shower it over his bride again. The elated guests were akin to the couple. The bride plucked the flower from her hair, kissed it and gave it to her groom, then turning, she tossed the bouquet high into the air only to be caught by an astonished passer by. She started to return it but was stopped by the bride "You caught it, you must keep it." she insisted.

Professional photographers were not present, for both the

wedding and the reception had to be planned on a very minimal budget. As with most young people of Eden and Sarah's age, money was a scarce commodity. Personal cameras however, were kept busy capturing all the moments of the day, including the surprise on the couples face as a horsedrawn carriage took its place in front of the chapel. "We can't have you hailing a taxi now, can we?" laughed the bridesmaid.

"Oh Sally, it's beautiful, but the cost?"

"Today is my best friend's wedding day, forget the cost."

"Well," Eden said with a mimicked air "then you must ride with us."

"I can't, the carriage is complete with vintage champagne. You know me with champagne, sharing it is not one of my forte's."

A footman ascended from the rear of the carriage and opened its door. Minutes later he walked towards Eden and Sarah, as an attentive butler would, carrying a silver tray laden, indeed, with two champagne flutes effervescent with their contents. "Congratulations to you both." he said as he transferred the glasses to their hands. Eden and Sarah took their place in the carriage and headed slowly down 23rd Street and into Virginia Avenue as the guests followed behind. The carriage took them past the Watergate complex and stopped in front of the JFK Center. There the party boarded a ferry and crossed the Potomac River to the Three Sisters islands.

Sarah and her friends had worked tirelessly in the days leading up to the wedding. A tent was erected on the largest of the three islands. Decorating it had been fun but time con-suming. The walls of the tent were pastel pink. Wisteria was roped around every support pole. The blossoms and leaves from dogwood trees had been collected in spring and dried to form a fragrant and romantic carpet to walk on. White linen cloths covered the tables and masses of rosebuds hung from the corners. White balloons covered the ceiling and fairy lights filled any available space. In the center stood a buffet laden with exquisite food. Waiters stood ready to serve the guests and a jazz quartet played their instruments in separate rhythms that united to create a spirited effect. The entire atmosphere having been created by a close team of friends, even down to the cooks, waiters and musicians.

The hours floated into the evening with each minute as marvellous as the next. The buffet had been met with resounding appetites, champagne had continually flowed and guests had tirelessly danced to the melodies of the band. A snow goose, which had wandered into the celebrations, had taken a liking to Sarah and where she went the goose followed, to the great amusement of the others.

Knowing that soon the ferry would sound its horn for the return of guests to the shore, it was unanimously decided that Eden and Sarah should be escorted to their houseboat, which was moored, on the other side of the island. The couple had decided to save the cost of a honeymoon and instead had rented a houseboat in which they planned to spend a week of solitude on the island.

The guests having left and the ferry horn sounded, Eden and Sarah stood arm in arm, their heads resting on each other. The warmth of the summer night blanketed them. The year was 1970, this July evening was no exception to the beauty of past summers. The dark blue-gray of the sky was a still back-drop to the twinkling stars. The reflection of the one hundred and sixty nine-meter obelisk of Washington Monument lay upon the river between the island and land. The tranquil ambience of the night a perfect ending to a sunny day.

Eden scooped his bride up in his arms and carried her into

the houseboat, setting her down on its verandah couch. "I'll just be a minute Sarah." he said as he disappeared inside. Sarah watched as the water lapped against the boat, while listening to Eden busy inside. Eden returned with a bottle of champagne in one hand and two glasses in the other. Sitting down beside her, he placed the glasses on the table, gently eased the cork out of the bottle and filled the two glasses. Sarah untied the ribbons from her hair, combing it with her fingers and lay back on the couch. Eden lay upon Sarah, champagne in one hand and a lock of her fair hair in the other. Sarah put her glass on the table and wrapped her arms around his neck. With one hand she loosened his bowtie and with the other unbuttoned his shirt. Her hands caressed his smooth, firm chest as they lay together, staring at the stars. As if both had had the same thought, they rose to their feet and gazed deep into each other's eyes. His hands stroking her beautiful face, went to the zip of her dress. As if opening the shell to see the pearl, he slowly eased the white satin dress over her shoulders and breasts kissing them as he did, while the dress slipped down her slender body and onto the floor. As his mouth sensually sucked her nipples and moved over her breasts, Sarah undressed him. Their now naked bodies pressed together, Eden picked her up, carried her inside and lay her tenderly on the bed. There they lay touching each other simultaneously and separately, their hands and mouths producing many orgasms before Eden's penis penetrated Sarah. Sarah's hands gripped his shoulders as they felt the ecstasy of the climax flood their bodies. Then Eden sat up, staring into her eyes and began touching her again. The passion of their lovemaking went on until long after the sun had risen. At length they fell asleep, their bodies interlocked, their foreheads nestling into each other.

Early that afternoon they were awoken by a flutter of feathers. Unbeknown to them the snow goose had been comfortably nestling between the two and was now amiable to some activity. "He must have followed us to the boat last night." Sarah said, as she sat up and swept the hair from her face.

"And, so, I'm making breakfast for three then?" Eden said with a grin.

"I think it's more like dinner for three." she laughed, pointing to the clock.

"How about, we take a bath in the river and Snowy here, can get dinner started" he suggested reaching for some towels.

The Potomac River was a luxury to bathe in and dinner was both romantic and comical. Sarah prepared a gourmet meal of grilled fish, green salad and melted camembert wrapped in pitta bread accompanied by a dry white wine. The table was laid with a white linen cloth and wildflowers that Eden had collected, which grew only feet away from the boat. The snow goose had ensured a place at the table and seemed thrilled at the menu but preferred the wild flowers to the green salad. When the meal was over Snowy nestled back in to his newfound bed while Eden and Sarah opened gifts and talked for hours into the evening.

The next six days on the island were like magic. Just Eden, Sarah and Snowy occupying a small piece of wilderness in the middle of urban Washington. By day, they talked and laughed as they walked the island and swam in the river, watched otters in the water and eagles glide above, picked wild flowers, bathed in the sun and played with Snowy. At night they shared their meal with Snowy, made sure he was happily in bed then sat arm in arm on the verandah talking and staring at the night sky, long into the evening, making love long into the night.

Too soon came the last sunset they were to see from the houseboat. The next day they were to pack and head for home. Home was a small apartment in inner D.C. that they shared with friends. Eden and Sarah were preparing dinner while Snowy was already at his place at the table, napping as he waited. "You know, Sarah, I didn't want to mention this at first but Snowy is by himself here on the island."

"I know, he can't fly. If he could he would have left with the others late spring. I was going to talk to you about him over dinner. I was hoping..."

"Yes, of course, though we will have to check with the wildlife department, not to mention the local vet." Eden said. "The same thought was on my mind."

"Oh Eden I'm so glad," she said throwing her arms around him "let's go and tell him."

"You tell him, I'll finish dinner. Oh! and tell him if I buy you flowers at home he's not allowed to eat them!" he answered kissing her on the forehead.

The next morning as Sarah packed, Eden organized a cardboard box for snowy to travel in, making sure it had plenty of holes and an abundance of wildflowers, should he get hungry. Sally and Matthew, the couple's flatmates, arrived promptly as planned to help Sarah and Eden get their belongings onto the ferry and back home. "Well, by the look of the both of you, marriage obviously agrees with you." Sally said, kissing them both.

"Now come on Eden, the ferry has seats. You don't have to sit in a box." jibbed Matthew.

"Ladies what do you think, when Matthew sings in the shower, maybe we could put him in the box."

"Actually, Eden and I were wondering if you guys could put up with another family member?"

Sarah said, pointing to Snowy.

"Putting up with him would be gorgeous, but could he put up with us?" Sally laughed.

"Ok guys and what's your name?" Matthew yawned as he bent down to pat the bird.

"Snowy." Sarah answered.

"Well, Snowy and the rest of you, we'd better move it or we'll miss the ferry." Matthew said as he stood up again.

CHAPTER
TWO

The next morning Sarah was slowly waking when the phone began to ring "Um, hello…" she mumbled as she tried to find her voice.

"Sarah it's me. I made you some breakfast, it's on the chest beside you. I thought I'd better ring and tell you in case Snowy got there first. I love you. I'll ring you later."

"I love you too. Don't work too hard." she said while surveying the already eaten breakfast with amusement.

Eden worked at Georgetown University medical center where he was approaching the end of his first year of residency. He had finished his medical degree at Georgetown University with the highest scores in the state. This didn't interest Eden as much as his love of medicine itself. His parents died when he was six months old. He was the sole survivor of a car accident that was the result of his father's apparent stroke while driving the car with his wife and son in it. As a child, never really knowing his parents Eden had done the next closest thing and created an image of them of which he looked up to and cherished. For years he had wanted to study medicine and more especially cardiology. As a child he believed by learning to cure people of such problems he could give something back to his parents. With age he still believed this but knew he would be giving something to himself as well, a fulfilment of his strong desire to save lives.

Like all university students in this era, Eden's education had been expensive. As with most students who were lacking wealthy parents, Eden had taken out a loan to put him through university. When he wasn't studying he worked as a member of a jazz band that played for many cafes and restaurants to earn money, most of which was sunk back into loan repayments.

Sarah had been the essence of their survival during this time and in many ways still was. She was a naturally gifted artist who had never taken an art class in her life. Her passion for the smell of oil paints and linseed oil, and the sight of a white canvas waiting for her to enliven it, was as intense as Eden's for healing. While Eden had studied medicine, she had painted. It was the sale of these paintings that had provided a roof over their heads, fed them, clothed them and helped pay the loan repayments. This was the first year that Eden had earned a weekly salary but as with most resident doctors their salary was eaten up by loan repayments.

Sarah put a dressing gown on and went looking for Snowy, to no avail. Knowing that all of them, at length, had discussed locking doors and generally being mindful of their new inhabitant, Sarah headed for the shower feeling sure that he would show his face soon. As she showered she wondered at the faint banging noise that persisted. Beginning to worry, she turned off the water and opened the glass door, as she stepped out to reach for a towel she tripped on Snowy as he happily walked into the shower. Nursing a sore toe she nodded at Snowy "Well you've eaten my breakfast and tripped me over. I am going to finish my shower and you can wait." she said, moving him out. The banging continued as she finished her shower and finally Snowy's turn came. Sarah watched as he flapped his feathers and danced under the water, poking his tiny head about and quacking in delight then emerging to flap his feathers dry all over the apartment.

Sarah and Snowy had the apartment to themselves, as was the routine on most days. Sally also worked at the Georgetown University Medical Center as a nurse and like Eden she worked erratic hours, through the night or day. Matthew worked as a journalist and a sixteen-hour day was standard practice for him. Eden and Sarah had answered an advertisement to share an apartment with the pair and a close friendship had ensued over the past two years. Though no one complained, they were each acutely aware that four people sharing such a compact apartment wasn't easy. In winter, it was bitterly cold, in summer, stifling hot. Most of the few appliances had ceased to work and the only view from the fourth floor was the beige brick wall of the opposite building. Despite these failings the rent was appropriately cheap which made the situation tolerable.

Sarah's studio, as it was jokingly called, occupied the hallway and as the others came home from work it was a welcomed delight to study and comment on what she had painted that day as they walked down the hallway. Sarah looked forward to this for each one saw something different in any one piece. Sally would look for realism, Matthew looked for communication and messages, and Eden's interest was in the brush stroke and feeling conveyed through the content. This particular day the painting she was working on was not for sale and the content was secret. She was working on a portrait of Eden which was to be a gift for his birthday, that being only a matter of weeks away. The day passed quickly, that evening they sat around the kitchen table sharing the pasta dish they all helped make and discussed the dinner party they had planned for the following evening.

The next day was a Saturday, the sun was shining and Eden and Sarah found themselves at the market before most shoppers had risen. The market boasted the freshest of foods and consumer goods of endless descriptions. Eden was carrying a dog's bed they had just bought for Snowy, it was comfortably lined on the inside and Sarah carried a wicker basket, both of which were being filled with groceries for the dinner party that evening. Eden picked out a bunch of orange tiger lilies and gypsilia for Sarah and popped them into the dog's bed. Their shopping now done, they sat in a little cafe sipping freshly squeezed orange juice and eating croissants with blackberry jelly and cream. A little boy who sat at the next table with his mother had intently eyed Sarah and Eden from the moment they sat down, noticing this they smiled at each other, "Shall we?" asked Eden. Sarah nodded. "I'll be back in a minute then." He grinned as he rose from the table.

Sarah, having asked one of the staff for a piece of paper, quickly drew an indistinguishable sketch of the little boy. Just as she was finishing Eden returned complete with a ping-pong ball. As they left the cafe minutes later they placed the ball and the sketch on the table in front of the child. "Wow!" was the response as he looked at his treasures.

"That's very kind of you, thankyou." his mother said.

"You have a beautiful son," Sarah told her.

Eden wrapped his arm around Sarah, smiling at the little boy and his mother "Have a good day." he nodded.

The two loved children and over the years they had handed many a child a small treasure.

The elevator door opened on the fourth floor and as they opened the apartment door, they were met with the sound of Matthew singing in the shower and Snowy banging on the door. They laughed at the disagreeable noise. "Hey Matthew," Eden shouted over the singing "if you keep it up we'll have to send you out for some aspirin, Sarah can feel a headache coming on already."

"Ok guys," Matthew said "I'll behave myself, but I reckon Snowy's making more of a racket than me." he laughed. As they unpacked the groceries Sally wandered into the kitchen

"Where's that smell coming from? You angels, you've brought back croissants."

Eden poured Sally some coffee and Sarah put croissants, jelly and cream in front of her.

"And to think I didn't want to get out of bed." Sally mused as she loaded jelly onto a croissant.

On this particular day none of them had to rush off to work, so they spent the day relaxing and preparing for the dinner party. Once Matthew and Sally were dressed for the day, the four headed off for a game of squash. Each of them had a knack for the game and took it very seriously, and as they darted around the court, their work and their concerns were erased from their minds. After three hours of unwavering squash they walked home, lunching on hot dogs on the way and congratulating each other on a good game.

The boys worked through the afternoon cleaning the apartment while the girls attended to the food in the kitchen, their efforts culminating in a drastic rush to be dressed before the first knock at the front door. Unlike the girls, the boys were first dressed; soon, the tiny apartment was filled with fourteen people, with sleepy Snowy alone in his new bed. The guests included young Tommy from the orphanage and his wife Anne. Over the years as children, Eden and Sarah came to see past Tommy's brutish facade and knew him only as a caring, intelligent and witty person. Tommy could and would make light of any situation, going to any length to make someone laugh, and for this he was loved. Then there was Doug and Melissa who owned and ran the art supplies shop that Sarah frequented. Their wealthy father had bought them the business though, to his great disapproval they were slowly paying him back his outlay. Also there was Bill, an ambitious young man whom Eden had met at Georgetown University. Their friendship had been cemented in 1968 when, after the assassination of Martin Luther King, Bill, Eden and Sarah devoted as many hours a day as possible to delivering groceries to church basements in riot-torn neighborhoods of Washington D.C. since that time, the three had been close friends and had kept in close contact. Bill rarely brought company with him to social gatherings, but was never without his sax. Bill and Eden had worked together in the same jazz band that helped earn extra money during their years of study. The balance of the party were more or less friends of Matthew's or Sally's, all had been together in this tiny apartment many times on such occasions and knew each other well.

As platters of crab quiches and smoked roe pate with French toast traveled the room, glasses were filled and genial discussions of politics, social issues and many others subjects quickly became the interest of the evening. Soon they found themselves seated around a beautifully set table. Eden carved a roast turkey filled with pine nuts and mushroom stuffing that had been bought at the market that morning for half the price from a friend of Eden's and Sarah's. To accompany the poultry, there was asparagus with minted hollandaise sauce, buttered new potatoes and creamed spinach. As they consumed their meals, repeatedly complimenting the cooks, conversation grew. "Mainstream of American politics? Who knows anymore." Doug responded to Matthew's question with a wry laugh.

"It's certainly not liberal democracy." Eden said.

"I think middle America is more content to listen to Agnew and some of them agree with him. I, for one don't, but I think the common interest is not in government initiative in fields where private enterprise has failed but more so in the young, the poor and the black, in as much as they should be kept in their place." said Matthew.

"Isn't it amazing though?" said James "Wherever you go people seem to have a good word to say for the creep."

"He's honest, I'll give him that but that's the only good words I have to say for him" said Sarah.

"I disagree. I mean at least he's thinking, which is more than I can say for the government, and he has bothered to tangle with the mass media, also he's actually using it rather effectively." responded Anne.

"Bill, what do you think will happen with the election this November?" Matthew asked.

"All bets are off! Nixon's ratings are down and yet there's no sign of a democratic resurgence. I think the Vietnam War divided and discredited a lot of liberals. The democrats were responsible for the war, and the republicans, no matter how conservative, won't let them forget it."

"Shit! the country's gone so far to the right, it's amazing." Matthew mumbled almost to himself.

"I think the problem with America right now is not so much disorder in the streets or in the universities, but that the voice of the silent majority, now it's being heard, is selfish and unforgiving." said Eden.

"You're right there," Bill nodded "but getting back to Nixon, he has shown some sense and judgment when it comes to foreign policy. He's not a sabrerattler. He's been sensible with the Soviet Union and he's interested in better relations with China. The trouble is his domestic policies. Inflation and unemployment are killing him in the polls and he's done nothing for social welfare and racial policies."

"Well I think he's totally preoccupied with deliberately dividing the people with the excuse of law and order, I think that's inviting disorder." responded Eden. "There seems to be a lot of fear and prejudice rather than confidence and common sense."

"Well, I think we all would agree Nixon is riding a right-wing tiger, and on that note, how does some cointreau ice-cream with chocolate orange sound to wash down that turkey?" asked Sarah "and while we're eating it I'll tell you about something that is both right and left winged with greater intelligence! Oh and we're off to a rally in the morning, the more heads, the better." she finished as she left the room.

The streets of D.C. as with the other states were filled with demonstrations against the war. Riot police usually accompanied these demonstrations and at the slightest provocation would respond with batons and tear gas. Students had been killed during the protests and the animosity between the young and the government was rife. The young hated the war and the idea of sending a young man off to witness and commit murder. The older generation found it easier to believe in 'fighting for your country' than be swayed by the real sadness and truth of a war. Young men who were crippled and maimed in the war would come home to their families only to sit around the dinner table with their saddened but proud parents and their brothers and sisters who were against the war existing. After having rushed off to a war for the cause of their country and putting their lives and sanity in danger they returned to the opinions that they should never have gone in the first place. Certainly they were given welcoming back speeches and a disability pension of sixteen or seventeen hundred dollars a month. As they relived the war in their dreams by night they adapted to their wheelchairs by day. In the end, many of these men attended the demonstrations against the war, often ripping off their medals and throwing them into the crowd, this gesture being enough to set off riot police. If they tried to demonstrate at a political speech or function they were quickly ushered away either quietly or with force as their maimed bodies and their opinions served only as a political embarrassment to the government. Division and unrest abounded the streets and its people.

The sweets proved to be so delicious that the only words that were audible were "oh" and "lovely" and "wicked". Bill, having finished his almost before it was put in front of him collected his sax and commenced playing one of his own compositions to the delight of all.

"Now, before I clear the table while you and Sally sit down, tell us what is left and right winged and intelligent?" asked Melissa with a grin.

Sarah left the room and returned with Snowy, who was still waking up in her arms "This is Snowy guys. He's both left and right winged and very intelligent!"

Snowy was unperturbed by the roar of laughter that ensued, but fascinated by the gleaming saxophone. He pecked at it and tried to nestle in the tube, but when Bill picked it up to resume playing it, Snowy flapped and squawked, apparently agitated by the sound. All were bent over with laughter with Bill adding to this as he lamented "Oh well, no sax tonight."

Half an hour later Eden, Sarah and Sally were seeing off the last of their guest's, while Matthew was preoccupied with snoring, having fallen asleep at the table minutes before. Back in the apartment Eden got Matthew into bed and found some scraps for Snowy to eat while the girls cleared away dishes. The basic jobs having been done they fell into bed agreeing to be up in four hours to attend the rally. Sarah however, had a sleepless few hours. She had felt unwell that evening and now felt a great deal worse. By the time the others awakened she was unconscious in a chair. Eden made sure that she was breathing, asked Sally to ring the hospital and carried Sarah to the car. As he pulled into the emergency entrance of Georgetown University Medical Center, two of his friends and co-workers, Simon and Ellen were waiting. Together, they transferred Sarah from the car to a hospital bed where they commenced checking her vitals. "Her temps forty three, BP's one hundred and eighty over one hundred and fifteen and her breathing is very labored." Ellen said looking at Eden.

Eden's anxious expression was the same as it always was on these occasions. Sarah's head suddenly moved at that point and she stirred into consciousness. Eden leaned over her and kissed her "It's ok Sarah, we're at Georgetown, don't talk just rest, I'm going to have you better in no time"

"The rally?" whispered Sarah as she looked back at him.

"No, no rally today darling, except the one to get you better. Now I've just got to talk to Simon for a minute and I'll be back, Ellen will stay with you."

"Hi gorgeous," Ellen said, patting Sarah's hair back "now I'm going to have to get mum to make some of those brownies for you, aren't I?"

Outside, in the corridor Eden and Simon were worried. Both paced, talking as they did. "In ten minutes we'll get her off to x-ray." said Simon.

"It's my fault," Eden said "yesterday Michael and I cleaned the apartment, usually we send Sarah out while we're cleaning but she wanted to help Sally with the cooking and so I thought if she just stayed in the kitchen, she'd be away from the dust. Dam, how stupid!"

"Eden stop, you do this every time. Yes, it might have helped if she was out, but are you going to know every time you walk into a restaurant or a cinema whether or not it's dirty, or whether it's just been cleaned? What's important right now is getting her better. You know that, the quicker she gets better, the less damage to her lungs."

"Can you book radiology? I'll get her up there now." Eden nodded.

After Sarah's first episode of pneumonia when she was six, she had been diagnosed with a condition called Hypersensitive Pneumonia, a condition common amongst farmers and anyone who had exposure to high concentrations of dusts from organic material at work or in the home. In Sarah's case, even the slightest exposure triggered pneumonia. The course of the illness had the same symptoms of a bacterial pneumonia but the duration of the illness was about four or five days, as opposed to a standard bacterial pneumonia which lasted around fourteen days. The greatest concern, with this condition was that with repeated episodes, a progressive, irreversible loss of lung function would occur over years.

As Eden and Simon stared at the light filled x-ray the shadows in her lungs were obvious. "We need to get her onto rullide straight away and do some blood tests." said Eden.

"You go and sit with her and I'll get the ball rolling." said Simon as he put his hand reassuringly on Eden's shoulder. "Get Sarah onto some glucose and tell Ellen to get you a coffee."

When Eden returned to Sarah's room she was sitting up and she smiled as he entered. "How are you feeling now?" he said as he sat down beside her.

"Better, Ellen's been on to me with pain killers and I feel much better. Oh Eden you look tired."

"I'm fine Sarah, I love you. We'll get you home in a few days."

"Will you stay with me?"

"Ellen's arranging another bed as we speak. Now, no more talking, I'll lie beside you while you try and get some sleep, ok?"

As Sarah lay there, her teeth chattering, Eden pulled more blankets over her and wrapped his body around hers. Soon she was asleep and Eden lay there staring at his wife's beautiful, pale face. A short time later Sally tiptoed into the room. "Good, she's asleep." she said kissing Eden on the cheek "How are you?" Eden stared back at her vacantly. "Ok, lets hit the canteen and get you some breakfast, you'll feel brighter then when Sarah wakes up. Oh, and I've brought a bag of PJ's and things."

"Thanks Sally, you're the best."

"Well, if I don't get some food into you, you won't be the best, now come on. Ellen will watch her while we're gone."

After eating, Eden picked up some flowers from the hospital florist and returned to Sarah. Sally was quietly unpacking Sarah's and Eden's personal things as she slept. "Beautiful." she said looking at the flowers. "Now I'm off back home. Michael and I thought we'd give the apartment a real spruce up while Sarah's here, that way she's not there while it's being cleaned and it will be impeccable when she gets back. Now, you make sure you look after yourself and my best friend while I'm gone, ok!"

"But aren't you on shift today?"

"Eden, you know everyone here adores Sarah, they've all been offering to swap shifts and do extra shifts for the both of us, so you relax and stop worrying"

Six days later Eden awoke to an empty hospital room. He had been on night shift all night and had climbed into bed beside his wife to get some sleep in the few remaining hours of the morning. As he walked into the canteen, his hair ruffled and his slippers back to front, he saw Sarah sitting with Simon and Ellen. As he walked up behind Sarah he wrapped his arms around her shoulders and kissed her "How's my darling today?"

"Eden, I was hoping you would sleep a bit longer, you looked so tired. Sit down and I'll get you a coffee." she said pulling a chair out for him.

"I've just been telling Sarah she can go home today" said Simon "and we've swapped your shift tonight, so today and tomorrow is all yours."

"Gee! I've got good friends haven't I?" Eden said smiling.

"Well, you've always set the pace. I mean how many favors have you done for us? Just make sure you catch up on some sleep pal and I've written a couple of scripts out for Sarah. so you'll need to pick them up on your way out, now, gotta go, or the patients will lose their patience and then I'll be in trouble, won't I?"

With those words Ellen gulped down the last of her coffee and jumped up. "Better be off too," she said "look after Sarah and Simon's right, you need sleep!"

Having had a coffee, packed and collected the scripts on the way out, Eden and Sarah walked out of the hospital and into the warm sun. As they approached the car Eden opened the door for Sarah and put the suitcase on the back seat. "I tell you what," he said as he climbed in beside her " why don't we pick up a picnic lunch, take it to the river and soak up some sun?"

"Sounds wonderful." Sarah said as she leaned over to kiss him.

Sitting on the grassy slopes at the Gorge end of Rock Creek Park, where the bridge crossed over to Georgetown, they ate their lunch while they watched some open air theater. After lunch they took a short walk through the park. Rock Creek Park was one of the oldest national parks in the world and was a favorite place to Sarah and Eden. Here, as they walked and watched hikers, bikers and horse-riders enjoy the hours, they often stopped to buy a bag of flour from Pierce Mill and to visit the Art Barn next door, complete with a gallery and workshop. The park was an oasis of vibrant green and a pacifier to many of the busy people who enjoyed it.

"A kiss for your thoughts." said Eden as they walked arm in arm, under the green leaves and beside the smooth water of the creek.

"I was just thinking how lucky we are, we have each other, good friends, a roof over our heads, you're doing well with your career and I'm enjoying mine and sometimes I wonder is it fair to be so lucky. Some of the patients I saw in the hospital have awful things wrong with them and as we pass the benches in this park we know someone will be sleeping on them tonight. Sometimes I think that if we all could and did share in the harder things, then everyone would be lucky. I know that such a possibility is a fantasy but I just wish it weren't. Then I wonder, is there a way we could all help each other more that nobody's thought about? The more I wonder, the more I see how complex it all is."

"Well most children grow up with parents, we lost ours as babies, so there's a piece of sadness we've had and that's the thing, it's all pieces of sadness. Yes, some have a bigger piece than other's, but if we all had the same size piece we'd all stop helping each other because we'd all be helping ourselves, and there would be no such thing as compassion for another anymore.

Appreciating how lucky we are makes us stronger and if we had to endure a greater sadness that too, would make us stronger. Strength and compassion will make life itself better for all of us."

"But do we give enough strength or compassion or, do we too readily just accept that we can't do too much more to help? I think, in the majority of people, strength and compassion plays a huge part in their thoughts and feelings, but tends to disappear when it comes to what they do in practice. I find myself constantly thinking of homeless people for example, but do I bring a homeless person home and give them a meal or a bed, no. Then I tell myself, one day in the future I will, but will I or am I just making my mind, my strength and compassion feel better? Then I think of being a part of or forming a group to help the homeless or the sick, but a group will give the homeless a bowl of soup and a couple of nights of shelter and pop in on a sick person every now and then to help, but a group won't do anything personal and real like giving a homeless person a home for good or staying with a sick person until they get better or die. So as an individual we want to help but we don't, and as a group we help, but not enough."

"I've never thought about it that way but you've got a point there. If you look at orphanages they are a group of people helping but what help do they give? They give the children food and a roof over their heads, but no personal time or love; how many individuals or families are there to take a child and give them that? They may think about it or want to, but they never do. So yeah, the individuals don't do anything and the groups don't do enough." he nodded.

"In that particular example the problem thickens because if you deprive a child of personal contact or love how does that child grow up and know how to give warmth or love? We love each other and our friends but would we be different if we had grown up in a real family?" Sarah continued.

"I'm sure we would have to be, but then you and I were lucky. We had each other during most of those years. Yet, is it just how much time and love you give a child that creates their adult character. If it is strongly dependent on that, how do you explain how two children for example, can grow up with the same parents in the same home and often turn out so differently in character? Obviously, individual personalities have a tremendous effect too."

"It's complex isn't it!" Sarah said to the sky.

"Maybe it isn't complex. There's the group, there's the individual, if each individual just helped one person who really needed help, imagine the impact. Doing that isn't hard or complex, the difficult part is getting society to realize they could do it. On that point, changing the subject slightly but along the lines of what we've been talking about, I need to talk to you about something. You know how, at the hospital, if you take two people with the same medical problem, the person who can pay, we help, the person who can't we send on, usually, only to be sent on and on? A couple of doctors are quietly helping, in, for want of a better word, backyard clinics. From what I've heard, they're doing a brilliant job. The cases are anything from a broken finger to a gunshot wound. A few of the staff at the hospital are carefully fudging the medical supply charts to get extra supplies in and handing them over to the guys going out there to help. It's all quite illegal but it's a way of actually helping these people who wouldn't get the help otherwise. The guys are doing their standard shift at the hospital and working outside the hospital a couple of hours, two or three days a week. The short of it all is, that they have approached me to see if I'm interested. I told them I'd talk to you."

"I agree with what they are doing but what are the consequences if they get caught?"

"Heavy, you can loose your licence. The real danger is if they are sued for malpractice, so they're covering themselves by operating, excuse the pun, on a first name only, that way they can't be traced. If the extra medical supplies are picked up it can be put down to theft."

"Well it seems to me you're always looking tired as it is, but if you really want to do this, then I'm proud of you. Does Sally know about this?"

"No, it's only guys going out, hopefully that will change, but the conditions are not as protected as in a huge hospital."

"So should we say anything, I mean, she is going to wonder where you're spending your time so many hours a week?"

"I'm not sure yet… then again I think we should."

"Well, it sounds like the sort of thing Sally would orchestrate herself, so I don't doubt she'd keep it to herself, anyway, when will you start on this new job?"

"They're anxious for me to start tomorrow, but I'll let them know that I can start in a week from now. My priority right now is getting you fighting fit, now let's get you home for a couple of hours rest before dinner."

"If you sleep for a couple of hours, I'll sleep better."

"In the aim of keeping the patient happy, I won't argue with that." Eden half whispered with that mesmerized look he often had as he stared into Sarah's blue eyes and met her lips with his. In his arms he held her close, as his olive hands ran through her soft blonde hair and came to rest on her slender hips. "You're my life and my soul Sarah." he said as his lips continued to caress hers.

As they walked into the apartment Snowy approached with great excitement to greet them. After focusing on him for a few minutes, the two found themselves in the shower with the hot water soaking their bodies as they tenderly touched each other and made amorous love. Having dried Sarah's hair and wrapped her in a dressing gown Eden settled her under a summer blanket and climbed in beside her. Three hours passed as the two slept soundly when they were disturbed from a knock at their door accompanied by Matthew's cheerful words "It's great to have you back Sarah! Oh! and dinner is served in twenty minutes guys and if you haven't heard anything I just said, then I'll just have to start singing, that's bound to do the trick."

Michael's words rang in their ears as they stirred.

"We're awake." they responded in unison.

"We'll be out in a minute Matthew." Sarah laughed.

"Oh, I've missed that laugh." was the response from the

other side of the door.

They sat down to a scrumptious meal that Sally and Matthew had prepared especially, to welcome them home. Matthew filled four glasses with champagne, bought especially for the occasion, then they toasted to Sarah's improved health. When the plates were empty Sally pushed her chair back and collected them, "Now I am going to get the dessert Eden, you make sure your wife sits in that chair and relaxes until I return." she said with determination.

Dessert was very simple, but as each of the four knew, Sarah's favorite. Sarah's first choice in the sweet range was inevitably sorbet and on this hot summer evening the others found it very appealing as well. They talked and laughed, laughed and talked, as the plates were emptied Matthew rose to his feet to collect them. He returned laden with another bottle of champagne and four freshly chilled glasses. "Now, another toast," he said as he filled the last of the glasses and raised it with the others "to my cherished fiancée, Sally and our future life together." The toast so astounded and thrilled Eden and Sarah that the sip of champagne that was required before words even, couldn't be sipped fast enough.

They were ecstatic as they threw their arms around Sally and Matthew. "Oh, I'm so happy for you both, that's wonderful!" Sarah said.

"Brilliantly excellent!" exclaimed Eden "Good on you both!"

"Thanks guys." Sally said with tears in her eyes "We're feeling a bit like we're on cloud nine. We've known for a week but we wanted you to be the first to know."

"Have you set a date?" asked Eden

"Eleven months away, on Independence Day eve." Matthew said as he took Sally's hands and kissed her on the forehead.

"You're perfect for each other, I love you both so much, I'm so happy for you." Sarah said wiping a tear from her eye.

"There's something else," said Sally "Matthew's been promoted to Assistant Editor."

"Great work!" Eden said giving Matthew a slap on the back.

"It's Assistant Editor on the New York paper though, which means moving permanently to New York, unless they throw me out in the first week, in which case it wouldn't be permanent. The job starts in three months, so I mean we both love the idea of New York but we'll miss you guys. Sally's already been checking the cost of train tickets, there and back, and it's not too bad, so with the pay rise I'll be getting, a couple of tickets every second month will be easy, so we'll be able to see each other, and I promise I won't sing when you're up."

"Or any other time." laughed Sally.

They sat and talked excitedly of the year to come, and of the year that was, until Sarah fell asleep on the couch. Her first day home from the hospital had been long, and annoyed at themselves for talking at such length, the others decided to make amends the next day.

CHAPTER
THREE

One week had passed, Sarah had fully recovered from her illness, Eden had completed his first week on his new job outside the hospital, Sally and Matthew had continued to make plans; Snowy seemed so settled in his new abode, it was as if he had never lived anywhere else. Sarah, Eden, Sally and Matthew sat with a group of friends in one of the many restaurants in the mall. It was the nineteenth of August, Eden's birthday, and everyone watched as he blew the twenty-five candles out on his cake. "Good blow old man." said Bill.

"Your turn old guy." Eden retorted with a grin.

"Now, now children, just make sure you both make a wish."

"But Sarah, Eden's got you, what more could he wish for?"

"I wish, you're as lucky as I am one day." said Eden with a determined grin.

Bill was studying at Yale and working part time for Senator Fulbright of Arkansas. When he was seventeen he was elected a Senator and went to the Boys Nation in D.C. He had shaken JFK's hand and had turned down a music scholarship in favor of attending Georgetown University and studying a Bachelor of Arts in international studies. Eden and Bill shared the same birth date and age, and on this particular birthday Bill's work for the Senator had brought him to Washington for a couple of days and as was usual, any out of work hours he had in Washington, were spent with Eden and Sarah and of course his saxophone.

The cake formalities over, both men commenced opening presents and seemed equally delighted with their gifts. Both were particularly delighted with one gift each. Eden had unwrapped Sarah's painting that morning and was so proud of it that he had insisted on taking it to the restaurant to show the others. The proprietor kindly hung it on the wall next to the table where they were seated for all to look at. Bill had brought the new saxophone his mother had given him for his birthday to show to his friends. The attentive proprietor noticed this too and requested Bill play a piece for his customers. By the end of the evening both men agreed they couldn't have had a better birthday.

The following morning the alarm shrieked at its typical time and Snowy reacted with his usual response of running in, jumping, landing and flapping directly on Eden's face. Thankfully, it was for this and numerous other reasons that Sarah had learnt to keep the bird's nails filed to a smooth ending. Eden sneezed, threw his hands around and grumbled beneath the feathers "Snowy! Now look, this is a bit rich at five in the morning." Wide-awake, Eden crawled out of bed and headed for the bathroom. Eden was very meticulous in everything he did, whether it be in the bathroom or the operating theatre. As he shaved he noticed Matthew had left the toilet seat up again. This did not irritate Eden, but not rectifying the situation, would have. Still shaving, he manoeuvered his foot to fix the lid and swore as he felt the razor cut into his skin "Shit, shit, shit!" Eden yelled as he grabbed at the tissues to mop up the blood. Undefeated by alarms, birds and razors he showered, dressed and was in the kitchen in time to grab his orange juice, coffee, and yogurt before he ran out the door.

Entering the hospital foyer he was just in time to hear his name come over the paging system. His face became the focus of discussion behind the busy desk. "Gee, shame he didn't get an electric shaver for his birthday."

"Could have got a cat."

"Alert, alert, home made joke. What do you get when you cross a razor and a cat? It makes me sore and makes me ow!

"Ok guys, can we keep it down a bit? I'm trying to return a page here. Yeah hi, Eden Parks, someone paged me?"

"One moment..."

"Eden, Kalowski here, how were the celebrations last night?"

"Great, thanks."

"Good, good, well I'll let you go then."

"Doctor Kalowski, ah, you paged me?"

"Oh yes of course, sorry. The short of it is I managed to fracture a finger at football last night so are you up for a bypass this afternoon?"

"Sure, just let me swap a couple of things around and I'll come up and get the chart and films."

"Good, good, I'll let you go then."

"Yes!" mouthed Eden as he hung up the phone.

This request was an undeniable honor, as Eden was well aware. For Doctor Kalowski to even know your name would be considered an honor in itself. Kalowski was known to be one of the country's best open heart surgeons, was president of the American Heart Association, and had written two books on cardiovascular disease, both of which had become semi gospels to Eden and others. Eden had assisted in many, but had never headed a bypass operation. Just to assist in such an operation you had to be either a senior resident completing your final year of thoracic surgical training, or a highly trained physician's assistant. Eden was close to, but not at either of, these levels yet.

The hospital had created the region's first services of integrated cardiology, cardiac surgery and vascular surgery. Over the years its reputation had extended the local region to serve nationally and internationally. The hospital had become highly regarded for its diagnostic expertise, clinical excellence and its dedication to offering patients a wide range of options to manage their cardiovascular diseases. "That wasn't Kalowski, as in our Kalowski, you were talking to was it?" asked Simon, who had walked in on the second half of the conversation.

Eden nodded "I'm finding it hard to believe it myself. He even asked me if I had a good birthday!"

"That wouldn't surprise me. I was just upstairs putting our name down for the echocardiography conference tomorrow and it seems the p.a. system did a fizzer again."

"Oh no, how bad?"

"About three minutes of the desk talk went all over the place, even the joke! So you'll probably get happy birthdayed to death today."

"Doesn't matter, I'll be so busy today anyway, I won't even

notice. Kalowski's fractured his finger and he wants me to head a bypass this afternoon."

"You're kidding! Well, I can't say I'm not jealous. Who's assisting?"

"Don't know yet, I've got to go up and get the chart and films later, then again, I'd better make it sooner. Better get my rounds done. Catch you for a coffee later?"

"Sure thing."

Eden's first port of call on his rounds that morning was Ben Strauss, a young man of nineteen years who had spent the last fourteen months desperately waiting for a donor heart, nearly dying in the process. Finally, a suitable heart was found and Ben had been whisked off to the operating theatre. As Eden walked into the room, two days after the surgery he was shocked to see Ben getting up out of bed. He rushed up to him, slipping his arm behind to support him "Ben, my friend what are you doing? It's too early to get up yet."

"I was just going to shoot some goals."

"No Ben, you've got to lie down now, there will be time for that later." Eden eased him back into the bed "If you lie down for me now I'll shoot some goals with you in no time."

Ben stared vacantly back at Eden but obliged by letting Eden settle him back on his pillow. Eden buzzed for the nurse as he held Ben's hand. Since the surgery Ben's blood pressure had remained unusually low, a factor that was conducive to post op delirium, in around ten to twelve per cent of patients, a day or two after the actual operation. A patient in this condition was in a state of confusion and often exhibited irrational behavior, which could in itself be dangerous to the recovery process. As the nurse entered the room Eden sent her rushing off for some haloperidol, a tranquilizing drug. Having administered the drug and checked other vitals Eden squeezed Ben's hand, who was now still and content, bending down and whispering "I'll be back to see you soon Ben."

As Simon entered the staff loungeroom later that morning, he found Eden busy with a pig's trotter "Gee, how about that coffee, I've been looking for you everywhere?"

"Um..."

"Forget it I'll be back in a minute."

Simon returned minutes later with two steaming coffees "Take a break." he said handing Eden a cup.

Eden put the pig's trotter down, stretched his back and lent back in the chair "I've gone through the films and I've just been doing some last minute suture practice on the trotter. I hope this patient is going to be in good hands," he said, sipping his coffee anxiously.

"You'll do fine, I mean, if anyone of us is up to it, you'd have to be at the top of the list."

"I hope you're right. How about I shout you some lunch, I always think better on a full stomach?"

"Sorry mate, no can do, I don't even have time for this coffee, I'm behind in my reports and I've lost count of how many more patients I've got to see by the end of the day. Tell you what, I'll make sure lunch is on tomorrow and you can tell me all about it."

Two hours had passed and Eden was in the scrub room. As he washed his hands and forearms with a disposable sterile surgical sponge soaked in antiseptic solution, his mind was racing through the coming operational procedure. Entering the operating room he was helped into a sterile gown by the scrub nurse. He took a deep breath and walked over to the mildly sedated patient ready on the operating table. "We'll have you out of here in no time." Eden said reassuringly "The anaesthetist will make you go to sleep now and I'll see you in a few hours."

"They tell me this is your first operation of this kind?" the patient enquired.

"Yes, I've assisted in many but this is the first time I've headed one."

"Well, don't you worry, I'm a great believer in firsts!" the man insisted with a wink.

As Eden smiled back at him, the man fell asleep. These few words from the patient had had a calming effect on Eden as he commenced the job at hand. He picked up the scalpel and made a long incision into the chest. Having exposed the breastbone Eden used the oscillating saw to cut through it. After dividing the thymus gland he opened the pericardium, a thin membrane, surrounding the heart. With the heart exposed, he passed large tubes into the right atrium and aorta, which were connected to the heart-lung machine. Then he inserted a large-bore tube into the aortic arch to return oxygenated blood to the aorta. "Turn the by-pass machine on now." he said gently "Oh, and some music would be nice." He began cooling the patient's heart by cold salt infusion into the surrounding pericardial space. "I'm going to have to insert a tube into the pulmonary artery to remove excess blood." he said as he instilled cardioplegic solution into the left ventricle. Like clockwork the heart stopped beating.

The isolation, dissection, mobilization and joining of the internal mammary arteries done, Eden directed the heart-lung machine operator to commence rewarming, in preparation for normal heart function to resume. He removed the aortic cross-clamp allowing blood to enter the heart chambers and checked the anastomosis for any potential leakage. The team of nine watched and waited for the heart to begin beating. Seconds went by to no avail "Ok commence defib!" Eden commanded. Two minutes later the direct electrical shock woke the heart up and all breathed a sigh of relief as it began to beat. As the heart idled, trying to achieve its normal beat, the heart-lung machine continued to operate, assisting the heart in taking over its normal function. Within minutes the heart was functioning properly. Eden removed the aortic tube and stitched the aorta and the atrium. The normal state of circulation having been restored, he reversed the anticoagulation and began to close up the chest.

After preparing the patient for transfer to the Coronary Care unit Eden left the operating room, ripped off his gown, threw it in the air and said "Beautiful!" as he caught it. The four-hour operation had seemed more like four days, and though every muscle in his body was exhausted and aching, he knew the jubilation of this moment would stay with him for many years to come.

That evening as Eden emerged from the lift and entered the apartment, he found it empty except for the sound of the water running in the shower and Snowy banging on the door. "Eden, is that you?" Sarah called out.

Now in the bathroom, Eden popped his head between the shower curtains and answered "It's me darling..., you're so beautiful."

"Oh Eden, you've cut your face again."

"Can't even feel it anymore." he said climbing in beside her.

"You look tired, and happy." Sarah said, wrapping her hands around the back of his neck and the other around his penis.

"I had a great day, I'll tell you about it in a while, right now I just want to feel you."

After the shower, Eden felt totally relaxed, the warm water having soothed his aching muscles. As he sat and waited for

Sarah to finish dressing, his mind slowly drifted over those minutes and hours in the operating room. The calmness that Sarah and the warm water had exerted over his body put him to sleep in minutes.

A short time later, Eden awoke to boistress knocking on the door. Sarah kissed him, whispered "Wait," and answered the door. A few minutes later she returned and took her place in his lap "You've been sleeping for two hours, you poor thing, you must have been tired! You said you had a great day and I had a lucky day. I sold three of my paintings for far more than they were worth, so I've taken the liberty of ordering some Thai take out, so, over a lovely dinner you can tell me what happened today."

"One day Sarah you will be so famous that people will hardly be able to pay for what they are worth."

"For you to be proud of me and for me to give something back to the world of art that I love, that's what pushes me each day I get up to start work."

"I'm already proud of you Sarah, but I know what you mean. As far as you contributing to art, I feel exactly the same about medicine. Now let's set the table and I'll tell you what I got up to today."

As Eden relayed the day's events, more particularly, the bypass, Sarah was astounded. Admiration was written all over her face as she listened to him meticulously detail the operation. "It's amazing, yesterday you turned twenty-five, this morning you get up, shower, eat and go off to work, and at the end of the day, what have you done? Saved somebody's life! That makes me feel more than proud of you. To have that ability is a great privilege, and to use that ability is a great privilege to others. You should always feel proud of that and special."

"About today, I'm glad you left out the part where I got flapped awake and attacked myself with the razor!" he said with a grin.

CHAPTER
FOUR

Four months had passed as if they were four days. It was Christmas Eve and Eden was on his first day of a much-needed holiday. His work and the expectations of him at Georgetown had escalated. Eden was uniquely gifted in his field, and the heads at Georgetown hospital seemed more aware of this than Eden himself. Sarah had agreed to put away her paints, and like Eden, was looking forward to a well-earned break. Her work had progressed to such an extent that she no longer simply had a flock of clients, but an additional flock of galleries, all wishing to exhibit her work. She was careful not to accept any of these invitations, for though an exhibition of her work was exactly what she wanted and had worked very hard for, she knew the first exhibition would be the first public eye image of her as an artist. In her mind the image she gave at her first public exhibition had to be perfect, she knew sooner than later she would have to accept one of these invitations; however, she intended using the interim to make sure that what she had to exhibit would be well worth it.

Sally and Matthew had moved to New York a month earlier and this Christmas Eve morning Sarah and Eden were busy packing to spend Christmas Day with them. Sally and Matthew had given them the tickets on their departure and all four were looking forward to a couple of days together in New York. The weather was bitterly cold and the snow plentiful. As Eden took charge of preparing a hot breakfast, Sarah was adamantly fitting as many sweaters as she could get into the two suitcases that lay on the bed. As the phone began to ring Eden yelled out "Can you get that Sarah, the eggs don't want me to leave them at the moment?"

"Hello, Sarah Parks speaking."

"Hi Sarah, it's David. I know you guys are on holidays, and sorry to ask but how would it be if we borrowed Eden just for a couple of hours this morning? We're sort of snowed under here, in the patient sense I mean. You could tell him after this we won't even know your phone number for two weeks, let alone ring it."

"You should be on holiday yourself David." Sarah laughed "I'll talk to Eden and if he is coming in he'll be there in half an hour, if not he'll ring you back in two minutes, although we both know the latter would be impossible for him. Have a good Christmas David and try to take a break."

"That was David." Sarah said entering the kitchen.

"Gee, he could smell food a hundred kilometers away."

"He doesn't want breakfast, he wants you to go in for a couple of hours this morning, they're snowed in."

"Oh no, I tell you what, I'll ring them back and tell them I don't have a spade," he said with a wink "Oh, I'm sorry Sarah, would you mind, the train doesn't leave until five-thirty so we should have time?"

"You can go when you've finished your breakfast, ok?"

"Yes, Mrs. Parks." he laughed wrapping his arms around her waist.

"Now you sit and I'll serve." He said as he pulled a chair out for her.

A couple of hours work had turned into five hours and as Eden picked the phone up in the hospital foyer to ring Sarah to let her know he was on his way home, he looked at his watch, it was three-fifteen, which luckily, still gave them ample time to make the train.

"I'll be there in twenty minutes Sarah, sorry for the delay."

"It's ok, everything's packed and I've got Snowy organized for the trip. Drive carefully home, I heard on the radio there's been some bad snow storms."

"Will do, I'll see you in twenty minutes then." he confirmed, before hanging up the phone.

Eden zipped up his jacket, walked out of the warmth of the hospital and into the cold, white storm outside. He paused momentarily as he watched two incoming ambulances, this sight he always found hard to walk away from. Annoyed at himself for this somewhat obsessive feeling he quickly stepped up his pace and headed for his car. Reaching the car he brushed the snow off the windscreen, grabbed the door handle, as the locks had long ceased to work and jumped in. Sitting in the driver's seat he slowly turned around and stared, he was speechless. In the front passenger seat beside him sat a frail, old woman with a terrier on her lap. She seemed very content and at ease, and was not at all perturbed by Eden's entrance. This in itself rendered Eden even more speechless. "Who was she and what was she doing sitting in his car?" he thought as he continued staring at her. Finally, he broke the silence "Excuse me, my name is Eden, can I help you with something?"

"Eden you say, what a lovely name." she responded with a bright smile "Yes young man, you could help me with something, I could use a warm blanket, my legs have gone quite numb on me in this cold."

Eden took off his jacket and placed it over her legs "Ah, you stay here and I'll be back with a blanket in a minute." he said reaching for the door handle and hopping out of the car. Outside the car he paused, shivered and scratched his head "This is different," he thought. He dashed back into the hospital to grab a blanket.

"If you don't get out of here, I'm going to stick you in an ambulance and send you back to your wife!" Simon said as Eden sped past him. "Eden," he insisted "That holiday of yours will be over before you start it."

"Don't blame me, blame the old lady sitting in my car."

"You do need a holiday don't you, maybe I really should call that ambulance?" he said as he feigned a worried look.

"I'm not kidding, I got into my car and found an old lady with her dog sitting in the passenger seat. She's just sitting there quite happily."

"Ok, well let's just say for one minute I believe you, what are you doing here? Are you just going to leave her sitting in your car and if she is sitting in your car, why?"

"I don't know why, maybe she thinks it's her car. Maybe she's waiting for someone. Oh shit, she's waiting for a blanket, I've got to go."

Eden found a blanket and ran back out to the car. As he jumped in he found the pair sitting as calmly as before. He leaned over and wrapped the blanket over her legs "Thank you Eden that's very nice of you." she said pulling a piece of the blanket over her dog.

"Ah, Ms…"

"No, no, young man, my apologies for not introducing myself. My name is Mrs. Spalding, but you can call me Esme."

"Well Esme, you're sitting in my car and I was wondering if you thought it was your car?"

"I couldn't be sitting in my car, I don't have a car," she volunteered, trying to be helpful. "No… I was walking my dog and we seemed to get a bit lost and then it started snowing, so I borrowed a seat in your car. I hope you don't mind." she said smiling at Eden.

"No, I'm glad you did, you shouldn't be out in this weather at all."

A knock on the window interrupted Eden's words and train of thought. Winding the window down he found Simon covered in snow, standing there with a plastic cup of coffee and looking quite bemused "Just checking everything is all right and I thought you might like a hot cup of coffee Ma'am to warm you up." Eden took the coffee and passed it to Esme.

"Simon this is Esme, she's a little bit lost so after you've had your coffee Esme," he said turning to her "I'll help you find your home."

"Maybe there's an address in Esme's handbag?" Simon said pointing to the bag at her feet.

"That is a very good idea young man." she said looking very hopeful.

Eden reached for the handbag and passed it to Esme. As she unzipped the bag and stared into it she responded with a bewildered look "Oh dear, dear, it's empty again. I never go out without my handbag, a lady without a handbag is by no means appropriate... but I have been known to lose it, so sometimes I empty it before I go out."

"Don't worry Esme, I'll drive you around for a bit and see if you recognise anything. Simon you'd better go in or you'll freeze. Can you give Sarah a call and tell her I'll be a bit longer in getting home?"

"Well, if you're sure?" he answered brushing more snow off "If you run into a problem bring her back and we'll find a bed for her overnight." he whispered into Eden's ear.

Eden nodded, wound up the window and waited for Esme to finish her coffee. This done, he set off, driving slowly around the nearby streets, feeling sure that at her age she couldn't have walked too far. Esme was not of much help, she managed to recognise her butcher and drug store but little else. Eden parked outside each store and took Esme in hoping the owners might know where she lived. They knew her very well but were quick to point out that she always did her own shopping and they had never had an occasion to make a home delivery with this customer. Both owners insisted she had become very absent minded in the last year, often paying for her shopping and leaving it in the store.

Eden helped Esme back into the car. By now both were getting worried. They continued driving around but to no avail. "Oh dear, I am causing you a great inconvenience aren't I?" Esme said fidgeting with her handbag.

"There is one problem," Eden said looking at the clock on the dashboard "It's five o'clock and my wife and I are supposed to be on the five-thirty train to New York tonight. She's at home waiting for me now."

"I am a silly old lady who's forgotten where she lives. I am not your problem you must drop me off right now and go home to your wife. I am sure to remember where I live soon enough and I certainly will not cause you any more inconvenience than I already have."

"No Esme, firstly, you can't walk around in this weather, and secondly, it's possible we won't find your place tonight. I think we should head to my apartment now and work something out from there. That is, if you're happy with that idea?"

"This is not like me, I am not one for causing other people problems and this I find quite disturbing, but I suppose you're right. Your poor wife must be quite worried and you must be quite annoyed with me by now. You have been very kind and I'm sorry to be causing you such concern."

It was five-fifteen when the lift door opened on the fourth floor and Eden gestured for Esme to leave the lift. The little dog barked as he trotted out into the hall, which made Eden wonder. Was the bark because of unfamiliar surroundings or was it because lifts and hallways were familiar to him. Sarah, having heard the bark, opened the apartment door and looked out. The expression on Eden's face was apologetic as he stared back at her. Sarah, however, looked quite relieved "Eden I was getting worried about you. I thought maybe you'd had an accident."

"I'm fine, I'm just sorry I'm so late. This is Esme, Sarah, and Esme, this is my wife Sarah." He introduced them as he picked Snowy up who had wandered out to see what was happening.

The terrier's tail started wagging and he barked excitedly as he stared at Snowy. Knowing it was impossible to speak until the dog was quietened the three entered the apartment, Eden signalled to Esme to take a seat, excused himself for a minute and took Sarah and Snowy into the kitchen and shut the door. The separation seemed to quieten the dog. Sarah took Snowy from Eden's arms and popped him into his travel box and shut the door. "Just in case he starts the dog off again." she said, looking quite perplexed by this stage.

"It seems I've ruined our trip." Eden said staring at his watch.

"I'm just glad you're ok, between the storm and the weather reports, I was getting really worried. Who is Esme?"

"Well, she says her name is Esme Spalding. After I talked to you on the phone I got into the car meaning to come straight home and I found her sitting in the car, in the passenger seat.

She told me she was taking her dog for a walk and managed to get lost and when the storm came she borrowed a seat in our car. She was cold, so I got her a blanket and Simon got her a cup of coffee, then I spent the next two hours driving her around hoping she might recognise where she lived."

"The poor thing!"

"Then, when I mentioned our trip to New York, she told me to let her out, she thought she could find her home herself and she was upset to be causing us concern. I knew I couldn't do that, it's freezing out there, so I suggested we come back here and sort something out. Simon mentioned finding her a bed at the hospital for the night if we couldn't find her place, but I didn't have the heart to leave her there and she'd have to be separated from her dog, so I brought her here."

"I think you did the right thing. As far as the trip goes, I don't mind if you don't. Sally and Matthew will be disappointed but we'll give them a ring and I'm sure they'll understand. In the meantime, we can give Esme the spare room and make her feel comfortable, being Christmas Eve we'll have a difficult time trying to find her place tomorrow, unless she can remember herself because everything will be closed. Oh, and Boxing Day will be a problem too."

Eden put his arms around her "I'm sorry about the trip and that I worried you."

"You shouldn't be sorry, you did exactly the right thing. You go and sit with Esme for a minute and I'll make some hot chocolate to warm us all up."

"After she's had a drink and a bit of a rest, I'd better take her down to the local police station, just in case she has a family out there that have reported her missing. With some luck we might find out where she lives and if she does have a family they'd have to be pretty worried by now."

Sarah and Eden looked at each other as Esme tapped on the kitchen door. "I am sorry Esme," Sarah said as she opened the door "Eden has just been telling me about the awful afternoon you've had and I'm just making a hot drink to warm you up."

"I wanted to apologise for the disturbance I've caused you young people and I don't want to cause you to miss your trip." she told them, looking upset.

"You've caused no disturbance Esme, we would much prefer to spend Christmas Eve with you. We have a spare room and after I do some shopping we can have a nice Christmas lunch tomorrow." Sarah responded with her typical warmth.

"You are both very kind."

"In the meantime," Eden said, "we will make sure we find your home as soon as we can. Now you sit down, keep that blanket around you and get some rest. We'll bring you a drink in a minute and get the spare room organized. Your little dog, would he prefer some warm milk or water?"

"Either would suit Charlie, he'd be very grateful. Thank you both."

"She's a real sweetie, isn't she." Sarah said as Esme trotted away.

"I'll give her that, I just wish her memory was more accommodating. Anyway, I'll go and check the spare room and I'll see you in there in a few minutes for that hot chocolate," he said rubbing his hands together at the thought of a warm drink.

Two hours later Esme was in bed, with Charlie settled on the floor beside her. A meal had been prepared and eaten earlier during which Esme insisted that she lived alone with the exception of Charlie and had no relatives to speak of. Given this, a trip to the police station seemed pointless. Sarah had found a pair of comfortable pyjamas and a dressing gown for Esme and had placed a jug of water, a transistor radio and a newspaper beside her bed but the soft snores coming from her room suggested she had fallen asleep as soon as her head had encountered the pillow.

Sarah and Eden went out shopping alternately and in such order not wishing to leave Esme by herself in the apartment. For Sarah, the change of plans meant shopping for food was a necessity for the fridge had purposely been permitted to get empty and she had to concoct a last minute Christmas lunch. What precisely Eden was shopping for, he insisted with a grin, was a secret. Upon Sarah's return, laden with brown paper bags of food, Eden helped her unpack, kissed her and ran out the door. Earlier, Sarah had phoned Sally and Matthew to explain their predicament and apologise which had under-standably been met with disappointment but the promise of spending a weekend together over the next month made both parties happier.

Sarah worked quickly and diligently in the kitchen preparing for the Christmas Day meal. On the bench was a small ham and two chickens, the last of the turkeys having been sold at this late point on Christmas Eve, chicken seemed the next best option. After stuffing the chicken and escorting them both to the fridge, Sarah took to the ham, and gave it a cherry-studded surface together with a rich cherry glaze. The ham now accompanying the chicken, she worked on a quick-mix pudding. Having crumbled a canned plum pudding into a bowl she added prunes, dates, sultanas, cherries and mixed peel, then combined it with a quarter of a cup each of sherry, orange juice and rum, finely topping it off with an egg, then mixed it all together and placed the contents of the bowl into a steamer, ready to steam for two hours in the morning. Freshly baked mince pies were wrapped in a tea towel to retain their freshness for the next day, baby potatoes were washed, ready to bake and baby carrots were peeled, ready to steam. When she had made a brandy custard and placed some fresh fruit and Christmas cherries into a bowl, she was content at last that Christmas lunch was prepared and would be worth the effort she had put into it. Pulling her apron off Sarah walked to the bathroom and washed the numerous ingredients off her face, no longer a walking sample of her cooking, she checked on their guest and lay back in a chair to wait for Eden.

Unintended sleep fell upon her and an hour and a half later she woke to find a Christmas angel on her lap and Eden sitting on the floor struggling with power adaptors and cables. "Close your eyes for a minute Sarah." Eden asked her. She obliged and waited. "You can open them now," he finally said with a relieved voice. Opening her eyes she was stunned by the fresh scented and beautifully decorated Christmas tree. As she stared at the beauty of it, the soft colored lights on the tree stared back at her.

"Oh, Eden it's stunning. How did you manage this?"

"Well actually, it more or less managed me. I've got needles in my shirt and pants, I got tangled, literally, in the lights and it had me stuck in the lift for twenty minutes but if you find it stunning then it was worth it. Now you've got to finish it and pop this angel on the top," he said, as he placed the angel in her hand, scooped her up and lifted her enough to manage setting it on the highest branch.

"It's beautiful Eden, really beautiful." she said still in his arms.

"No, it's beautiful you're really beautiful." he said as he carried her into their bedroom, shut the door and laid her on the bed.

After they had made love, unlike Eden, Sarah could not sleep. She had an idea in her head and responding to it then and there, she knew would put her mind to rest. After watching Eden for several minutes as he slept she got up, put on some warm leggings and a sweater, and went quietly into the kitchen to make a warm cup of milk. While the cold milk slowly succumbed to the heat of the flame, she found her camera and loaded it with a new roll of film. The polaroid camera was her pride and joy, it was a gift from Eden last Christmas and she cherished it. With it she could photograph scenery or events that were impossible to take home with her and then transfer that image to canvas. She had used it sparingly though, for the film was expensive and she sometimes felt that using a photograph to transfer an image was somewhat akin to copying an image.

Camera in hand, she tiptoed to the door of Esme's room. "Charlie," she called in a whisper. The sleepy terrier lifted his head slowly and looked at her. With one ear up, the other down and his head at an angle he looked at her for a minute then sensibly decided to lay his head back down and continue sleeping. Sarah shrugged her shoulders and went back to the kitchen returning in a few minutes with a leftover slice of the meatloaf they had had for dinner that evening in a bowl. As she reappeared in the doorway the terrier sensed her presence and looked up at her again. Seeing the bowl in her hand spoke many words, he checked his sleeping mistress and then bounded off the bed and happily followed Sarah, or more so the bowl, into the kitchen. As he jumped at her feet, she laid some newspaper on the kitchen table and then put the bowl and the terrier on the newspaper. She waited until he had eaten and then patted him. The meal had made him alert and her patting relaxed him long enough for her to take a few steps back and take a shot of him as he sat in a perfect pose looking straight at the camera. Having checked the photo she patted him again and lifted him to the floor. "Ok Charlie, you can go back to sleep now, thanks."

The terrier headed back to his bed and Sarah having collected her hot milk took the photo and headed to the hallway. She slipped one of her painting sweaters on over the one she was wearing and placed a small white canvas on the easel. Giving the canvas an off-white background she sketched the frame of the terrier upon it. For the next hour she continued to paint, with photo in one hand and brush in the other. Finally, as she swallowed the last of the milk, she stood back and studied the silky-gray dog that looked back at her with his alert blue eyes. "Esme will be pleased," she thought to herself and with her idea now exacted in her mind she happily went back to bed and fell asleep.

The next morning, the snow still falling, Snowy and Charlie ensured that nobody would sleep in on Christmas Day. With vigorous honking and a driving bark, they had discovered each other once again. As they bounced around on the loungeroom floor, Sarah, Eden and Esme were busy slipping on dressing gowns to go and check on the pair. Standing in the loungeroom they watched and giggled at the endearing sight. Suddenly, the giggling, quacking and barking stopped as Esme put her hand to her mouth and exclaimed "Oh!"

The dog stopped playing and ran to his mistress's side and Sarah and Eden jumped up "Esme are you alright?" Sarah asked anxiously.

"I haven't seen a tree like that in ten years," Esme answered in a trance "Every year my dearest Samuel would bring me home a fresh green tree on Christmas Eve and I would decorate it. Then Samuel died and so I haven't seen or smelt a tree like that since."

"Well," Sarah said as she took Esme's hand "I'm glad you can see this one. Now you sit down in this chair next to the tree and I'll get you a cup of tea."

"And I'll fix us all some breakfast." Eden offered, still smiling at Esme's reaction.

Esme was a diminutive and frail woman. She had lived a wholesome and happy eighty-nine years as she had proudly told Eden and Sarah over dinner the prior evening. She had that magical beauty that few old women have, in that her appearance had retained a unique charm, which made her a definite eye catcher to this day. Her long, silver-grey hair was tied in an elegant bun. Her petite face was both attractive and dainty. Her eyes were soft and housed a bright twinkle and her demeanor was that of a fluttering lady. The beauty of her silky terrier made them an interesting and handsome pair.

After breakfast Esme had her first bath since she had left her home, wherever it was. Eden had locked Snowy into his travel container for Esme's bath knowing that his usual banging would probably come as quite a shock to an old lady trying to have a quiet bath. While Eden washed the breakfast dishes and Sarah busied herself putting the pudding on to steam and attending to other food, Charlie sat intently outside the bathroom door waiting for his mistress. Later, as Esme was taking rather a long time, the terrier saw fit to take a break for a minute and thus ran around looking for something to play with. Having found a toy he happily brought it into the kitchen and sat chewing it and throwing it into the air as Eden and Sarah worked. A few minutes passed before Sarah noticed the game and as she did she bent down and plucked the shoe from Charlie's mouth "Now Charlie," she said with a smile "I don't think Esme wants you to ruin her shoe. I'll get you some meatloaf instead, you can have a chew on that." she said as she popped the shoe on the top of the fridge and proceeded to wash her hands in the kitchen sink. Eden, having observed the situation, went to the fridge to get the meatloaf and as he opened the door his eye caught the inside of the shoe. Picking it up he read out aloud "9th on 7th Avenue – the 14th floor…"

"Pardon?" Sarah responded.

"There's an address written in this shoe," he answered scratching his head and reading it out again "9th on 7th Avenue – the 14th floor…"

Sarah clapped her hand's together "I'll bet that's Esme's address. She'll be thrilled."

With these words Esme entered the kitchen and as Charlie ran up to her she waved a finger at him "Now Charlie! What have you done with my shoe this time?"

Eden handed Esme the shoe "Charlie was playing with it and it's a good thing because we found an address in it!" he told her excitedly.

"Oh yes, these are my walking shoes. I always keep my address in my walking shoes, I never know when I might get…" with these words she stopped and the realisation of the significance of the address came to her. Just as Sarah had done she clapped her hands and then bent down and scooped her dog up "You're a clever dog Charlie, you are, you're a clever dog." she said kissing him repeatedly.

As Charlie enjoyed his kisses, Sarah kissed Eden on his ear as she whispered into it "And you're a clever boy too."

Looking up from Charlie, Esme stared at her hosts "You have both been so kind and I will never forget it. I have managed to forget where I live and forget that I'd written my address in my walking shoes, should such an occasion arise but I will never forget what you have done and with your blessing you must let me repay your kindness. If Samuel were here now he would be proud to shake your hands and I myself would be proud to give you both back some of the help and hospitality you have granted me."

"If you would share our company over Christmas lunch before we drive you home, Sarah and I would enjoy that very much. Having your company has been a pleasure so there is no more thanks necessary." Eden insisted.

"You are both too kind and to be your guest for lunch would be the best Christmas I have had in ten years." she said as she brushed a tear from her eye.

As Eden, Sarah, Esme, Snowy and Charlie sat down to lunch two hours later, Eden and Esme never ceased to marvel at Sarah's creation. The meal was so undeniably perfect that all ate as if they hadn't eaten in a week. Through all of this, Esme proved to be like an inquisitive child wanting to know everything about Sarah and Eden. All of her questions, they happily answered, from when they had met to what they were doing now. Were they happy in their apartment and how did they meet Snowy? An hour later, having eaten and talked a great deal, they left the table and settled around the Christmas tree. Eden reached under the tree, pulled out a parcel and handed it to Sarah. Sarah eased the paper off making sure not to rip it, a habit she had always had and as she took the lid off the enclosed box she discovered an envelope embossed with gold writing that read "The National Gallery of Art". Her hands shook as she reached for the envelope and opened it. Inside she found a gold embossed card that welcomed her as a member of the gallery for the next twelve months. Throwing her arms around her husband she said in a stunned voice "I'm so lucky. I will cherish this Eden and they won't be able to keep me out of there. Thank you."

"As long as you take some time out for me and Snowy, that's what I was hoping. I figured we should at least get you in the door before your work gets there first." he said with a wink.

At that moment Snowy seemed to be in the spirit of things as he plucked up the ribbon of a little box and dumped it in Eden's lap. "What's this Snowy?"

"He watched me wrap it, maybe he knows it's yours." Sarah explained.

Eden opened the box and as he pulled out the gold watch he was equally as stunned as Sarah had been by her gift. "My very first watch, oh Sarah it's beautiful, thank you." he said as he commenced wrapping it around his wrist with pride. "Would anyone care to know the time?" he enquired proudly.

"I think it's time for Esme to look at her present." Sarah laughed, and excused herself to leave the room for a minute. "Happy Christmas Esme from both of us." Sarah said as she gently placed the painting on Esme's lap, upon her return.

Esme stared at the painting in disbelief while Eden looked at his wife knowingly. This was the way that Sarah had always been, she could not forget anyone, ever, that was her way. "I'm sorry the paint still needs a little more drying time Esme but we hope you like it."

"Oh dear, I am quite overwhelmed." she responded with a faltering voice. "It is like looking at Charlie in the mirror."

"I know what you mean Esme. Sarah's work never ceases to overwhelm me."

"Charlie here, was quite an accommodating subject, thankfully, after a bit of meatloaf, that is." She told them as she patted the dog.

"When I get home I shall put it on the wall next to Samuel's picture. You are both too, too kind."

The three spent a couple of more hours sitting around the tree, talking and laughing, trading stories and experiences and watching Snowy and Charlie play together. "I don't think I've ever laughed so much in my entire life," giggled Esme "and I've lived a long time."

"Well my new watch tells me you must be getting tired and I'm sure we must be tiring you out."

"Indeed, on the contrary, I think not having you both around to enjoy will tire me out. I haven't been this happy in a long time, well, since I had my Samuel at least."

"Eden and I will miss you, we've had a lovely Christmas Day with you. After we take you home, if you'd like, maybe we could visit you every now and then?"

"That would be a real treat for Charlie and me!" she responded, looking thrilled at the prospect.

An hour later, Eden, Sarah, Esme and Charlie walked into the lift of Esme's apartment building. "Which floor, Esme?" Eden asked as he went to press one of the buttons. Esme's face suddenly had that blank look again, of which Sarah and Eden had come accustomed to.

"Your shoe, Esme." Sarah volunteered trying to help.

"Of course," Esme nodded as she took off her shoe and looked in, "the 14th floor, dear," she said. As they walked out of the lift Charlie barked, just as he had done once before. "I was right," thought Eden to himself "He was barking at the familiarity." They walked down the corridor until Esme stopped outside a door jammed with mail. "This is my apartment." she alerted them, as if pleased with herself for remembering "I always get the most mail." The three bent down to collect it and as they rose to their feet Esme's hands were so fully occupied with mail and Charlie's leash that Eden asked for the key. "It should be open," she confidently volunteered "I always leave my keys in the fruit bowl, that way burglars would never find them, I feel." Eden glanced at Sarah, noticing she looked as worried as he was and then opened the door.

Esme's apartment was small but enchanting. The floor was home to many antiques, the walls were covered from bottom to top with gold lined paper, windows were imbedded within lush, gold velvet curtains and white lace and the gold ceilings surrounded by their white cornice proudly exhibited matching chandeliers. Above the white, marble fireplace hung a large oil painting of her husband and to the right of the fireplace on the floor, sat what was obviously Charlie's bed. The apartment had ducted heating, which was to explain its stifling warmth. As Esme turned the heating off and opened windows, apologising for the heat as she did, Sarah found the kitchen and put the parcels she had been carrying down, picked up the jug she had found on the bench, filled it with water and turned it on. "Esme," she called out "I've put the kettle on, can I make you a cup of tea?"

"No, no dear, you have both done enough for me. You and Eden take a seat and I'll take care of the tea." she called back.

As Sarah walked back into the loungeroom she found Eden peering into a fruit bowl. "She's right Sarah, her keys are there amongst the fruit!"

"Let's talk about it over tea with her." she suggested.

"Good idea. She seems to have everything else organised though, I mean the place is immaculate."

"I don't know. I was just putting some of the left over food in the fridge. On one shelf she had some washing and on a another shelf there was a pile of magazines. Anyway, we'd better talk about it later. I'll go and see if I can help in the kitchen." she concluded getting up from the elegant armchair she had been sitting in, only to quickly sit down as Esme entered the room.

Esme had prepared some tea and sliced some of her own homemade fruitcake. While they were drinking their tea Eden located some tools and with Esme's direction hung the painting of Charlie exactly where she wanted it. Sarah raised the issue of the keys and gently suggested Esme must lock the door and take her keys with her. This suggestion, she appreciated and agreed with, but something, nonetheless worried her. Sensing what it was, Sarah asked "If you have a spare long chain from your jewellery box I'll show you a trick that I've used in the past."

As she returned and handed Sarah a chain, Sarah slid the chain through the key ring and as Esme caught on and lifted her hair at the back of her neck, Sarah slipped the necklace on. "Now if you just pop that under your blouse, nobody will know it's there and they can't get lost."

Esme was delighted "And if I forget they're there, the jingle will remind me." she volunteered and jingled the keys.

A short time later as the tea was finished and too much cake had been eaten on top of Christmas lunch, Esme's guests rose to leave. In a little over twenty four hours the friendship struck between them was strong. Sarah and Eden seemed to worry about her as if she were their own mother, if they had known one, and Esme wasn't looking forward to being without their company. "If there's anything you need Esme our telephone number is just by your phone," Eden reminded her.

"Oh, and there's a bit of meatloaf in the fridge for Charlie," Sarah mentioned kissing Charlie goodby as he sat contentedly in his owner's arms.

Esme saw them to the lift and twenty minutes later Sarah and Eden walked hand in hand out of the lift, in their own apartment building. Both had hardly spoken on the way home. "I hope she doesn't get lost again." Eden mumbled, breaking the silence.

"I can't stop thinking the same thing." Sarah responded.

"Look at us," Eden laughed "We've spent the last day worrying about her and we're still at it."

"You're right, I'll tell you what, let's make it an Esme worry free zone for the rest of the evening."

At that moment the phone began ringing. Eden picked it up "Eden Parks speaking…"

"Hello Eden, it's Esme here. I just wanted to check that you both arrived home safely?"

"Yes, thank you Esme, we've just walked in." Eden told her as he winked at Sarah "Are you ok?"

"Oh yes dear, I'm fine. Well, I'd better let you go then. Say hello to Sarah for me. Goodby dear."

"Goodby Esme. Look after yourself." Eden hung up the receiver and laughed "Now look who's worrying now." He concluded with a grin.

"She wasn't going for a walk again, was she?"

"Sarah! What happened to the Esme worry free zone?" Eden blurted out, now laughing incessantly "This is so ridiculous but ironic nonetheless." he conceded.

CHAPTER
FIVE

Sarah and Eden spent the few remaining hours of Christmas Day quietly. After a small supper they took a short stroll and then headed happily back to the apartment. For both, there was a sense that suddenly their busy year had caught up with them. They sat up for an hour and discussed some of the things, apart from sleep, they would enjoy doing over the following twelve days of their holiday. The first thing they must do, was unanimously agreed to, that they would sleep in the next morning, the second, which was again equally agreed with, was that they would finish discussing the must do's, in the morning. Having made these decisions they headed to bed and were asleep before Christmas had ended.

The next day, having complied with their first decision they boarded a bus en route to the mall. They stood on the steps of Lincoln Memorial and viewed the two miles of brilliant green laden with snow that led to the pure white dome of the

Capitol. The mall was a vibrant stage that hosted school marching bands, picnickers, runners, kite flyers and frisbee throwers. Surrounding the stage were magnificent museums and galleries with the focal point being Washington Monument. At this time of the year, pageants took center stage and the trees shared their branches with hundreds of Christmas lights. As they walked hand in hand they savored this splendor, felt the warmth of the people and watched snowballs fly through the air. They sampled hot dogs and drank hot chocolate and by the end of the day both felt exuberant and energized.

It was early morning when Eden and Sarah took their place in the queue at the White House east gate on Executive Avenue. Each day, White House staff would hand out a daily allocation of free, same-day, timed tickets and the recipients simply had to be early so as not to miss out. Quite by accident they had never toured this huge home that housed the head of state and to do so, they knew would relieve Bill who could not comprehend how two American citizens could call themselves such without having had this experience. After a stringent security check the tour entered through the East Wing lobby, passed the Garden Room and along a corridor lined with portraits of former first ladies. The tour was preceding quickly, but unlike the rest of the group Eden and Sarah managed to take a quick glance into the Library, the China Room, the Vermeil Room, and the oval Diplomatic Reception Room, all of which led off from this corridor. Realising they had separated from the others, they cautiously took a guess and climbed the stairs from the lobby, and by chance found the group entering the Green Room. "So it's definitely green," Eden whispered to Sarah "but it looks like all they do is sit here."

"You are quite right sir. The green room, is indeed green, it was once Jefferson's dining room, but it currently serves as a sitting room!" the tour guide interrupted with a pained face.

"If she doesn't cheer up she'll turn green." a robust woman said as she nudged Eden with unintended strength, in his chest.

"Ow! I mean how are you?" he responded in a semi shriek.

"Eden, you're being watched." Sarah informed him as she pointed secretly to a surly looking security guard.

"Don't worry, I'll behave myself now." he winked.

True to his word, he did behave himself as they entered the Blue Room but as they entered the Red Room, he couldn't resist. "Well, at least they're not square." he whispered again, as they perused yet another oval room. The group then proceeded to the State Dining Room, which was modestly sized and could seat one hundred and forty people. In this room Sarah became the talkative one, almost dancing with excitement as she spoke.

"Oh, look Eden, that's the George Healy portrait of Lincoln, he painted it from photographs and memory because he only ever saw Lincoln once. They say it's the best likeness of him ever painted."

"Really." Eden responded as he approached the painting and studied it.

On the way out they passed through the Cross Hall, complete with its portraits of more recent presidents, and then through the marbled lobby and north portico. The tour was completed with a walk around the outside fence, where Eden and Sarah took a few minutes to study the exterior view across the south lawn where the presidential helicopter arrived or departed.

It was late morning when they walked through the door of

740 6th St NW, and were greeted with the tempting smell of Burmese cooking. The thought of a Burmese lunch had taken them into Chinatown where the food was good and inexpensive. The restaurant was quiet and as they enjoyed their prawn appetisers, papaya salad and Burmese curries they decided they would walk to a nearby cinema and see a film before returning home. Three hours later they walked through their apartment door and collapsed in a couple of chairs, all the walking and fresh air having tired them. A few minutes later Sarah begrudgingly climbed out of her chair to answer the phone that had begun to ring. Returning to her chair minutes later she yawned and mumbled "That was Esme. She wants us to have afternoon tea with her tomorrow."

"Well the thought of veging out in a chair with a cup of tea and a bicky actually sounds appealing right now." he responded, and then paused "Gee I must be getting old."

"Up you get." Sarah said as she pulled Eden to his feet "Let's have a shower and put that theory to a test."

The next morning as Sarah entered the kitchen she found Eden playing touchdown with a ball of dough. "Is this recreation in the cooking sense or the sporting sense." she asked with a grin.

"You proved my theory wrong yesterday so I'm feeling pretty young again and I figured I'd get some exercise in while I'm making some scones."

"Ok, just promise me you won't play touchdown with the scones at Esme's place?"

"You whip me up a bowl of cream and it's a deal."

Hours later the three of them were enjoying scones, fruitcake, biscuits and tea. Esme was vibrant and quite obviously thrilled to have their company. As Sarah and Eden relayed their activities of the past few days, she responded with frequent giggles. "Your repertoire at the White House sounds quite like my Samuel. He was always making me laugh, in fact I can probably credit my age to that. You see, I believe that laughter is a natural medicine. You must never lose your wit Eden, to have a good wit is indeed a blessing!"

"I couldn't agree more Esme, although the security guard nearly lost something."

"And so did I," Sarah giggled "When I saw you playing touchdown with the scone dough."

Esme's eyebrows arched as she chewed the scone in her mouth with renewed interest. "I thought they seemed rather springy." she said with a wink. "Now I must show you both a little secret of mine. I've been quite busy myself the last few days." she told them as she rose to her feet.

They followed Esme out of the apartment to a neighbouring front door. "Now if I can just find the right key…" she said as she fingered through her keys. The first key she offered the lock complied with it and the door opened to a large sunny apartment that smelt strongly of new paint. Whilst unsure of the significance of the apartment Eden and Sarah followed her around as she pointed out each room. She showed them a sunny practical kitchen with an island bench, a bathroom with separate shower, a bath and toilet, two amazingly large bedrooms with walk-in- wardrobes, a large open plan lounge area and finally a large sunroom surrounded by windows offering a stunning view of city parkland. There was wall-to-wall peach colored carpet and peach colored curtains to match. Having concluded her tour Esme clapped her hands together. "Well, I do hope you like it?" she asked looking for their response only to have them look at each other questioningly.

"It's a lovely apartment Esme." Sarah volunteered "It's sunny and spacious and the coloring is just gorgeous… It's great isn't it Eden?"

"Absolutely." he responded with determination.

"The tenants you get will be delighted." Sarah assured Esme, now feeling confident that this was the essence of her question.

"So you do like it, that's wonderful! Now I don't need this key anymore and you most certainly do." she told them as she handed the key to Sarah.

"Oh, I'm sorry. I think Eden and I have misunderstood you, we're not sure why you want us to have the key."

"No my dear, you're quite right. I haven't explained at all, have I? You both must think I'm quite mad. Let's have another cup of tea and I'll explain everything to you."

As they sipped their steaming tea, Esme explained that the apartment belonged to her and had been left empty and unused for some time. Over the past two days she had enlisted a tribe of tradespeople to fix numerous things and brighten it up. She had apparently had a sleepless night the day before as she lay all night trying to think of a way to repay them for their kindness. After much thought she decided they might enjoy a rent-free apartment in which to live. Also, she admitted, the idea of having them as neighbors pleased her immensely. Eden and Sarah sat quietly through this explanation and their faces responded with even greater amazement. Noticing this, Esme put her cup of tea down and said "Oh dear, I've confused you again, haven't I?"

"No, quite the opposite Esme," Eden said, as he glanced at Sarah looking for her confirmation "it's just we're a little overwhelmed at your offer."

"That's right," Sarah nodded "Also if you had us living in your apartment you would be losing a sizeable sum of rent each month."

"But I have no need for the money and as Samuel would tell you if he could, I was never an avid spender of it, in all of my life. I have grown quite fond of you both and what I would enjoy is your company over a cup of tea, when you can manage the time. I know you both work very hard and I wouldn't want to be a disruption."

"Given that we've grown fond of you, I know we'd both welcome any disruption but Sarah's right, your offer is way too generous and we could still drive over and see you regularly anyway."

"Let me put the kettle on for one last cup of tea and while I'm making it, you could both discuss it and hopefully change your minds." she asked with an almost pleading expression.

She trotted off with Charlie in tow and Sarah and Eden did as they were asked and fell into a discussion on the issue. By coincidence Esme seemed to take rather a long time over her tea making and after a lengthy discussion, they decided to accept her offer. The offer was indeed exciting to them but the generosity of it was difficult to accept. This said, they decided they didn't have the heart to reject it for Esme's sake. Esme returned, put the tea tray on the table, clasped her hands together and perused their faces inquiringly. "We'll have to swallow the tea and run Esme, it seems we've got some packing to do!" Eden answered her.

"Oh, I'm so excited!" she exclaimed.

"Thank you Esme," Sarah said kissing her on the cheek "This is really very kind of you. It will be a treat to live in such a lovely apartment and wonderful to be your neighbor but we'd like to make a deal. We've accepted your generous offer and we would like you to accept some help from us when you need it. If you need some errands run, shopping done or meals cooked then we would enjoy being able to do that for you."

"But you're both so busy!" she paused "but... if it means

you'll stay, we have a deal." she agreed.

Three hectic days ensued as Eden and Sarah packed at one end and unpacked at the other. Eden hired a trailer, which made the entire process both economical and quick. At length they said goodbye to their old home and were somewhat ready for their first night in their new residence. Snowy had coped well with the move and on establishing his new home came complete with a shower door he was quite at ease. Sarah and Eden however, were exhausted. Moving a studio to another location, they discovered, was a painstaking job. Despite their best efforts, one painting was badly damaged. The upset this caused was compounded by the fact that the particular piece had already been sold and was due to be collected the following day. Sarah quickly rectified the problem by phoning the buyers and offering to paint a larger version of the painting, for the same price, within the following four weeks.

It was 31 December, 1970 and despite the fact that they had just moved in, Sarah and Eden decided to take a break from unpacking boxes and spend a part of their first evening in their new home celebrating New Years Eve in the same way as many Washington citizens did. They braved the snow and caught the train to the Old Post Office at the corner of 12th Street and Pennsylvania Avenue, NW. A piece of Victorian romanesque, the seventy-year-old building had survived a proposed demolition, thanks to public outcry and was more commonly referred to now, as the Pavilion. With its soaring glass-roofed atrium, the Pavilion housed dozens of little shops and restaurants and was renowned for its open stage concerts on New Year's Eve. After adding to the food consumption and enjoying the show, they took the glass-encased elevator to the 9th floor and another to the 12th to take in the view from the three hundred and fifteen foot clock tower. Being the third tallest structure in the city, the view of Washington on this New Year's Eve was indeed breathtaking and a perfect accompaniment to the evening. Feeling revitalised by dinner, the show and the stunning view of their city they decided to pick up some champagne and count the New Year in at their new home.

Back in the apartment, champagne in hand, they listened to the people in the streets below as they cheered "…three, two, one! Happy New Year!" Arm in arm, they took a sip from each other's glass, and spent the first few minutes of the New Year with their mouths kissing and caressing each other. "I love you." Sarah whispered as his lips roamed her neck and his hand drew her waist tight to his.

"My heart and soul is yours darling and every day, I am so thankful for that. I love life and the world, but without you I can't imagine loving it at all. You are my life."

Over the next hour neither spoke but communicated with touch as their bodies and minds made love to each other. Later, as Sarah sat in Eden's lap, they sipped champagne, talked and watched the stars twinkle back at them, through the sunroom window. Soon they were in their bed fast asleep.

The next day they worked fastidiously, unpacking, sorting and organizing. The pile of empty boxes was beginning to outdo the pile of full boxes and the apartment was looking more like their own. At midday, Esme arrived pushing a trolley laden with sandwiches and tea and Sarah and Eden sat down to a well-earned rest. In no time, Esme sensed they were anxious to continue, so feeling content that they had eaten, she left them to complete their work. By late evening their work was done and after surveying their efforts they semi mumbled to each other and staggered to bed.

The next morning Sarah woke up early to the sound of Eden working in the kitchen. As she lay with her eyes half open she decided she must get up and help but the comfort and warmth of the bed seemed to insist that she needed more sleep. Giving in to the latter, she went back to sleep only to be woken fifteen minutes later to what seemed to be total chaos going on in the kitchen. As she turned to look at the clock she was shocked to see Eden beside her fast asleep. "It must be Esme." she thought to herself and as she reached for her gown and nudged the sleeping body next to her "Wake up Eden, I think Esme's making breakfast."

"It's too early to go next door." He mumbled.

"In our apartment Eden, Esme's in our kitchen."

"What?" he mumbled as he sat up and watched Sarah allready hurrying to the kitchen.

As Sarah reached the kitchen, she suddenly felt faint and as the room blurred in front of her eyes, she felt something hit her in the face. Within a second she fainted and crumbled to the floor.

"Oh, shit!" came a worried voice from near the stove.

"Hi Esme..." Eden said half asleep but cheerfully as he entered the kitchen, tripped over his wife and went crashing to the floor.

"Oh, gee, shit!" the voice spoke again.

Eden clamoured to his feet, rubbing his head and Bill rushed over to help him "Bill what are you doing here?" he asked still rubbing his head "Where's Esme?" he paused "and where's Sarah?"

"Sarah's behind you," Bill answered, his voice now quite shaken "I was making you guys breakfast and I hit her in the face with the omelette."

"You're kidding!" Eden said in disbelief.

"I wish I were." Bill muttered.

Eden bent down and picked Sarah up "Can you get the omelette off her?" Eden said, nodding towards the still intact omelette that lay on her chest. Bill quickly obliged. "and don't throw it out, I've got somewhere else to throw it when Sarah's ok!"

Eden carried her into the loungroom and lay her on the couch "Get me a bowl of cold water." he yelled out. Bill brought the water in promptly. Eden dipped his hand in the bowl and began flicking the water in Sarah's face, calling her name as he did. Within thirty seconds her eye's opened "What happened?" she paused "I think something hit me in the face." She finished looking bewildered.

"Hi Sarah," Bill said leaning over her "I'm the guilty one. I was flipping an omelette and the damm thing had a mind of its own and landed on top of you I'm afraid."

As she observed their worried faces and envisioned the sight of being clouted with an omelette she burst into hysterical laughter. Two minutes later, it seemed not one of them could stop laughing. Eden managed to wobble through his hysterics into the kitchen and returned, still bent over with laughter and with tears coming out of his eyes, with the offending omelette. "Hey Bill" he called "watch out, the damn things got a mind of its own again." he warned as he spun the omelette towards him.

Bill responded with perfect timing, catching the omelette as it traveled towards him by sticking his thumb through the middle of it. "Now it's a holy omelette with a mind of its own." he laughed as he demonstrated his handiwork.

"I've got to stop laughing," Sarah said, clutching her sides "I'm going to make some breakfast and it won't be omelettes!"

"I'll give you a hand." Bill offered as he opened a window and sent the omelette spinning into the fresh morning air.

"Is it safe?" she called back "your help?"

"Well my hand is but I don't know about the food in your house!" he grinned.

"I tell you what, you get the coffee going and I'll give Sarah a hand." Eden said slapping his hand on Bill's shoulder "you do know what you're doing with a kettle, don't you?" he chuckled.

Bill resigned himself to the coffee, sugar, milk and cream, while his friends quickly prepared a breakfast of muesli, toast, boiled eggs and orange juice. They were still laughing and chattering as they sat down at the table to eat. "So how did you let yourself in this morning?" Sarah asked.

"I flew into Washington two hours ago, I'm doing some work for Joe Duffy on his senatorial campaign and knowing how you both love my visits so much I thought I'd have breakfast with you, you see I've got to fly out tonight."

"Oh, what a shame!" Eden jibbed.

"Anyway, I went around to your old place and discovered the new address on the door so I came around here and a very sweet lady who couldn't seem to remember her name, was collecting her mail next door and after I explained who I was, she let me in. You guys were in noddy land so I thought I'd do you a favor and make…"

"Omelettes fly around the room." Eden jibbed again.

"A nice hot breakfast!" he continued, pulling a face at Eden.

"Well, that's very thoughtful Bill." Sarah winked.

"So who's the duck next door?" Bill asked.

"She's not a duck, she's a lady, her name is Esme Spalding. Gee, when you get voted in to some top job and I know you will, you'd better not refer to people as ducks, it wouldn't look good if you go around saying 'hey duck, have I got your vote?'" Eden laughed.

"We met Esme a week ago on Christmas Eve. She was out walking her dog, got a bit disorientated and couldn't remember where she lived, so Eden brought her home and she stayed with us on Christmas Eve. The next day we found her address and helped her home, she lives by herself with a little dog. Anyway, she really appreciated our help and over a few days we had made good friends so she amazingly offered us this apartment to live in, rent free as a thank you for our help, which Eden and I found quite overwhelming, but we figured if we accepted then we can be there for her a little bit because she lives by herself and since she lost her husband ten years ago she's been pretty lonely. Also, as you found, she's a bit forgetful, so we think she could use a bit of watching."

"Well good on you guys, you know it's sad, a lot of people wouldn't have bothered. I think that's great. Oh, and I had another reason to visit you guys. To say congrats mate!" he said slapping Eden on the back.

"Congrats for what?" Eden looked confused

"You don't know, I thought as much. Wait a minute." he said getting up from the table.

He went over to his bag and pulled out a magazine. As he sat down he dropped a copy of *Time* magazine in front of Eden "I was reading it on the plane and I was proud of you, so I thought I'd say congrats in person. Go on, turn to page six!"

Sarah leaned over and watched as Eden found page six. Both stared at an article entitled 'Young Achievers, most likely to succeed'. Eden ran his finger down the print and stopped in surprise when he found his name. As he rubbed his chin he read out aloud 'Eden Parks, twenty five, of Washington D.C., graduated from Georgetown University in 1968 with the highest scores in medicine ever recorded in the United States of America in the past quarter of a century. Mr Parks is currently completing his second year of residency at Georgetown University Medical Center and is tipped to be at the realm of surgical excellence in cardiac and transplant surgery and research of the future.' Eden sat back in his chair, ran his fingers through his uncombed, black hair and mumbled "Wow." to himself, seemingly in deep thought.

"I'll second that!" Sarah said as she wrapped her arms around him and kissed him.

"I didn't know that myself," he said, "I mean, I knew I had the top score in the state but I had no idea that it was the top score in the whole country and the best in twenty-five years. Maybe they've got it wrong."

"Eden, you're talking about *Time* magazine. They don't put facts in there without triple checking them. Ring the journalist if you like and check with him." Bill insisted.

"Yes," he paused "you're right. Gee, that's not bad."

"Eden, it's brilliant! I'm really proud of you." Sarah said, with an expression of pride on her face.

"I reckon I made it one of the best breakfasts you've had in a while with that bit of news." Bill grinned "Really, I was thrilled to see that. Major congratulations mate. You can operate on me any day but no research on me, ok."

"Research you, no, but an operation or two, or three, might help." Eden laughed "Only joking, you're the best, you know that. Thanks Bill for bringing that over, although, I'm never going to eat one of your omelettes again, who knows where you might have thrown them."

"Anyway, don't cry, I've got to get out of here and pretend I'm working." Bill said as he jumped up, grabbing his bag and another slice of toast "Oh, and by the way, I think I'm finally hooked."

"This I've got to hear. You hooked?" Eden said, feigning shock.

"Actually I think the terminology is I'm in love. Her name is Hillary, she's a Wellesley College graduate from Chicago, she's intelligent and stunning, and she actually loves me."

"She sounds wonderful Bill."

"She is wonderful Sarah, you'd love her and talking of that I've told her all about you guys and she's busting to meet you. The next time I'm in D.C., I'll bring her with me and we'll have dinner."

"She's really got you, hasn't she?" Eden said "Well, that's made my day. Look after her Bill, better than you look after your sax."

"Gee, that's a tall order! No, honestly, if I had to throw my sax away for her, I would. There you go, that proves I'm in love." he mused, almost to himself "Catch you guys soon, gotta go and big congrats again mate." He repeated as he flew out the door.

Sarah and Eden had six days of their holiday remaining, after Bill had left they decided to celebrate Eden's 'commendation', which they felt was an apt way of describing it, by going out to lunch and asking Esme out with them. They showered, dressed and tidied up the breakfast dishes then knocked on her door. Esme's ever cheerful voice called out "Come in, the door's open."

As they walked in, Sarah went straight over to Esme who was sitting at her desk surrounded by piles of mail and busy writing, put her arm around her and said "Esme, please promise us, you will keep your door locked all of the time? If you don't I'll have to get Eden to stand guard outside your door instead."

"You're quite right dear. I am sorry. In my younger years things were much safer and I find I live in the past in that respect. I simply won't leave it unlocked again!"

"Good for you, Esme." Eden said looking as pleased with her answer as Sarah did.

"Sarah and I are going for a walk and then we were hoping to take you out to lunch if you're free?"

"Oh, that sounds lovely. I'll pack this up straight away, tidy my hair and get a suitable hat.

Oh, it does sound exciting. I shall be ready the moment you are back."

"While you're getting ready Esme, have a think which restaurant you would prefer, then we'll head off there." Sarah said.

Esme had chosen the Old Ebbitt Grill, situated near the White House, on 675 15th St NW. As the three sat at the white linen covered table with vibrant miniature red roses as the centerpiece, Esme chatted excitedly. "My Samuel was a bank manager, you know. I was very proud of him. A part of his responsibilities was to entertain the bank's clients so we were always dining in the best of establishments but when Samuel and I had some free time to ourselves we always came here. The Old Ebbitt we called it then. The Ebbitt is twenty-five years older than I am, but I must say it still seems as lively as I feel today. Oh dear, I have missed it, I haven't been here since I lost my Samuel. When you said to choose a place I decided it was time I visited the Old Ebbitt again, I think Samuel would be pleased."

"In that case, we will just have to come here again and again." Sarah insisted as she passed her a menu.

"It sounds to me like Samuel was a very lucky man Esme." Eden said.

"You know, in the fifty-eight years we were married, there was not a day go past that Samuel didn't tell me the same thing." she told them as she tried to remove a tear from her eye, without them noticing "But I always felt, and I still do, that I was luckier."

"I know what you mean Esme." Sarah agreed smiling at Eden.

Eden reached for Sarah's hand and squeezed it "Now let's see if the food is as good as it was when Esme was last here."

All were very impressed with the quality and taste of the meal. Esme and Sarah chose the Maryland rockfish, while Eden settled for the grilled chicken salad. During the meal a tall, slender, white haired man in his sixties, approached their table. For a minute he stood still, staring at Esme. "Esme Spalding," he said with a pondering gaze across his face "what a pleasure to see you again. It's a while since I saw you last. How have you been?"

"It's very kind of you to ask sir. I have been well and I hope the same can be said for yourself?"

"Indeed the same can be said, I'm glad to say and Charlie, is he well?"

"Quite well, thank you."

"Perhaps you could bring him by the surgery, he always enjoyed my attention. Ah, I do apologise for my manners," he said turning to Esme's company "David Withers is my name and you're?"

"Sarah and Eden Parks." Eden answered.

"A great pleasure to meet you both indeed. Now, Esme, can I look forward to seeing you and Charlie over the next few weeks? Or could I visit you both at your convenience?"

Esme looked quite perplexed as she smiled at the man "Thank you for your interest sir, I shall check my engagements and be sure to let you know."

In lieu of her answer, he clapped his hands to his chest "Oh dear, I've left my jacket at my table. Mr Parks, if you would be kind enough to come with me I shall give you a card that has my current phone number, then Esme will be able to get in touch?"

Eden got up and followed him to his table. He waited as he searched through the pockets of his jacket, finally producing a business card. "May I ask, are you a close friend of Esme's?"

"My wife and I have known her a short time but I believe Esme would consider us close friends."

"Well I have been Esme's physician for the past twenty years, or to put it more correctly, I have tried to be. You see Esme is one of those people who doesn't have the inclination or wish to have their health checked regularly, if at all. I was her husband's physician for ten years and tended to him before he died and ever since, I see very little of Esme. Constantly I have found myself worrying about her and for this reason I gave her a surprise home visit three months ago. She didn't seem to know who I was at the time and I noticed several other worrying factors. I gave her my card and asked her to come into the surgery for some tests but I never saw her after that. On the card is my address and details, if you and your wife could get her in for those tests, it would put my mind at rest."

"May I ask the nature of the tests?"

"I have reason to believe it's possible she is suffering from Alzheimer's disease and is probably approaching the mid stage of the disease."

As Eden studied the pattern on the carpet his eye's glazed over and after a fictitious cough to cover this, he looked up "We'll make sure that you see her within the week. Now I must excuse myself and be getting back to my table. I appreciate your interest in Esme."

That evening Eden relayed the conversation to Sarah. After much dialogue and many tears they decided to focus their energy on the steps that would be of benefit to Esme. Feeling drained by the thoughts that were swimming through their minds they went to bed early and were determined to have Esme in the surgery the next day.

The following morning they suggested to Esme that it might be nice to visit her friend David Withers and take Charlie with them. Esme, who always seemed to be amiable to any of their suggestions was happy to comply. Entering the surgery, an hour later, they found a waiting room full of people. They had just taken a seat when David came out, noticed them and put them at the top of the list by beckoning them into his room. "Hello Esme, what a treat it is to see you again," he told her with a huge smile on his face "and here's my little friend, Charlie." he continued, patting the dog as he spoke. "Now Esme, if you could take a seat here I'll just ask you a few questions and get you to do a few things for me." David moved his chair close to and opposite Esme and sat down. "Now Esme could you close your eyes and place your hands on your knees?" Esme did as he asked. David then stroked her right hand and asked her which hand he was stroking. Esme indicated her left hand. Then he stroked the right cheek on her face and when questioned which cheek she indicated her left cheek. David continued this several more times but was unable to elicit a correct answer from her. "Now Esme could you open your eyes and we'll repeat this a couple more times?" he asked.

With her eyes open, Esme still could not provide the right answers and seemed to be unaware of this herself. David then went on to ask her a few everyday questions. "Who is the president of the United States?"

"Mr Nixon."

"What's today's date?"

Esme scratched her head and smiled embarrassingly "I'm not sure."

"The month?"

"December." It was January.

"What year is it?"

"Nineteen…" she paused "something…"

Then he asked her to memorize three short phrases 'red shoes, black box, 300 Broadway', she repeated the phrases and he then asked her to spell 'home' and 'world' forwards and backwards. Esme could not manage this, nor could she manage to count down from one hundred to eighty, when asked. Finally, she was asked to repeat the phrases she had learned minutes earlier. 'red' was all she could remember.

"Well Esme, I think you have been very generous in letting me take up so much of your time today. If I could just ask one last favor of you? I just need one x-ray, which is very quick and simple to do."

"If it's simple and quick we could do it now Esme and then we could have some lunch at the Old Ebbit again." Sarah prompted.

"That would be wonderful." she said smiling at Sarah "Mr Withers we must hurry up with this x-ray or we will all be getting quite hungry!"

True to word, the x-ray took no time at all and half an hour later they were on their way to lunch. Before leaving the surgery Eden had quietly arranged to discuss David's diagnosis that evening over the telephone. Lunch, was again, a success as was the rest of the afternoon which was spent shopping. When they returned home Eden and Sarah saw Esme to her apartment, helped unpack her shopping, organized a cup of tea for her and then quietly left her to recuperate after the hectic day that it had been.

That night Sarah and Eden waited anxiously for David Withers to call. By nine thirty their patience was ebbing. "I can't stand this anymore Eden, let's ring him. Maybe he's forgotten."

"You could be right but I think we should give him another thirty minutes and then," he startled as the phone interrupted him. "that will be him." he reassured her "Eden Parks speaking."

"Yes hello Eden, it's David here, sorry to call so late."

"Not at all."

"I have just finished looking at Esme's x-ray and I'm afraid to say it shows what I had expected.

Her brain shows widespread loss of nerve tissue in the cortex. The x-ray also shows that the channels that circulate cerebral spinal fluid in the brain are enlarged which indicates that brain substance has been lost and fluid has filled the gap. The x-ray, together with her failings in the examinations today confirm overwhelmingly that she is suffering from Alzheimer's disease."

"Should Sarah and I talk Esme through this and explain what's going on?"

"Naturally she must be told. Given that she seems to be very fond of you both, it would be much better for her if it was to come from you. Also she has no living family, so between the three of us, there will have to be some thought given to an appropriate institution for her in the future."

"I can't see us doing that. I mean we haven't discussed any of this yet but I'm sure Sarah and I can look after her."

"You need to look to six months from now. By then, she will more than likely be a deadweight both physically and mentally. She will probably be confined to a chair, need bathing, toileting, feeding and whereas she knows she is forgetting things now, by then she won't even know she has forgotten anything. Basically she will need twenty four hour care, and this, to say the very least is completely draining on the carer."

"Nonetheless, I still can't see us putting her in a home. I'm sure there's social services available that could help. I mean her dog and her home is her world, how do you take that away from somebody?"

"Um, well the disease itself will take all that away, over time, sadly."

"Look, we'll talk to Esme and we'll do a lot of talking ourselves and in a few days, we'll get back to you."

"If you need me in between, you've got my number."

"Yep, thanks."

Sarah and Eden sat talking long into the evening and by the time they took themselves to bed it was early morning. Already, they felt mentally drained. Both agreed they couldn't and wouldn't consider a home and yet they knew the option they preferred wouldn't be an easy one. Their minds were made up however, this they would tackle themselves. It was early afternoon when they woke, in no time they found themselves sitting down with Esme and talking her through the information they had learnt. Esme however, insisted she was fine and simply refused to condone the thought that she had this illness. Her forgetfulness, she insisted was only an old lady's bad memory and she anxiously wanted them to accept this. Finally, for her sake they pretended to accept it, believing that if she was happier to see it this way then what was the point in arguing with or subsequently upsetting her further. They had done the right thing and told her, now the only other consideration was that she be happy.

CHAPTER
SIX

The remaining days of their holiday passed quickly and as Sarah set to work, to repaint the damaged painting, Eden showered, ate, and left for the hospital. As he entered the hospital foyer and approached the reception desk he was greeted with cheers from his co-workers. His first response was to look around to see who they were cheering at and with this to no avail, to study his clothes to make sure nothing was on inside out. As Simon walked out and joined the cheers, Eden's confusion was answered. Simon was the only doctor in the entire hospital who was permitted to wear civvies, although nobody knew why. As such, his typical wardrobe consisted of a pair of denim jeans and a T-shirt, usually white. Eden stared at Simon's T-shirt and realised that the words from the article in *Time* magazine had been copied on to it. "I've worn this T-shirt five days running, with some washes in between of course!" Simon announced to Eden, in front of his co-workers.

"That's great Simon, but how about making this the last?" Eden asked, looking less than impressed.

"If you promise to wear yours, it's a deal." Simon responded as he reached behind the desk and tossed Eden an identical one.

"Ok! I promise to wear it." Eden conceded, as he mumbled to himself "At home."

After numerous pats on the back and congratulatory words, he was left to continue down the hall to the staff room, change and get on with his day's work.

The day proved to be more than hectic, and by early afternoon Eden was running well behind. In situations like this, in the past, he had mastered a technique of jogging from room to room. Jogging now, around the corner with charts in one hand and fruit salad in the other, he came to an abrupt stop as he collided with the chief of staff. "There's no need to rush through your work, you'll give yourself a hernia. 'At your own ease' I always say 'at your own ease'. If it doesn't get done, it's not good enough but at least you don't have a hernia." he winked "Now, I've been looking for you, two things:" he said, taking the salad from Eden's hand and studying it "we would like to speak to you in the boardroom at three o'clock tomorrow, Dr. Carmichael has asked me to ask you to take over one of his ops this afternoon. Here are the charts, any other queries page him and remember 'at your own ease.'" he mumbled with a mouth full of fruit as he walked away with Eden's lunch.

An hour later, as Eden scrubbed in, he couldn't help but notice how calm he felt, in comparison to his last op, this, he found very pleasing. The patient was in for an abdominal aorta resection and replacement, to repair an injury to the aorta that could not be repaired by suturing alone. The operation itself was a simple one but it was one of the few remaining surgical procedures for which speed was essential.

While he waited as the patient was anesthetized, shaved and scrubbed with soap and antiseptic, he directed a nurse to put some classical music on. As the music played softly, he cut through the skin, fat, fascia and muscle, and, requesting retractors, he spread open the incision site. He ligated the bleeding vessels and exposed the damaged portion of the aorta. He had chosen not to construct a temporary bypass, but instead, rely on speed to avoid damage to portions of the body that would lose their blood supply once the aorta was clamped. He knew if he was too slow the blood supply to the spine would be destroyed, and paralysis of the lower body could occur. With the damaged section clamped off, he cut between the clamps and removed it, leaving cuffs to which the graft would be attached. He inserted the graft and clamped it into place. Then he unclamped the aorta and making sure there were no leaks he closed the body wall in layers and bandaged the incision. "Good work guys, we're done! Now Mrs Spinx here needs to finish her nap."

Two hours later as Eden entered Mrs Spinx's room, he smiled to himself as he stared at the huge family that was quietly and cheerfully gathered around her bed. Mr Spinx, the patient's husband was the first to notice him "Dr Parks. Everybody, this is Dr Parks. This young man is the one responsible for fixing our Rose. I will never forget what you have done for my wife today and for that I thank you from the bottom of my heart. My little ballerina here," he continued as he took his wife's hand "is my life. Without her I don't know where I would have been the last thirty years. Today, you have let us continue our lives together, and for that, again I and all of us thank you."

"Well, I'm glad to say your wife will be fighting fit within a few weeks." Eden responded as he patted Mr Spinx on the back and winked at his wife.

"Now I must ask for just five minutes with you Mrs Spinx, then I'll leave you alone with your family."

Mr Spinx ushered everybody out and having kissed his wife on the forehead, left to join them. "So you are a ballerina?" Eden asked as he began examining Rose.

"Many years ago, yes. Ever since, I have been very fortunate to teach the subject."

"I'm sure your student's would consider themselves the fortunate ones."

"Oh yes. A good few of them have assured me of that, I'm lucky to say."

"Your blood pressure's good, pulse rate is amazing, we should be able to get you off that drip in a couple of hours. Now I'll just check a couple of reflexes and then let you have your family back."

"I didn't want to say anything in front of the others, but since I came to, from the anesthetic I seem to have no feeling in my legs and to say the least, I feel a bit unnerved. When is it going to come back?"

This was the last thing Eden expected to hear. The operation had gone both smoothly and quickly. "How, on earth could she have no feeling in her legs?" he thought to himself. Nonetheless he felt gripped with panic. Somehow the expression on his face indicated the opposite to his patient as she lay staring at him, still waiting for a response. Instinct told him to hide his apprehension and fear as he commenced testing her reflexes. "Just let me do some checks first?" he requested calmly with a smile. His alarm grew as she failed to respond to any of this. "Now, Mrs Spinx, I want you to sit back, relax and try and eat something. I'll be back in one hour and I want to hear what you've had to eat. Oh, and if you could limit everyone except Mr Spinx to twenty more minutes of visiting, then some rest would be in order.

With pre-op, op and post-op reports under his arm, he made his way to the staff room, leaned over the sink to splash some water on his face, poured a coffee and threw himself down at a table where he surrounded himself in the facts pertaining to Mrs Spinx's case and what had happened in the operating room. He went over and over her previous medical history looking for anything that might have caused complications. He checked and rechecked the duration of the procedure, each time staring at the clearly written 'seventeen minutes' that stared back at him from the op report. He had used a sutureless, ringed graft, which he knew was the most recommended for this procedure. Unsure of where to look further for an explanation or reason he felt at a total loss. According to the paperwork in front of him this complication shouldn't exist. If paralysis was present now he knew one hour from now most likely wouldn't change this. "How was he to explain this to Mrs Spinx?" he thought to himself. As these thoughts spun through his mind, so too, did images of Mrs Spinx walking into the hospital and leaving the hospital in a wheelchair. "Was there something that he had done or not done that would have caused this?" he asked himself over and over. He felt distraught and his love of medicine suddenly seemed transposed by fear of it.

The door to the staffroom flew open as two doctors barged in deep in a discussion. "Hey Eden," one of them said "you're just the one to ask. We're discussing the merits of…gee you look awful! Are you alright?"

"Far from it, either of you know where Carmichael is?"

"Sure. He'd be in theatre right now. I mean the man is actually doing three transplants in one day, can you believe it? Why do you ask? What's up?"

"Don't have time to explain, gotta go!" Eden answered as he gathered the reports and ran out through the doorway.

Noticing the crowd at the lift, Eden took to the stairs. He darted up the three flights, past Kalowski's secretary, to her annoyance and into his room. Kalowski and a young woman sitting at the other side of his desk were obviously startled as he appeared. "Ah Eden... I don't believe you've met my daughter, Christine. Christine this is Eden Parks, one of our finest doctors, although he's much like you, he works too hard." he stated, waving his still bandaged finger at both of them.

"Talking of work, I'd better go Dad." Christine said as she collected her coat and purse " It's been a pleasure to meet you Eden. Bye Dad, I'll catch you on the weekend." she called back as she left the room.

"Sorry, I didn't mean to interrupt." Eden said.

"Not at all Eden. Now I can finish my whiskey," he said as he retrieved his whiskey glass from under his desk "I'm supposed to have a bypass in a week and Christine has got quite worked up about my whiskey consumption. Not that it's anything more than medicinal, but women just don't want to believe us on certain things, do they? Let me get you a glass. Actually, you look like you need the bottle!" "Thanks, but I really don't drink the stuff."

"Well it'll just have to keep you company then." he insisted placing a glass beside him "Now you look worried. What's the problem?"

"The short of it is, Carmichael asked me to do an abdominal aorta R and R early this afternoon which I finished about three hours ago, but forty five minutes ago when I checked on the patient she complained of no feeling in her legs which the reflex test I subsequently did confirmed. The procedure was timed at seventeen minutes and it all went, to my knowledge, smoothly. The patient is sixty-one. The procedure was done to correct an aneurism and she is otherwise healthy. I've gone through the reports and charts and I have no idea why there is any paralysis. I was hoping you could have a look at these," Eden asked handing him the reports "and find where I went wrong. I'm supposed to get back to her in ten minutes and I don't know what to tell her."

"Ok, shush for a minute and have some of your whiskey." Kalowski said as he polished off the last of his drink with serious thought and pressed one of the buttons on his intercom "Ah Rebecca, no calls for ten minutes please."

As Kalowski put on his glasses and began to read, Eden sat with one leg shaking, trying again to go through the events of the procedure in his mind. All of his thoughts however, kept being disturbed by one question, "What was he going to tell Mr and Mrs Spinx?" He watched the clock on the wall as fifteen minutes painstakingly ticked by. A further fifteen minutes traveled around the clock before Kalowski finally looked up.

"Well this is both interesting and a shame. All I can tell you is that I concur with you. I can't be more specific than that. I mean the standard time for this procedure is nineteen minutes, you did it in seventeen which is better than ideal. Choosing speed as opposed to a bypass, we both know is the best option. The appropriate graft was used and apart from the fact that she is an ex-smoker I can't see anything in her medical history that could have pre-empted the paralysis. If your thinking you had something to do with it, then I'm as guilty as you, because I would have done the procedure in exactly the same way and with the hundreds of aorta R and R's I've done, I could do one right now with my eyes shut."

"That's a relief," he paused "although somehow I don't feel any happier. She walked into this hospital and I've got to tell her that for some unknown reason she's going to spend probably the rest of her life in a wheelchair... or not necessarily! Sorry! Can you give me five?" he asked without waiting for a response.

Eden tore down the staircase, ran down the corridor and paused for a moment "Hernia," he said to himself, as he began to walk instead. "stuff this!" he concluded running again "I'd prefer a hernia to mimicking a snail." Entering their room, he found the Spinx's playing scrabble. "Hi, I'm going to be with you in fifteen minutes. Can I just check something with you? Have you moved house, or done or been through anything else out of the extraordinary in the last twelve months?

The Spinx's looked quite perplexed as they gazed at Eden. "No, not that I can think of." Mrs Spinx responded.

"Nothing at all?" he reiterated, looking disappointed at the response. Mrs Spinx shrugged, sensing his disappointment. Eden scratched his head and mumbled "I'll be back soon." as he left the room.

Heading back to the stairs he stopped and turned as Mr Spinx called out behind him. "Dr Parks. There is one thing you might want to know. Two years ago we lost our son. He joined up and went off to Vietnam. He was killed over there, he was only nineteen," he said with watery eyes "he was our only child. My wife has not been the same since and it's something she finds hard to talk about so that's why she didn't mention it. Is that any help to you?"

"I'm very sorry for your loss Mr Spinx but yes that is a great help to me. Has your wife mentioned to you that she has no feeling in her legs?"

"Yes, she said you would explain why and when it's coming back. It is coming back isn't it?"

"I think I'll have something fairly positive to tell you in ten minutes. Bare with me and I'll be back."

"You're a good lad. Thank you."

Eden strode back into Kalowski's office looking tired but happy. "I've just had a word with the patient and her husband and I think I've got it." he said sitting down and taking a gulp of the whiskey beside him.

"What, the cause of the paralysis?" Kalowski asked looking doubtful.

"Yes. You see at one of the conferences I went to they mentioned a study done recently called the Social Readjustment Rating Scale. A couple of doctors from the University of Washington, Thomas Holmes and Richard Rahe compiled some data indicating stress levels associated with certain events in people's lives and the effects of this stress on their mental and physical health. To get to the point I feel pretty sure the paralysis is just an illusion. I noticed on her medical history report that this is the first time she's ever had surgery and I've just discovered that she lost her son two years ago and apparently that hit her pretty badly. I think her mind, not her body is causing the paralysis. If you agree, I'd like to explain this to them and see if someone from psychiatry can't help her budge some feeling into her legs. I feel sure I'm right."

"Very interesting," Kalowski paused "I've got a friend who is excellent with this sort of thing.

Good work Eden. You go and talk to the patient and I'll ring and see how soon I can get him over here."

Eden spent the next thirty minutes explaining all to the

Spinx's who were both thrilled and relieved to hear this. An hour later he popped in, before leaving for the day to check on their progress. Mrs Spinx was eager for him to study her toes and as he did he was greeted by a zestful wriggle. "Well, that's made my day!" he smiled appreciatively "Keep at it Mrs Spinx, you're doing great. I'll pop in first thing in the morning and see what else you've got to show me."

When Eden walked into the apartment, half an hour later, he found a note on the island bench waiting for him. Sarah had run out of lime green paint and had gone out to pick some up. He grabbed a carton of milk out of the fridge and gulped down most of its contents, then he headed to the bedroom to lay down for a bit while he waited for her. As he lay staring at the ceiling, his mind was racing. The experience at the hospital was new to him and had shown him a side of medicine that he hadn't been acquainted with. "To think you've helped or caused a person to never walk again is monumentally overwhelming," he thought to himself. His love of medicine had subsided so quickly when he initially learnt of the paralysis, and this, in itself had frightened him. Medicine had always been something he trusted and relied on and today, for a short time, he had lost that trust. "If you can't rely on or trust the human body, how can you rely on or trust medicine?" he thought to himself. Today, he had learnt something invaluable. "If an accountant adds up a long list of amounts he's not going to know the total of the list until he gets to the bottom of it. He's following the principles of accounting but every set of figures is different. You can follow the principles of medicine" he thought to himself "but every person is different. What does the accountant do when the figures won't balance, does he fear them? No they interest him more. Principles won't necessarily give the right answer so judgment offer's its services. Likewise, the principles of medicine are always there but without the use of judgment one shouldn't expect them to balance." Today, he feared that medicine had let him down, but as he lay staring up at the ceiling he knew he had let it down. He had been too quick too blame medicine for not doing what it should and too slow to accompany the knowledge of what he had learnt over many years with the judgment it needed. Eden had always seen knowledge as something to treasure but without judgment the knowledge was of no use. With his eyes starting to close, he felt a kiss on the forehead. "Mrs Spinx's got her legs back and I've got judgment…" he mumbled, half asleep. A while later he awoke to the smell of dinner cooking. He fingered the folded piece of paper in his hand. Undoing it he read "Mrs Spinx's got her legs back — you've got judgment — I love you."

Over dinner, Eden relayed his day to Sarah and listened intently as she relayed hers. Later, they sat in a chair together and savoured each other's company. The days were always busy and the evenings were a time they cherished. Their love for each other was almost too strong and each of them knew this. They had always been there for each other, not themselves. Their love wasn't what many would deem 'sensible' and this Sarah and Eden were acutly aware of. Both loved their lives, careers and friends, both knew too well they couldn't and wouldn't want to live without the other. The closeness they had was as imperative to each other as the air they breathed. They were dangerously dependent on this closeness and to make it safer was impossible for neither wanted to. Their love was not selfish, but natural, neither had asked for such closeness, it had just happened. To the world, they would give paintings to look at and health to enjoy, to themselves they could and would only give each other.

The next day as Eden sat outside the boardroom waiting to be called in, Sarah sat at a small table near a window in the Chez Grand-Me`re restaurant waiting for one of Washington's top and most innovative gallery owners to arrive. As Sarah nervously sipped her mineral water Eden sat in deep thought with one leg shaking. Within a few minutes Sarah's appointment arrived looking as eccentric as she had been led to believe. A short, thin man with white hair, dressed in black with a black beret on top of his head and despite his hair color, in his early thirties. "Sarah darling, sorry to keep you waiting. It is a true pleasure to meet you!" he informed her, waving his hands around and beckoning a waiter in the process. "Maurice, your freshest snails dear, for two, and a fine red to match." he ordered.

"Thank you but I ate earlier." Sarah volunteered.

"Then you must simply poach some snails from my plate. One cannot leave this fine establishment without a snail or two in their belly. Isn't that right Maurice?"

"That cannot be argued with, Madam." the waiter nodded to Sarah.

As Sarah took a sip from her glass, trying to distract herself from the thought of even looking at, let alone, swallowing one of those little animals, her husband entered the boardroom. A dozen men and a great deal more paperwork lined the huge, oval table and as he took his seat he realized he knew all but three of them. He nervously reached for the water jug as he felt their eyes surveying him. "Thank you for your presence Eden, we'll get straight to the point." the Chief of Staff offered. "We are all overly aware that to have you at Georgetown Medical Centre is one of our greatest assets, and as such, we would like to offer you a proposal that we believe would suit both your's and the hospital's potential. Firstly, we would like your presence at all future board meetings, as a member, of course. Secondly, when your final year of residency is up, we believe in a matter of weeks, we would like you to head the cardiologist team and," he paused as they waited for Eden to stop choking on a sip of water he had swallowed "if you are interested," he continued "we would like you to familiarize yourself with our research programs and give one of them your expertise." Eden was stunned, as they waited for his response he shifted in his chair, gulped some more water down and wondered if he had lost it. "I must have misheard them." he thought to himself "No, I don't think I did."

"Dr Parks?" somebody prompted.

"Over here..." Eden answered in deep thought "I mean, sorry, um yes, ah! the research. Do you think the hospital might be interested in me setting up a new field of research? It's just that out of hours I've already been working on the possibility of producing a man-made heart."

"And you don't think that's biting a bit much off?"

"Well, I think we all know it's inevitable and like with all things, you've got to start somewhere to get to an end. If the board was to consent I don't think there would be a lack of organizations interested in funding it, and any developments would give the hospital great exposure."

"You're thinking like a board member already. Ok, let's go over it in more detail at the next meeting and vote on it then."

"As far as heading the cardiologist team, thank you, but I would like to decline the offer. I have a tremendous respect for Dr Kalowski and I don't believe I can give you what he can."

"Sorry Eden, we've left you a bit in the dark there," Dr Kalowski responded "you see, you remember I mentioned my need for bypass surgery next week? Well after the op I'd like to spend my days with my grandchildren. I've given this hospital enough of my life now and what's left I'd like to give to my family. We all feel that you are the most suited to taking over my position. There are others, of course, whose noses will be out of joint, given your age and the relatively short time you've been with us, but pleasing the staff isn't our priority, as I'm sure you understand. On a personal note I'm counting on you to fix me up when I'm on that table!"

"I'd be honored, and I'm honored, thank you, at your proposal. I'll work hard not to let you or the hospital down."

"Good, then on behalf of all of us welcome aboard and we are equally honored that you accept! I'll have my secretary go over your new package with you at your convenience. Now we seem to be done here so I'll see you all next week!"

Papers were gathered in a hurry, as each member left the room they made sure to give Eden a slap on the back offering congratulatory words. Ten minutes later Eden was still sitting in the boardroom by himself and was no less stunned when his pager beeped him back to reality. He smiled as he read the message 'I love you, call me when you've got a minute.' Quickly he scribbled down the number and headed off to the staffroom to return the call.

"Good afternoon, the Chez Grand-Me`re, can I help you?"

"Yes, could I speak to one of your diner's, Sarah Parks please?"

"Certainly sir, one moment!"

"Eden, I meant to tell you that I was having a meeting with Ben Zacov today" Sarah said excitedly.

"Gee, really, that's not bad, what happened?"

"Well he's just left and the worst of it is he talked me into eating snails but the amazing thing is they weren't actually bad, they were delicious."

SONIA ROWLEY

"What did he say about your work?"

"He hates it."

"Sarah! Come on." he shrieked, feigning exasperation.

"I'm sorry," she laughed "he's offered me an eight week, sole exhibition in his gallery. He wants to make up a gorgeous catalogue. He showed me a sample and you couldn't ask for better. The best of it all though, is the list of people he's organizing for the opening night.

You won't believe some of the names on it! Anyway the pressure's on now. I've got four weeks to get ready and hopefully do some justice to it all."

"Sarah, in four weeks they won't know what's hit them. Gee, I'm proud of you. The exhibition will be the best they've seen. You sure picked a gallery, I mean Ben Zacov, wow! I tell you what, if you really like those snails, go home, take a break from painting, if you remember how to," he paused and laughed "I'll leave now, then we can go shopping for a dress for the opening night and have snails for dinner at the restaurant, although I think I'll have to work myself up for the latter."

"Oh Eden, that sounds perfect, I'll book a table on my way out. I might be a bit late getting home though, I've got a couple of things to do on the way."

Eden left the hospital a short time later, his head still spinning with the day's events. On the way home he stopped to pick up some champagne and two bunches of flowers. He arrived home first, decided to have a warm shower before popping in on Esme to give her one of the bunches of flowers. Esme was pleased to see him, within minutes she had left her work at the desk and prepared a pot of tea. "The flowers are lovely, Eden, thank you." she said as he handed her a vase.

Somewhat on cue Sarah walked in with more flowers for Esme. Surveying and surmising the scene, she laughed

"You're just too special Esme! This is why we have to double up."

"I think I'm too lucky." Esme said with a wink "Now you've both been at work all day so sit down and let me pour you some tea."

An hour later after a great deal of laughing and conversation between the three, during which Sarah and Eden had managed to whip up a casserole and pop it in the oven, they left.

Later, they sat in the warmth of the restaurant and toasted to Sarah's coming exhibition. "You know the whole time I was talking to Ben I kept thinking that reaching this point is really your doing. Watching you work so hard has always tended to push me to do the same."

"No Sarah, you have a special gift and that's why you've reached this point. A million people could push themselves as you've done but they would never get there because they don't have that gift."

"That's another thing, I never stop wondering whether one of my parents may have been an artist?"

"Could be. What we do know for sure is they'd both be proud of you."

"Ben told me he likes to have each of his exhibitions dedicated to something. I want to dedicate this exhibition to you, if that's ok with you?"

"Careful, you don't want to ruin a good thing." he laughed "No, really, that's pretty special, thank you."

"Sir, Madame, our finest snails for your enjoyment." the waiter interrupted as he placed their meals in front of them.

"Now I'll dedicate the art of eating snails to you" Eden whispered "how on earth do you do it?"

"Just pretend they're not snails, and you'll like them! Eden,

I've got something else to tell you," she paused "but after all my babble, tell me about your day first."

"No, you go first."

"After you tell me about your day," she insisted with a smile.

"Well yesterday, I told you about Mrs Spinx, the lady who got her legs back, oh, and when I checked on her today she was almost ready to walk! Anyway, I forgot to tell you that I was asked to be in the boardroom today at three o'clock. I sat outside for ages waiting, finally they called me in, the room was awesome, to say the least. As it turns out they told me I was an asset to the hospital and they had a proposal for me."

"Really!"

"Yeah, and it's not a bad proposal, I mean I nearly fell out of the chair. Did I mention yesterday, Kalowski is having a heart bypass next week?"

"No, is he ok?"

"He seems to be great! Except he wants me to do the op. Anyway, he's resigning in a couple of weeks to spend more time with his family and they want me to be the new head of cardiology. That's why I nearly fell out of my chair."

"Wow!"

"They also want me on the hospital board as well as being involved in one of the hospital's research programs. I mentioned my interest in developing a man-made heart, but I think they thought I was mad, nonetheless, they're happy to discuss it and vote on it next week."

"Eden, this is amazing! I'm stunned, literally!"

"Don't worry, so was I, in fact I think I still am a bit."

"Well congratulations doesn't even seem appropriate does it? If this is where you're at, at twenty-five, where will you be at thirty-five!"

"I'll be a professional snail eater by then, maybe?"

Sarah topped the champagne flutes up "Well I think a toast is overdue 'to the capabilities of medicine with Eden Parks in it!'"

"We have had a big day haven't we? I have learnt one thing though."

"What?"

"I definitely don't like snails!" he laughed "now, that's my day so what's the other thing you were going to tell me?"

"Well, this bit of news is going to make the day and our whole lives significantly bigger, in fact you might want to check you're sitting properly in the chair." she warned him as her eyes began to cloud over.

Noticing this, Eden was worried "What is it Sarah?" he said as he leaned over and took her hands into his.

"Remember the last time Bill came over and omelettes were flying around the apartment?"

Eden nodded "Well, that morning I was walking into the kitchen and before the omelette even hit me I suddenly felt faint. With all the joking later I didn't think much about it, but ever since I've been having lots of faint spells. At first I put them down to tiredness, you know, with the move, worrying about Esme and my work, but today, during the meeting with Ben it happened again and I know I've been sleeping well the last couple of nights. I'm babbling again, aren't I?" he didn't answer as he gazed into her eyes. "On the way home today I went to the doctor and he confirmed what I'd been thinking. We're going to have a baby in eight months." Sarah's eyes clouded more as she stared at Eden waiting for his response. Eden's grip tightened around her hands while the rest of his body seemed motionless, with a look on his face that Sarah had never seen before. His next action was even less typical "We're going to have a baby! This is my beautiful wife Sarah and we're going to have a baby!" He exclaimed, rising on his feet, to the rest of the room. As the diner's cheered and clapped he sat back down as if he didn't even realise that he'd told the entire room and with his own eyes clouding, said "I love you Sarah," he paused wiping a tear from his eye "and I love you too!" He grinned as his eyes met with Sarah's stomach "Oh Sarah, I couldn't be happier!" Then with a sudden realisation he asked "Are you happy?"

"Aside from wanting to cry, I couldn't be happier either. The next eight months seems almost too long to wait."

"It seems a long time now but we'll be so busy getting everything perfect, it will go in no time. In fact, we'd better start tomorrow, we've got to think about names, toys, cribs and…"

"Eden, we've got eight months not eight days. Anyway, after today I feel exhausted, let's head home. You've got a late shift tomorrow so maybe we could treat ourselves and sleep in."

"You're right." he conceded signalling the waiter "Could we get the bill please?"

"Ah, no sir, the manager insists your meal is on the house, it's not every day we share such delightful news. Congratulations to you both!"

CHAPTER
SEVEN

The next morning they enjoyed sleeping in, but over the ensuing fortnight they were to have no such luxuries. Even the evenings were spent working and grabbing a snack for dinner. At length an evening came that they could spend together. As Eden entered the apartment complete with flowers, and a little jump suit that he had shopped for in his fleeting lunch hour, he could hear Sarah crying softly in the bathroom. Putting the flowers and jump suit down he went in. There she was sitting in the bath scrubbing at the paint on her arms. "What's causing the tears?" he asked, running his fingers through her hair.

"Oh, I'm just so tired, maybe I should just go to bed and stay there for a week, and I can't get this stupid paint off!"

"Well if you went to bed for a week I'd have to come with you or I'd miss you too much." he said with a wink "Now, let me deal with that paint." With a bottle of linseed oil out of the cabinet he dabbed some on a face washer and gently eased the paint off. "There, my beautiful, paintless wife." he said as he washed her back with a soapy sponge.

"I don't feel beautiful and what if I'm a hopeless mother? I mean I can't even get paint off my arms. How many people can't get paint off their skin and you come home and find me blubbering, I'm not even a good wife so how can I be a good mother?"

"You're right, you're not a good wife. You're a perfect wife. I mean I should know. As far as being a hopeless mother, that's impossible. With everything you do, you aim for perfection which never ceases to amaze me, that's why our child is going to have a brilliant mother.

Wait a minute and I'll be back." he said, returning a second later with the little jump suit. "Look at this." he said, as he dangled the suit in front of her "You and your body are hard at work making a tiny human being to fit into this. That's the most special thing on the earth but it's very tiring too, so if I were you, I'd be pretty teary as well, but I can't do what you're doing so my job is to make you as unteary as possible, and that's what I plan to do. So, are you unteary yet?" he asked as he put his arms around her.

Clothes and all, she dragged him into the bath and laughed as she said "I love you."

Wiping the soap out of his eyes, Eden grinned "I'll take that as a yes."

The weeks passed quickly, rolled into months, in what seemed to be no time at all, Sarah was six months pregnant and looking very much so. She had suffered little morning sickness in the first three months and relatively no other complications, the only exception now being that she felt huge and that her usual quick step had been replaced with a less than quick waddle. The opening night of her first exhibition had proved to be an occasion that both Eden and Sarah and more so, the art world, were determined not to let end. The mention of her name and work had escalated rapidly among the right circles. Ben Zacov, despite his airy ways, had become a close friend to them and for Sarah, he became her most honest and valuable adviser when she needed guidance. Galleries across the country were desperate to have her work on their walls, auction houses were using her name, and the sale of her work as drawing cards to fill their rooms on auction nights. Her work was selling for ten times more than it had a matter of months ago. Orders reached such a high number that it became common knowledge that for the privilege of acquiring a piece of her work, one could expect to wait up to eight months. The apartment had long since been barren of easels, boards and the smell of paint, since all had been moved to a modern studio, only a few blocks away. An assistant attended the studio three days a week and was kept busy checking supplies, cataloguing the work and attending to framing, among other things, thus leaving Sarah free to focus on her work. Amid all these changes, Sarah's main attention never diverted from Eden; although the child now wriggling inside her seemed to be instinctively coaching its mother in diverting her attention between husband and child for the coming months.

Eden had settled into his new role at the hospital admirably; now occupying a large office with an ensuite of his own overlooking three neighboring city parks. On the walls hung three of Sarah's paintings, in one corner there was a pram lined with bears and colorful toys hanging off the handle, complete with an abundance of soft blankets. It was ready and waiting in the event that dad could have his son or daughter with him, at work for short bursts. Along with his new job came a personal secretary who soon made it clear that she was a diligent worker and who seemed to have a natural rapport with both Eden and his patients. Shift work had been replaced with more regular hours, though they were seldom less than twelve in a day. His research proposal had been, to his surprise, unanimously voted in, with numerous organisations showing huge interest in funding it. Eden's vast transition from second year resident to Head of Cardiology had gone so smoothly that the only difficulty he seemed to encounter was in remembering that the salary he was now earning was as equally, vastly different.

Contrary to David Wither's expectations, Esme's Alzheimers had, thus far, failed to take a stronger grip on her mind. She was well and truly her usual, highly forgetful self, but no more forgetful than in the past. Her health, according to Dr Withers, had actually improved over the past six months. Sarah and Eden had managed to make Esme amiable to regular, eight weekly, medical checks and the reports from these checkups were pleasing to all. Her somewhat erratic blood pressure had settled to normal for her age, her blood test results were better than normal for her age, she had put on a comfortable amount of weight and she had more color in her face, than David had seen in years. She was spending less time at her desk the past six months in preference to spending her time with Sarah and Eden and was busy shopping for little parcels for the new arrival whom she saw as the grandchild, she never had. Once a week, without fail, Sarah and Eden left their work to have lunch at the Old Ebbit with Esme; every third night, over the past months they dined together. Sarah had employed a cheerful mother of nine adult children, in her early sixties to spend two hours a day in Esme's apartment attending to cleaning, ironing and generally, to Esme herself. Her daily visits had become yet another source of friendship for Esme. Charlie too, had blossomed under Snowy's wing. Apart from being at his mistress' side he was now used to daily romp abouts with his feathered friend.

Sally and Michael had come down twice from New York to visit, as had Sarah and Eden, gone to New York, to do the same. Sally had left nursing in preference of attending medical school; Michael's title at the newspaper had changed from Assistant Editor to Editor. Michael had managed to extract a week's annual leave, and Sally simply intended to take a week off from university to stay with Sarah and Eden in the first week of their child's birth. The intention, apparently to help out, as all were happy to agree they were more looking forward to attending to the baby, than to Sarah and Eden.

Bill was to be the child's godfather; this he saw as the biggest responsibility of his life, as yet. Suddenly, political issues relating to the very younger generation, had become intensely significant to him. At least once a month he would stay over with Eden and Sarah and each time he came equipped with an additional piece of furniture for the baby's room. Sarah and Eden had met Hillary on three occasions and decided they couldn't be more impressed with her. Bill's outlook and attitude had remarkedley matured under her influence and his vibrant happiness was obvious to all. His breakfast cooking had digressed from omelettes to scrambled eggs with all agreeing they were less prone to take flight.

It was late on Sunday morning, and already on this mid-summer day, the temperature had risen to thirty degrees. Sarah and Eden, together with about two dozen close friends, had celebrated their first anniversary, the night before. The party had gone on long into the evening. Esme was the first to leave, though she had insisted on staying to midnight; the last of the guests had left at four in the morning. Everyone had had a wonderful time, especially Esme who was thrilled to illustrate her dancing skills. After sleeping in, Sarah and Eden had breakfast, showered and began cleaning up the apartment. Snowy was a big help as he trotted around, apparently taking delight in picking up bits of rubbish in his beak and dropping them into the bin. Sarah and Eden weren't quite sure if this was a game or whether he was mimicking them. Nonetheless, apart from being a help, it was entertaining. "You know, there's enough cold leftovers here to eat for a week." Sarah called out from the kitchen.

"Great, that means a week of no cooking!" Eden called back.

"I might go and see if Esme wants to come and have some lunch with us."

"Good idea. Hey Snowy, do you want to go and have a play with Charlie?" Snowy dropped the piece of rubbish in his beak and did a dash after Sarah as she went out the door.

Sarah knocked on the door but got no response. "You know Snowy, I bet she's still in bed. I wouldn't be surprised after all that dancing." She said as she opened the door with her key. She was surprised not to find Charlie on the other side "Well maybe Charlie's got the tired bug too." she said to Snowy "Come on, let's get them up!" As Sarah walked into the bedroom, she froze, a matter of feet from Esme's bed. "Esme?" she tried to say but no voice came out. She was motionless as she stared at Charlie who was laying across his mistress's chest, and quietly whining, stopping only to lick her on her face, before he began again. With tears streaming down her face, Sarah walked to Esme's side and knelt down beside her. "Oh Esme." she cried as she kissed her on her forehead. Charlie began to lick the tears off Sarah's face, stopping to lick his mistress in between. Sarah clasped Esme's hand and tried to warm it by rubbing the back of it, talking to her soothingly as she did. "Esme, you can't die, you have to wake up. Charlie needs you and I need you. After Eden, I love you the most in the world and I can't say goodbye yet. please wake up? I've said goodbye before, to a mother I never knew. You've been there for me Esme and I don't know how to say goodbye to that. I can't lose you! Oh Esme, I'm sorry, I'm being selfish. You probably want to go and be with Samuel again. I'm sorry, I hope you're with him right now. I love you and I will always love you." Sarah kissed her hand and lay it on the bed to rest and then wiping her hand dry, she reached over and gently closed Esme's eyes. As she rose to her feet she picked Charlie up and held him close, as he quivered in her arms, she quivered in her heart. "It's ok Charlie, Esme's happy and we'll work very hard at making you happy." Turning to leave, she found Eden standing in the doorway. "Esme's gone Eden, she's with Samuel now."

"I know Sarah, I know you loved her but you're right, she would be happy now and of everything Esme deserves the most, is to be happy." he said as he wiped the tears from her face.

They sat in the sunroom, arm in arm, over the next two hours, neither speaking, comforting each other in silence, then as Snowy came over to tempt Charlie off Sarah's lap Eden got up to call David Withers. Over the next three days there were many tears and as much preparation as Eden and Sarah organized Esme's farewell. Charlie, Eden, Sarah and David Withers were, to their surprise, all that made up the tiny gathering at her funeral, this being vastly ironic as Eden and Sarah were to discover over the coming weeks. Esme was put to rest with Samuel and it was for Esme and Samuel's sake that Eden and Sarah were able to accept her departure, knowing that she would always be a void in their lives but that she was with Samuel, which was what she would want.

The next week was difficult for Eden and Sarah; neither could eat nor sleep properly. The death of someone they were close to was new and unknown to them. They had lost their own families when they were too young to know; they had only experienced the security and love of having each other. For both, Esme had been akin to a maternal figure and because of this their grief was compounded. Their days were occupied with going to work and the evenings with comforting each other.

The following week they received a phone call from a quietly spoken, middle-aged man, who identified himself as Esme's solicitor and repeatedly apologized for not having rung them earlier. That Esme had a solicitor was news to Eden and Sarah, but between the three, an appointment was agreed on, for the following morning.

Entering the reception of the city legal firm they were directed to take a seat amongst the many other clients waiting in the busy practice. There they sat quietly and in deep thought for the best part of an hour, until eventually they heard their name called. "Mr and Mrs Parks, Ian Grant, we spoke on the phone." he said as he shook their hands. "My apologies for keeping you waiting. If you'll come this way we'll get you seated with a cup of tea or coffee and get down to business."

Sure enough as they sat in the beautiful, glass-enclosed office, the solicitor's secretary promptly busied herself organizing the beverages. "Firstly," he began "my condolences on your loss. Since my father has just retired and I've taken over the main of his clients, I had the pleasure of meeting Esme a matter of weeks ago, when she wanted to make some changes to her will. I enjoyed every minute of the short time she spent with me and I could see, then, why my father has always spoken so highly of her. I'm sure you both must miss her considerably. Nonetheless, our job now is to get the ball rolling as regards to her wishes, so I should begin."

"Before you do I'd like to explain that Sarah and I live next door to Esme, in an apartment that she owns. Esme was insistent that we were not to pay any rent and given the circumstances Sarah and I will vacate the premises within a fortnight. We do ask though, that her dog Charlie, can leave with us, that's what Esme would want and Charlie wouldn't be happy anywhere else."

"According to Esme's will that's her wish entirely, so good, Charlie's organized and in good hands. As far as your apartment, Esme in fact owns the building and of all the eighty-three tenants there, none of them are paying rent. Are you aware that Esme was an extremely wealthy lady?"

"We knew she was comfortable, but wealthy, no." Sarah responded.

"I'll explain from the beginning and have my secretary organize some sandwiches, because if you'll bear with me, this may take a while."

After requesting some sandwiches and fresh tea and coffee, Ian Grant continued. "The first thing I should tell you is that Esme has left the entirety of her estate to you both..." he paused for a moment as he noticed the blood draining from their faces and having reestablished eye contact continued "included in her estate is this firm and all of its staff and as such, we are now all working for you. Over the years, Esme has channeled a great deal of her wealth into one area, charity.

She bought this firm nine years ago and has paid our wages and costs ever since, so that we're here for the people who can't afford legal representation. We are here for the poorest of the D.C. community, if they need genuine help, we help them without sending them a bill at the end." he paused, taking a breath. "Let me know if I'm going too fast for you. According to my father, Esme and her late husband Samuel, grew up in wealthy families and both inherited a great deal of money. Samuel was the manager of a highly respected and profitable bank, aside from this he had a passion for investment and the money market. Apparently, Samuel's mind with money was like Edison's with light. Shortly before his death, he and Esme were said to be one of the wealthiest couples in the country. When Samuel died, Esme sold the mansion and purchased the apartment building that you are living in now. They had never cared much for socialising, apparently preferring each other's companionship instead and so their huge fortune, was and has been unknown to most. Esme, herself, has lived a quiet existence ever since. Over the years, she has occupied herself with channeling millions of dollars into numerous charities, though none of the heads of these charities or indeed the benefactors have ever met her or even know her name. None of the people in her apartment building are paying rent, none of them know that she owns the building and so, none of them know just how far Esme's kindness extends. You see, she insisted on helping anyone and anybody but she preferred her help, to be kept as quiet as possible. Now you both look somewhat stunned by all of this, as I'm sure I would be in your position, so can I suggest, if you are agreeable, that I leave you for twenty minutes or so, to have a talk between yourselves, before I continue. My apologies again for keeping you waiting in the reception, we only learnt of Esme's passing two days ago and, as such, we have been up day and night, finalising and sorting her affairs, to pass on to you. My father and Esme were very good friends, but just before he retired, he had a stroke so I have more or less spent the time since, acquainting myself with her affairs and trying to please her as much as my father did. Anyway, enough said, I'll give you that breather I mentioned."

With that, he left his office, shutting the door behind him as he went.

"Do you think they'd mind if we went for a short walk?" Sarah whispered unintentionally with a tired voice.

"You're looking a bit pale but if you're up to it, let's go. The fresh air might do you some good."

The walk was devoid of conversation but not stupor. Their minds, already exhausted from their grief, were now shocked and stunned with this new reality. So much had happened since they had met Esme and, it seemed, her departure from this earth had no wish to encompass these happenings.

As they resumed their seats half an hour later, Sarah's face had some color in it and they both felt better for the fresh air. Ian Grant was waiting and anxious to continue. "Now, up until a month ago, Esme's will directed all of her estate to go to charity and to be slowly dispersed by myself over the next two decades. Her recent amendments were so extensive, however, that we drew up an entirely new will. This will directs, all money and assets, other than those promised to charities before her death, be passed on to you both only. Most wills I deal with every day note certain stipulations, Esme's will contains none of these, suffice to say, to be used as you both see fit and that Charlie was cared for by you as I mentioned. Now, we have sifted through her finances, as they stand today. Being as diverse as they are, it will be at least another week before we have a more accurate estimate. We have, however, a rough calculation of its worth. Collectively, there is around ten million in fixed assets and a further twenty-one million in liquid assets. These figures don't include the five million, which again is a rough calculation, that is owed to charities, this firm included. Now sixty per cent of the fixed assets are being used as charitable outlets, for example, the apartment building you live in. Esme owns the building and provides free housing to many people but this asset, costs continually in its maintenance, electricity bills, water bills, etc. Likewise, this firm, Esme owns the building and the company, but both have continual expenses in operation. So despite there being no stipulations in the will, you will, excuse the pun, both have to choose whether to sell or keep these assets and whether you want them to continue on a charitable basis. If the latter is so, there would be continual costs that you would have to meet. Now the other forty per cent of these fixed assets are profit earning, and bring in a sizeable sum, year after year. If you were to choose to keep the charitable assets going, the money from the profit earning assets would offset the costs. Now, all of this in such a large dose, is, I'm sure, probably hard to contend with. Nonetheless, my job is to put to you the crux of Esme's affairs as they stand and the crux of your inheritance. As I mentioned these figures will be more accurate in a week but if I may, again, offer a suggestion, that you take a couple of days or a week to mull over what I have told you and make some decision as to your wishes."

"Thank you, Mr Grant for your time and your hard work. I hope your staff and yourself try and get some rest over the next few days," Sarah said, with her gentle smile.

"Please call me Ian?"

"I think Eden and I would prefer to pay Esme's personal

effects in her apartment our first attention, but we will make every effort to get back to you shortly regarding the rest."

"Of course. That reminds me, however, I omitted to say that all of your staff here and myself are naturally at your complete disposal, should you require any assistance at all."

Sarah and Eden left the building and from a pay booth downstairs, they each made a phone call and organized the rest of the afternoon off. They were tired before they went to the appointment, losing Esme had had a tumultuous effect on both of them, but after sitting in the solicitor's office for three hours or more, and taking in this information, they felt consumed with fatigue. As they passed a cinema and noticed 'Little Big Man' with Dustin Hoffman was screening they decided that some time out watching a film might relieve their spinning minds. Eden purchased two tickets and guided Sarah through the dark cinema to a seat. As they tried to absorb themselves in the film they found the exercise fruitless and within twenty minutes they left the cinema and decided to continue their walk. "Gee, I miss her Eden."

"I know."

"Now I know why she was always so busy at her desk. You know, I asked her once about it and she just said she was finishing off Samuel's work. I didn't understand it then, but I do now."

"What do you mean?"

"Well Samuel worked hard to earn that money but they never really spent much of it on themselves, so Esme has been busy putting all of Samuel's hard work to use, spending the money on something worthwhile."

"You're right. What an amazing couple. People like that have got to be a real find in the world. Here's Esme helping all these people and only three people go to her funeral. If people had known what she did there'd be hundreds and hundreds of them there."

"And if someone did her a favor, like helping her find her way home she was just so appreciative."

"Well, I think we should try and cheer up a bit, that's what Esme would want. If she could be so cheerful without Samuel then we should learn from that and besides we've got this little one on the way, how lucky could we be."

"We couldn't be any luckier and you're right, we've got a lot to learn from Esme."

The following week was occupied with a great deal of discussion about Esme's estate and her wishes. Eventually, having made numerous decisions they found themselves once again, eating sandwiches and drinking tea and coffee in Ian Grant's office. On this occasion, Ian sat, more or less quietly, waiting for them to convey their thoughts.

"We've given everything you said a great deal of thought and we feel Esme would be pretty happy with our decisions. The details are still new to us but we've worked out some basics. This firm, we would like to see continue exactly as it has over the last nine years. Aside from that, you seem to have Esme's interests at heart, we don't have a solicitor and we would be pleased if you could be there for us with any legal advice we should need in the future.

Regarding the rest of the estate," Eden paused "ah, where do I begin? Oh yes, the rest of the fixed assets. Our feeling was to make the non-profit assets equal to profit earning assets, that way, both should constantly balance each other out. As to which ten per cent to deplete from the non profit assets will be the difficult question and some form of compensation would have to be worked out for those people affected. As to the twenty-one million, we would like to invest two thirds of it in similar ways as Samuel did and have all of the earnings, except for administrative cost of course, directed to designated charities, with a special emphasis on, some proportion of, going to medical research. Did I put all that correctly Sarah?"

"You did well," she said with a wink "but you forgot one thing…"

"Ah, Esme's story! I knew I'd forgotten something. This is our favorite part," he said grinning at Ian, who was looking perplexed. "We would like to use some of the money to research Esme and Samuel's life. Their childhood, their young adulthood, their marriage and after. Basically, we want someone to write a biography on them. A book that is guaranteed to be published and made accessible in most book stores."

"What a brilliant idea!" Ian exclaimed slapping his hand on his desk "They could even make a film out of it!"

"Well, I don't know how Esme would feel about that, you see the reasons are twofold. Firstly, Eden and I wanted people to know how special they were and what they did for so many people, and secondly, we thought the profits, could go to charity as well," Sarah explained.

Over the next few weeks, Eden and Sarah's life suddenly encompassed the huge workload that Esme had happily dealt with for years. For both, this workload kept their minds busy, thus softening the grief they felt for her. Contrary to Ian's advice, they staved off asking for help in these early weeks, preferring to use the opportunity as a learning process for themselves and learn they did. Suddenly, money took on a new dimension, as did people who needed it and they were determined to know what they were doing in both respects. Their evenings were spent sifting through boxes of paperwork that Eden collected from the solicitor's office every couple of days.

As the ensuing weeks presented themselves, only to dash past quickly, their child was fast outgrowing its home of the past eight months. While her child became more and more energetic inside her, Sarah became less and less energetic. For the first time in years Eden and Sarah grew accustomed to spending their evenings simply relaxing. Though this was new to them, both were aware that this was imperative to Sarah. They listened to music, took long baths together, played scrabble, read book after book on child rearing and talked endlessly about their little son or daughter to be. At night, as they lay in bed, Eden couldn't sleep unless he had one arm wrapped around Sarah's shoulder and the other around her stomach, that way as he said, he could enjoy feeling the kicks and thumps of his little child as he fell asleep.

After what had seemed an eternity of waiting they found themselves waking on the morning of their child's due date. Eden leaned over and kissed Sarah, talking to her stomach as he did "Hey, you can come out now," he said, then pausing for a minute "if you come out now I'll show you all your new toys!"

"Eden," Sarah laughed.

"Maybe he or she wants to sleep in."

"Good, that means I've got time to have a shower first," Sarah laughed again.

As Sarah headed off to the shower, Eden headed for the kitchen to get breakfast started. As he reached for the frypan he heard Bill's typical knock at the front door and responded with his typical answer. "We're definitely not at home Bill."

"Now would I visit you if you were at home?" Bill joked back.

"Now, now, children," Sarah said as she entered the kitchen.

"Well, I came over here to meet my godchild, but I can see I'm early, never mind, I can wait." he said, pulling the apron off Eden.

"What are you doing?" Eden asked.

"I think you'd better leave breakfast to me," Bill laughed.

"Why?"

"Eden, you just took two eggs out of the fridge and put them in the bin."

"I don't know about you, but Sarah and I don't eat the shells."

"Well it might help if you ate the contents. You forgot to crack them over the pan before you put them in the bin," Bill grinned as he put the apron on. "It's alright, you've got a good excuse to be distracted, I'll give you that. Now you look after your wife while I fix breakfast."

After breakfast Eden and Bill tidied up while Sarah occupied herself with checking and re-checking the baby's room. This checking process seemed to be catching, for no sooner had Eden and Bill finished their work, they too, seemed to find this a necessity. "Ok guys, I think we all agree the baby's room has been thoroughly checked. Why don't we sit down and have a game of scrabble?"

"We could go for a drive to the hospital and give the little one a hint," Eden volunteered.

"That's not a bad idea," Bill said looking enthused.

"And I thought pregnant women were supposed to be the crazy ones! You guys are unreal. You know that reminds me of a joke I heard the other day, 'women like the simple things in life.'"

"What?"

"Men," she grinned.

Finally the scrabble board did come out but as the day

passed they found this was to be the only coming. After dinner, Bill reluctantly left, having written down a list of about ten phone numbers, which he insisted they dial if anything was to happen in the next twenty-four hours. The next twenty-four hours came and went to no avail as did the next twelve days.

With the baby, now two weeks late, they woke up knowing that their child would be born today. The day before they had been told that an induced labor was necessary. The placenta would have done its job well over the past forty weeks but would have been less adequate since, thus the baby would need to be properly nourished, outside, in the real world.

It was the first day of November and the air was cold as they pulled into the hospital carpark. Eden quickly found a space to park and within minutes they were at the reception desk booking in. They filled out a long admittance form and watched as the woman wrote out two hospital wristbands, placing one of them around Sarah's wrist and the other safely with the records, ready to place around the baby's wrist later. With the paperwork complete they were shown to one of the birthing rooms in the hospital where Sarah changed into a nightie and climbed into bed. Though half an hour late the doctor finally appeared with an energetic and beaming look on his face. "Good morning, Mr and Mrs Parks, lets get started then." Within minutes he had ruptured Sarah's membranes, inserted a drip and then left, after ordering the midwife to page him when there was any sign of labor. For the next twenty minutes the midwife chatted to them incessantly and then disappeared to have some breakfast. The room was quiet as they sat there, trying to distract each other from their nervousness. Both remained undistractable though, the events of the next few hours were too enormous for them, to be distracted from them.

Within no time Sarah was complaining of feeling uncomfortable and ten minutes later she was asking Eden to look for the midwife. Eden tore out of the room and, as luck would have it, found the woman in the next room chatting with another staff member. "Sarah's feeling labor pains, we need you back!" he interrupted them.

"Oh, no, no, dear. It's too early for that," she responded before she quickly resumed her conversation again.

Eden's head was spinning and it was because of this that he reluctantly accepted what she had said and returned to Sarah to relay her words. "Well, this might be my first time at childbirth but I know the labor has started, I've been feeling contractions for ten minutes now. I think you'd better go back and tell her that early or not, I am having contractions and the labor has started."

The midwife looked doubtful as Eden relayed Sarah's words, minutes later, but this time followed him reluctantly back to the room.

"Now, I've just been telling your husband that it's too early for anything to be happening yet dear," she insisted as she checked the drip.

"I can feel contractions," Sarah insisted in return.

"Ok let me check if there has been any dilation and that should answer our question," she answered as she commenced doing so. "That's amazing, you're in labor dear and not much longer to go by the look of things. You should have said so."

Sarah and Eden traded exasperated expressions and in their minds both were wondering at this woman's abilities. As the midwife left the room to page the doctor, another two young nurses entered. Both busied themselves attending to Sarah and doing what was needed to be done to help. They seemed to know when to talk reassuringly and when to be quiet. Ten minutes had passed and things were moving quickly. The contractions had intensified in pain and were more frequent. As Eden held Sarah's hand and mopped her forehead, she was now looking somewhat panicked, like a scared little animal. "Wow, this is harder than I thought," she mumbled.

"I'm amazed at how brave you're being!" Eden responded as he stared into her eyes and then kissed her on the forehead.

As she listened to his words and stared back at him the panic released itself from her expression. At each contraction she began to look into Eden's eyes while Eden kept his grasp of her hand and continued to mop her forehead. Ten minutes later he watched an expression come over her face that he had never seen before. Her eyes were glazed and vacant and it was as if, in mind, she had left the room. He knew the pain was about as intense as it was going to get now and that the baby was only minutes away. Seconds later he felt someone grab his arm and as he turned around he noticed all the people in the room, including the obstetrician. The room was abuzz with busy staff and one of the nurses was directing him to have a look at his baby's crowning. "No, I'll be there in a minute, I need to stay with Sarah at the moment." The nurse smiled knowingly and busied herself again amongst the others. Minutes later he heard the obstetrician call excitedly "Here we go, come on little one." Eden leaned over and saw his child for the first time, a little girl, with a bewildered look on her face, as she worked her way into the obstetrician's waiting hands. He was numb with love and happiness as he stared at her tiny body and when Sarah tightened her grip on his hand, he knew this love and happiness was real and would be there with the three of them, for the rest of their days. With the most careful gentleness he had ever exacted in his life, he took his daughter from the obstetrician's hands and placed her on Sarah's chest. The love in Sarah's eyes was as remarkable as the tiny person who nestled into her chest, with her bright eyes fixed on her mother's face. Eden offered his daughter a finger to clasp, which she gripped thankfully and with the other hand he wiped away the tears that were streaming down Sarah's face and seemed oblivious to the tears that made their way down his cheek. "Aren't you beautiful!" a nurse said, running a finger across their daughter's forehead "What's her name?" she asked, looking at Sarah and Eden.

"Jane," Sarah answered.

"Well, if I could borrow Jane and Daddy for a minute, we'll get her weighed and wrap her in a blanket and have her straight back here in a couple of minutes."

While Sarah waited, a nurse came in saying she was doing her best to keep the crowd of visitors waiting outside, at bay. "I've told them that you've had a little girl and they're all ecstatic," she said "You let me know when you're up to it and I'll let them in," she continued.

Minutes later, the room was quiet as Sarah and Eden sat on the bed holding their daughter in their arms. "She's more beautiful than I could ever have imagined," Sarah whispered to Eden.

"She is," he whispered back. "She's precious."

"It's like a dream, isn't it?"

"The fact that it's not a dream is as overwhelming as looking at her."

"We adore you Jane," Sarah told her, as she stared into her daughter's eyes "and we love you more than we can explain, surfice to say, our hearts have melted. You are precious and you will always be precious and you are indeed a gift from God. Our little Jane, we will always love you more than life itself. Nothing will ever be more precious to us."

CHAPTER
EIGHT

I t was a cold winter day as the sun tried to break through the steel gray of the sky, to no avail. As Eden stood on the white marble steps of Washington Heart Hospital, the solid gray background of the towering building behind him, seemed in harmony with the sky. A huge contingent of media, clad in thick coats, had taken up residence on the steps of the hospital, over the past forty-eight hours, determined to be the first to hear and run with any news on the health of the vice-president, who had been admitted two days earlier. Eden's appearance was a welcome relief as they grabbed their mics and cameras and surrounded him with instant precision. "Dr Parks, can you tell us how the vice-president is?"

"Dr Parks, is it true, the vice-president suffered a stroke?"

"Is it true he had a visit from the president?"

"The vice-president has asked me to relay his warm wishes

to you all and assure you that he is feeling well and in good health," Eden answered, smiling gently back at them.

"Doctor, can you tell us why he was admitted?"

"His admission was due to a suspected stroke, but after exhausting all avenues of testing procedures, we have been pleased to inform the vice-president that he did not experience a stroke but more so the effects of working too hard and so both the staff and myself at Washington Heart believe that with vigilant rest over the next fortnight, the vice-president will be in excellent health."

"Did the president visit him?"

"No but at the president's request he has been kept fully informed of the situation."

"Will the vice president's future in politics be affected?"

"Not at all. He should be back at work in a fortnight and the only necessary change to his work, as we have informed him, should be the inclusion of a bit of 'r and r' each week, which, of course, is what we all need and should strive for."

"When will he be discharged?"

"I am not at liberty to divulge that, but I can repeat, that by all accounts, he is in fine health.

Now, if you will excuse me, I can see my wife and daughter waiting patiently for me to escort them to lunch. We're celebrating my daughter's twenty-first birthday. I wasn't late when she was born and I don't plan to be now. Thank you."

"If I could, Dr Parks, just ask one last question? How does the vice-president feel having the world's top cardiologist attending to him?"

"Well," Eden smiled "you'll have to ask him that. Again, thank you for your time."

As Eden made his way over to Sarah and Jane, he was followed by a couple of cameramen anxious to get the three on film but thwarted as Eden politely waved them away. "How's our birthday girl then?" he asked kissing first Sarah, then Jane on the forehead.

"Now come on Dad, we had a deal, remember!" Jane laughed her mother's laugh.

"What?"

"Eden, Jane's twenty-one, she's not a girl any more."

"Oh, yes, that deal, ok. How's our birthday lady? Is that better?"

"Much better, good boy," Jane grinned back.

"Well, don't look at me Eden, she has your humor, you taught her."

"Mum's right Dad. Alright, I didn't say boy and you won't hear that again," she joked "Where are we having lunch?"

"At the table."

"Dad!"

"Ok, you drive and your mother and I will direct you," he said handing her the keys.

"You're letting me drive, after the last time?"

"Ah, I've been doing my best to forget that," he nodded.

Jane had grown to be the image of her mother. She had her mother's pale skin and her delicate, sculptured face, with large, soft blue eyes and dainty lips. Likewise, her nose was tiny and dappled with the same freckles. She had her mother's height and delicate build. The only perceivable difference was her hair, though its color and texture was the same, Jane preferred to treat her hair to a mass of tight curls rather than its natural straightness. Her beauty was so mesmerising that it had precisely that effect on both the people who knew her and those who were strangers to her.

Also, like her mother, Jane had shown, from an early age, a natural affinity with art and all it encompassed. She had proved to be a gifted artist with a brush but had a greater interest in sculpture and, as such, had just completed studying under the instruction of Yves Montreaux in Paris. During this time her love of sculpture had intensified, as had the nature of her work. Her sculptures communicated a wide magnitude of messages and expressed an even wider magnitude of feelings. As Yves put it, quite aptly, to Eden and Sarah, on one of their many visits to Paris to see their daughter, 'Jane has one interest and one passion, for both they are sculpture and only sculpture'.

The two years that Jane had spent in Paris had been difficult for the three of them. Jane adored her parents and always seemed to be at her happiest when around them. For Sarah and Eden, their life for the past twenty-one years had evolved around their daughter and they were, as many of their friends would say, totally devoted to her. The three were each other's best friends and none took too well to being separated. Nonetheless, the two years had given each one of them a taste of the inevitable separations that come with a child growing up. During this time, they had, however, managed to see each other at least every second month. Either Jane would fly in from Paris for a couple of days, or Sarah and Eden would travel to her. These visits had had a twofold effect, apart from alleviating their missing each other, they were the only time each of them actually stopped working and took a break from their busy schedules. Together, they roamed the streets of Paris or, alternately Washington; eating in fine restaurants or having simple picnics in beautiful places. In the evenings they would enjoy the nightlife of either city or simply don aprons and share a kitchen and conversation as the three worked on a home cooked meal, which usually culminated in a game of scrabble later. They savored these visits and no sooner than one had ended they were looking forward to the next. Eventually, these visits had come to an end as Jane completed her two year study and returned to Washington, taking up residence in an apartment that her parents had bought for her only streets away from their own home.

After a quiet lunch in Jane's favorite restaurant, they walked up and down the Watergate Mall, going in and out of boutiques looking for an evening gown for Jane. Sarah and Eden had organized a surprise twenty-first birthday party that evening. They had described it to their daughter as dinner with a couple of guests and insisted she have a new dress to wear. While Sarah and Jane discussed one dress after the other, Eden took a moment to check his e-mail on his handheld pc. As he paced the parquetry floor, reading the messages off the screen he bumped into something. Promptly turning around he said "Excuse me madam, I do apologise," but madam's eyes refused to acknowledge him and as Eden realised he had apologised to a mannequin he quickly spun around to check for any observers of his conversation.

"It happens all the time," an assistant graciously volunteered, trying to divert the smile off her face. "the truth is, I talk to her all the time, she makes a good listener."

"Well, at least she doesn't get bored then," he responded with a smile as his attention shifted to the gown the mannequin was wearing. Pure white and shimmering it just reached the ground, it was stunning, sophisticated and elegant. He called Jane and Sarah over "Look, what do you think?" he asked them, indicating the gown.

"Dad, it's gorgeous but, so is the price tag!"

Eden bent down and checked the tag. "Ah, ha," he mumbled with surprise "Do you like it?" he asked both of them. With a nod from both he continued "Good, we'll take two of them," he instructed the girl "Two size tens should do."

Their shopping now complete they left the mall and headed to Jane's apartment. Pulling into the carpark they found six men waiting for them. "That's funny, I wasn't expecting anyone," Jane said.

"It's a surprise dear," Sarah answered "a little something your father and I have been working on for your birthday. We'll go up, make some tea and then we'll explain it to you."

Fifteen minutes later nine people were sipping tea and coffee and talking, with great enthusiasm, about the plans that lay all over the dining table, in front of them. Three of the men were architects, two were builders and the last was an interior designer. All were present to discuss Jane's birthday present, a studio, or at least the proposed plans and design for a studio in which she could create her sculptures. Yves from Paris had been flown in and consulted and all had been working on the plans for weeks. Jane looked deliriously happy as she discussed the plans. "I don't know how to thank you both," she said throwing her arms around her parents "I can't believe it, it's wonderful!" She was glowing with youthful excitement "I can't wait to work in there, in fact I might have to move my bed in, in case I never want to come out," she laughed.

"We've only just got you back from Paris, we're not going to lose you to this studio dear." Sarah insisted with a wink.

"Now, the location?" One of the architects asked smiling at Jane "We suggested to your parents that they purchase the adjacent apartment, that way we can take out both of these walls and you can work from home. Is that preferable or would you prefer some distance between the two?"

"No, it sounds perfect."

Each of the nine people in the room threw themselves into discussing, deliberating and designing the proposed studio as if it would be their own, over the ensuing hours. In no time Sarah was startled as she glanced at her watch. "Gentlemen, I'm afraid we'll have to continue this tomorrow, would four o'clock be convenient? We're taking Jane out to dinner tonight and I had no idea the time had passed so quickly." Having agreed that four o'clock was suitable, they wished Jane a happy birthday again and were on their way.

"We'll run and get ready and be back in half an hour. You pour a glass of champagne, have a hot bath and pop that beautiful gown on. I love you sweetheart, happy birthday," Sarah said taking her daughter's hands into hers and squeezing them.

"You, my dear, are our world, happy birthday darling," Eden added as he kissed her "and as for you, let's get your coat on and I'll pour you a glass of champagne when we get home."

"And a warm bath?"

"Absolutely."

Sarah and Eden returned home to the flurry of caterers, florists, musicians and many other busy people. They had spent weeks organizing a huge party for five hundred guests to celebrate their daughter's birthday. The people dashing about had been well organized and versed on last minute preparations and had everything going smoothly, to Sarah and Eden's delight.

The house was a huge mansion in the prominent suburb of Bethesda. Eden and Sarah had become one of America's most wealthy couples and could more than afford it. Over the past two decades, Sarah's paintings had brought in millions of dollars. What Eden had said years ago 'one day people won't be able to afford them' had long become a reality. At auctions and private sales buyers fought to acquire a piece of her work; the more they fought, the more they paid. The love of painting was something that Sarah had always had, the fame and the wealth that had come with it, still, never ceased to overwhelm her. Eden, likewise, had done well. In all circles of medicine he was unanimously regarded to be the world's best cardiologist and the most successful in cardiac research. He was now working at Washington Heart at Washington Hospital Center, the nation's busiest cardiac facility, and had been with them for over a decade. The hospital performed more than ten thousand cardiac catheterizations, seventeen hundred open-heart operations and an average of twenty heart transplants annually. Eden had become known worldwide, for his work in stents and intravascular ultrasound and more notably, for his goal of creating a man-made heart, a goal which was nearing completion. He was now the President of the American Heart Association and had written a number of books on cardiovascular medicine. With all of these successes came a huge annual income each year. This, coupled with Sarah's earnings had created their worth.

Over the years Sarah, Eden, Ian and others had worked tirelessly to make a fortune out of Esme's estate contributing also to benefit hundreds of charities and to medical research. A biography of Esme and Samuel's life had been written, published and read in many homes across America. Though she had never met her, their daughter thought of Esme as a grandmother figure and had grown up wanting to know all she could about this special woman. Sarah and Eden had christened their daughter, Jane Esme Parks and so Esme's name still lived on as did her loyalty to helping others.

An hour later, Eden, Sarah and Jane were on their way to the restaurant of which they didn't intend to arrive at. "Oh no! Sarah moaned "I've left my purse at home. I'm sorry Jane, would you mind if we stopped on the way to pick it up?"

"Of course not. You know, I knew something was missing, I just couldn't put my finger on it."

As they drove through the security gates of the mansion, Jane couldn't help noticing, on such a cold, dark night that all the lighting was off. "Gee, there must have been a storm, the powers off."

"I've got a torch in the glove box, we'll get inside and see what's happened." Eden responded and he winked at Sarah.

They pulled up, fossicked for the torch and made their way through the front door. The house was pitch black and all the staff seemed to have disappeared. "Where is everybody? Did you give them all the weekend off?" Jane asked.

"I didn't, did you Sarah?"

"No. Maybe they're in the dining room with some candles. Let's check there."

Using the torch they found their way to the dining room and as they walked in Eden flicked the light on. Jane was stunned as five hundred or so people yelled out in unison "Surprise!" With a dazed expression she stood motionless for a second, with everyone's eyes upon her. Then she smiled her mother's gentle smile and said "Hi guys." Seconds later Jane had a glass of champagne in her hand, as did her parents and everyone else in the room Eden then proposed a toast to Jane.

"Happy twenty-first birthday, darling," her father said before he kissed her as everyone raised their glasses in response to Eden's words.

With the surprise and toast over, music, laughter and chatter transposed the room as everyone began the festivities of the occasion. "Twenty-one years, it seems like just yesterday when you were born," Bill said as he hugged Jane "and I thought I was the luckiest man in the world to be your godfather. Look at you, a perfect lady. For twenty-one years you've been in my heart and that's where you'll always be, happy birthday princess. Now do your godfather a favor and have the first dance with me?"

"Happy Birthday darling," Hillary said as she kissed Jane "you'd better give him the first dance or he'll be devastated."

"And it's no wonder I've always loved you guys," Jane smiled "now that first dance?" she remembered and wrapped her arm through Bill's.

The room was a picture of beauty, with its vast marble floor, fountains and lustrous chandeliers above. Opaque balloons carpeted the ceiling, ice statues shimmered under the lights, while the floor was covered with women adorned in elegant gowns and men dressed in black and white. The atmosphere was vibrant as everyone danced and mingled. Numerous guests had flown in from overseas, including Yves and the guest list was as dazzling as the surroundings. The staff, many of which had watched Jane grow up, attended to their needs with instant exactness.

Eden and Sarah were kept busy being perfect hosts and Jane was kept busy with a constant stream of young men wanting to dance with her. Finally, Eden had his turn and made the most of it by dancing his daughter through a trio of consecutive dances until yet another young man interrupted even his turn. "Now I can see what your father means when he talks about the two beauties in his life. I'm honored to meet you Jane," he said, as he took her hand and kissed it. His eyes stared deeply into hers and as she involuntarily succumbed to his undiverting gaze she seemed immobilised by it.

The man that Jane was staring at was unnaturally handsome, as if one could travel the world and would never find such looks again. An intense masculinity displayed itself in his tall, slender body. The color of his skin seemed to favor neither an olive nor a pale complexion but a perfect cross between the two. His straight, blonde hair had the same softness as his blue eyes and his handsome face seemed to command equal attention. Jane had seen many beautiful things in her life but this vision served only to stun her. At length she looked at the floor as if normality would resume when she looked back up, but no, there he still was, as handsome as the moment before. Finally Eden, somewhat nervously, broke the silence. He had never seen his daughter so absorbed that she was rendered speechless before. "Jane, this is Michael Berther, he's just joined the team at the hospital a month ago. By all accounts we're very lucky to have him, too."

"A compliment that I hope I live up to!" Michael responded as he continued to stare into Jane's eyes.

"Coming from my father it is more the truth than a compliment." she said as she finally broke her silence and her eye contact. "I've had the benefit of his honesty all my life, you'll see what I mean when you've known him a bit longer." She concluded smiling at her father and then Michael.

"My mother always told me that integrity is the finest asset a man can have and I do admit to having noticed that in your father already. I feel very privileged to be working with him and I must say the same for meeting you."

"That's very kind of you."

"Not at all, it's the truth," he laughed "the truth is also that I would love to have one come a hundred dances with you and though my truth is probably bordering on being presumptuous now, at least I can blame honesty for it."

Jane looked at Eden and then Michael. "Well, with all this honesty I would be amiss in saying that I wouldn't enjoy that too."

"Don't keep her too long, I believe the cake is appearing soon," Eden alerted them as he left the pair to look for Sarah.

As he slowly made his way through the huge gathering Eden stopped to check on one of the twelve strong security contingent, that, as always had accompanied Bill and Hillary on their outing. Like the others that stood conspicuously around the vast room his eyes moved with exactitude noting the tiniest movements of anything and anyone. "I hope you've had something to eat?" Eden asked him.

"Ah, no sir."

"Well, I'll see to it that the staff get each of you a plate immediately. Say, you haven't seen my wife around, have you?"

"Yes sir, she was with the first lady, five minutes ago."

"Good, thanks. That will give me a starting point." Eden said, ready to head off again.

"Sir, allow me," he offered interrupting Eden's departure and addressing his cuff-links "Agent Brougan here, can anyone see Sarah Parks at the moment? Ok thanks. Your wife's by the fountain sir."

"Good on you, appreciate it," Eden said with a wave as he headed over to the fountain.

"Eden," Sarah called as he came into her view "I've been looking everywhere for you."

"Ditto" he responded with a wink. "I had one of Bill's agents track you down."

"We should use flares next time!" she laughed. "Have you seen Jane?"

"I have!" Jane volunteered as quickly as she had appeared.

Ten minutes later, all cheered as Jane blew the candles out on her cake. "Now, a wish darling," Sarah said.

Jane pondered, as everyone waited "I can't, I already have my wish," she told them wrapping an arm around each of her parent's "I'm holding on to it now. Thanks Mum and Dad. I love you. Glasses ready? Then a toast to my parents, the two people I admire most in the world!"

Vibrant cheers again filled the air. "And another toast," Bill called as he kissed Jane on the cheek "Ok, I'll wait. Top them up again." he grinned. "Firstly, a toast to Jane, a true princess, who has always been in my heart and will capture the hearts of anyone who is lucky enough to know her! And secondly," he continued as the cheers subsided "And no! I'm not waiting this time, a toast, to my oldest, and I'm not including you there Sarah, and dearest friends, Sarah and Eden. I know that everyone here adores you guys, as I do, but I thank you. Your friendship has been a blessing and a privilege over the years. My life would not have been the same without you and I know Hillary will second that! Love you Sarah," he said as he kissed her on the cheek " and love you Eden but you're not getting a kiss! Ok?"

"I'm glad to hear it!" he laughed.

The party continued as if nobody had any desire for it to end, but end it did and the following day Jane, her parents and a small group of friends enjoyed savories and champagne and then helped Jane in her mammoth task of opening all her presents. By four o'clock they were back in Jane's apartment to resume their discussion on the studio. Two hours later, with all three being suitably tired, Sarah and Eden decided to head home and have an early night, while Jane decided that the latter, appealed, likewise to her.

The following afternoon as Eden walked out of theater, having just completed a successful heart transplant on a fourteen year old girl, he congratulated Michael on his assistance during the operation. "Thanks," Michael responded "but gee, I can't get over the way you work."

"What do you mean?"

"Well, most surgeons will walk into theater with one thing on their mind, to fix a problem, you're the only surgeon I've ever seen that seems to have a personal affinity with the person lying on the table. It's like you're operating on your wife or your daughter every time. Anyway, that's something I'd like to feel. Then again, I'm a bit of a whiz kid with my hands and we both know that's the most important thing!"

"If a surgeon loses a patient on the table, or the surgery leads to a bad complication, have you ever seen that surgeon go and sit somewhere quietly alone, look despondent or be quieter than usual?" Eden paused, "likewise, if a difficult operation has been successful, have you seen a surgeon looking pretty buoyant and spirited?"

"Sure."

"If they didn't have an affinity with the patient they wouldn't have these reactions would they?"

The fact that this new colleague didn't already feel this surprised Eden. "Then again, maybe he's too young to know what he feels yet," he thought. "As to his 'whiz kid' hands", he thought it best to ignore this ostentatious comment. "Anyway, I'm late for a lecture, I'm supposed to be giving so I'll see you around." he concluded to Michael.

"Oh, just one other thing," Michael said as he took his gown off "I was hoping you might go over the data on some research I'm thinking of starting. It's just that I'd really appreciate your thoughts on it. The only free time I've got is tomorrow evening."

"I'm a bit tight for time too. I promised Sarah I'd be home for dinner tonight and I'd planned to stay back and write a couple of speeches tomorrow night," he paused "Ok look, I'll do the speeches tonight and fit you in tomorrow night. How does eight sound?"

"That's great, I really appreciate it Eden, thanks. I'll see you then."

With that they parted, Eden to his office to get his lecture notes and Michael to his office to make some calls.

Like Eden, Michael was a gifted cardiologist, though nowhere near Eden's ability, although in Michael's mind, he would dispute this. He had recently left another Washington hospital, citing better prospects as his reason. Washington Heart had happily taken him on knowing his ability was excellent and should even, improve. He had been interviewed and scrutinised by the hospital board and though he had voted for him, Eden had sensed some reservations. "Why?" he had thought to himself, he didn't know. Maybe it was his lack of personal details that worried him. Interviewing a prospect-ive surgeon, who would represent the hospital and be paid a great deal of money, was not only based on ability but also history. Michael had talked his way out of many of their quest-ions, as if he had a definite reason not to answer them. This had worried Eden to a degree, though the others seemed unperturbed by it. In the end, he had decided to let his guard down and ignore these reservations. "The young man cert-ainly has ability and it appeared that his work at the hospital has his sole concentration," he had thought to himself.

The extent of Michael's family was one brother. He and his younger brother had spent their early days growing up in a poor family, watching their alcoholic father beat their mother. Finally the beatings had culminated in her death. A month later, having escaped arrest by going on the run, they had news that their father had drunk himself to death. Michael, then sixteen, had worked and put himself through medical school, raising his brother as he did.

Having finished med school and worked as a doctor ever since, Michael and his brother had been able to live comfortably. Michael had rented a good apartment and had insisted his brother live with him for as long as he wanted. James, his brother, had always been more interested in being a socialiser than a student and as such had never really achieved anything, certainly not earning a wage. A large part of James's socialising included gay men. Though Michael respected his brother's sexual preferences he had been constantly irate at his perilous promiscuity. Seven years earlier, in 1986, his worries were met with the news that his brother was HIV positive.

Having reached his office, Michael shut the door, keyed in a number on his mobile and sat back in his chair. "The Royal Men's hospital, can I help you?"

"Yes, could you connect me with the Sister in charge on ward three please?" he waited impatiently, tapping his fingers on the desk as he did.

"Sister Maloney speaking…"

"Sister Maloney, how are you? It's Michael Berther here. Tell me, what's the status on my brother James?"

"James Bertha, let me see," she paused "oh yes, your brother is doing very well. He has been resting and we believe most of the inflammation is down."

"And the surgery?"

"Definitely tomorrow."

"Good. Now I need to know exactly when he'll be due out of surgery. I'd like to be there for him when he wakes up."

"He should be out at seven so if you're here by eight he should be just waking."

"Excellent. Now if anything changes I'd appreciate knowing straight away, you've got my contact numbers, and please, straight away if anything changes."

"We'll keep you informed, Mr Berther."

As Michael folded down his phone and slipped it into his pocket, he whispered "Perfect." to himself. Everything was going as planned and this rendered him happily, at ease. He had organized a private room for his brother. The staff at the hospital seemed entirely accommodating to any requests he put to them and this compliance, as he was well aware, he needed.

Three years ago, in 1990, Michael had tired of James's constant companionship and had organized a suitable apartment for his sole use. Michael had always felt an obligation to provide his brother with anything he needed but that had never included friendship or love. He had rarely even seen his brother over the past years. David would forward his existing bills and estimates of future necessities to his brother who would, in return, forward a cheque. It was the estimate of the up and coming hospital bill that had alerted Michael to his brother's confinement on this occasion, not his brother. Likewise, it was through this avenue, two months earlier, that Michael learnt that his brother had been finally diagnosed with AIDS. David had spent two weeks in hospital with Pneumocystis carinii pneumonia, a common medical condition in patients with AIDS. On this occasion, David was in for an appendectomy, after, according to the staff, having spent weeks with an inflamed appendix.

For Sarah and Jane their afternoon had been hectic. It had begun with lunch in the warmth of the Old Ebbitt with Ian Grant as their guest. Since Esme's death, Sarah and Eden had made it a tradition to have a meal there at least once a month. After lunch, the three had an appointment with Jane's neighbor to discuss the purchase of their apartment. The discussion had proved to be entirely fruitful, due mainly to the fact that

Sarah and Ian suggested that double its worth would be an appropriate figure in their minds to cover any inconvenience. Jane's neighbors had found this so overwhelming that they insisted on moving out within the week. After that, Sarah and Ian spent a couple of hours, in Jane's apartment, sifting through the latest batch of paperwork from the charity investments, that needed signing, while Jane rushed off to an appointment with her architect.

Later that evening, as Sarah sat in her dressing gown, reading a recent book that had been published on her work, while she waited for Eden, the phone rang. "Jane," the housekeeper whispered as she handed Sarah the phone.

"Hello darling. How did your appointment with the architect go?"

"Great. I'm in the car on my way over, is Dad home yet?"

"No, but I don't think he'll be much longer."

"Well I'll give him a call and see how much longer he's going to be. I'll be there in about three minutes. I've got someone with me who wants to meet both of you."

"Tell him I'm very much looking forward to meeting him as well. Darling... did I just assume correctly when I said him?"

"Actually I'm not sure!"

"Pardon?"

"Just joking. The someone is a surprise anyway, so my lips are sealed."

Within minutes Jane parked in front of the house. Sarah glanced at the savories that had been hurriedly placed on a platter and stared past Jane as she strode into the room. "Hi mum," she greeted her and kissed her on the cheek.

"Darling, where's your friend?"

"In the car, asleep."

"Really!"

"Sorry I'm so late," Eden apologised as he rushed in "where's your friend?"

"In Jane's car asleep." Sarah answered looking puzzled "Are you going to wake him up?"

Jane nodded "I'll be back in a minute."

"Fancy falling asleep like that," Eden said to Sarah

"Maybe he's had a long day. Jane certainly looks excited though."

"Mum, Dad, meet..." she paused "where have you gone?" she asked as she left the room again.

By this point Eden and Sarah looked so bewildered that the sight of them was comical. "We're back. To stay!" Jane told the goose in her arms.

"Oh, look Eden, isn't he gorgeous! Is this your friend!" Sarah laughed "I thought,"

"I know," Jane grinned "No, he's your friend."

"Where...?" Eden began.

"From the same place Snowy came from," Jane interrupted to answer "You see, when we lost Snowy I could see how upset you both were, so, a little while after, I got in touch with the Island Ranger, gave him my number and asked him if he ever came across a lame goose could he give me a call. After all this time, I had a phone call two hours ago and I dashed out to pick him up. He's got a much better home here than on the island and if you guys are away, I'll goose sit him for you."

"I love him already," Sarah smiled as she took the sleepy goose from her daughter's arms and patted him "Eden can we?"

"I'll get a new bed tomorrow." he smiled knowingly, looking as pleased as Sarah.

"What are you going to call him?" Jane asked.

"What about Junior?" Eden volunteered "It could be short

148

for Snowy Junior."

"Junior it is!" Sarah agreed.

Early the next morning, after his daily run, Eden returned with a bed for Junior. The goose was hesitant to try it out but suddenly had no qualms when Sarah laid some flowers in it. In he got and happily stayed, the transition was made.

As Michael drove to the Royal Men's Hospital, where his brother was being treated, he half listened to the incessant chatter of the D.J. on the radio. The only piece of this chatter he actually took in was the news that it had been the coldest November day on record, over the past fifty years. "The coldest day," he said to himself "maybe for Eden Parks but not for me. In eight weeks it will be the New Year. 1994 wow! Eden will be gone and I'll be God!"

In the warmth of the hospital, Michael made his way to ward three. The ward was dimly lit as were the patient's faces as they slowly walked or rode the corridor, either on their feet or in their wheelchairs. Many of them were accompanied by a mobile drip and some, by a nurse. The bleach white of the nurse's uniform was the only unbeige color to be seen, just as their faces wore the only smiles to be seen. Michael was entirely unaffected by the people and their surroundings with his concentration focusing only on one objective, locating his brother. Rather than approach the desk, he sidled past any available staff in favor of finding his brother's room as surreptitiously as he could. Things, he knew, would be less complicated if his presence remained undetected. It seemed, however, that his brother had the same wish, for as Michael passed each separate room, his brother's presence seemed elusive. Just when he was starting to look somewhat annoyed by the situation, a voice from behind enquired "Can I help you?"

"Yes, it appears you can," he coolly responded. "I'm looking for my brother, David Berther, one of your patients."

"Well, if you can wait half an hour or so, he might be up to a quick visit. You see he's just come out of theatre so he's still heavily sedated."

"I've been speaking to Sister Maloney the last twenty-four hours, you see, I'm his brother and she assured me that I could be there, for him when he wakes up."

"If Sister Maloney has ok'd that, that's fine. Come with me."

Michael followed her to a secluded room where she threw the door open and eyed the patient. "This room is great for post-op. It's really peaceful here," she explained to Michael.

"I'd like to sit quietly with him until he wakes. I'm sure you're busy, so don't let me keep you."

The nurse looked surprised "Of course!" she answered as she headed out of the room, pausing a moment to say "By the way, your brother's operation went very well. I'm sure you were wondering!"

"Yes, well, it's a pretty straight forward procedure, so I assumed as much. Anyway, thank you, I appreciate the information. I'll just sit here quietly with my brother now," he reiterated as politely as he could manage.

Relieved to be alone, at last, he stood, staring at his brother. Gone was the handsome young face, instead, it was sunken and hollow. His closed eyes were cushioned upon dark, concave circles. His face was composed more of bone than flesh. What flesh that remained was jaundiced and covered in sores. His hair was brittle and clumps of it were missing. A once strong, masculine body, now a wasted figure under the blanket. Though he was shocked, Michael felt no emotion. As a very young child he had known emotion, but his father had seen better to crop that. This had been the only thing, in

Michael's mind, that his father had actually done, to benefit him. It was easier to accept and deal with the sorrows of his childhood if he didn't have to contend with the feelings that went with those sorrows. In his later years, he had found that having no emotions was a staple to survival. He trusted this detachment and the sanity that it brought him.

Fifteen minutes had passed while he stood at his brother's bedside, and as his brother's hand suddenly twitched, Michael was startled back to his mission. "Damn!" he snapped as he looked at his watch. Quickly he checked the door was shut and locked it. "Now, with all the things I've done for you David, at last you can do something for me," he whispered as he took a small silver flask out of his pocket, as he had done on his way over to the hospital and once again he checked the temperature. Content with the setting he opened the flask and withdrew the large sterile syringe that it housed. Within seconds he had punctured a vein in David's left arm and watched the blood vacate his brother's body and fill the connected syringe. Slowly, he removed the syringe, capped it and returned it to the ready flask. With the flask now safely in his pocket he was excited. "Thank you David. You've just increased my career prospects one hundred per cent. Eden, my only competition, will, thanks to you, have the pleasure of sampling your blood. Then I'll have the pleasure, that belongs to me anyway, of assuming his job, with all it encumbers and all it brings."

Minutes later, Sister Maloney and the nurse walked in, only to find that their patient's visitor had disappeared. "That's strange," the nurse said.

"Very. He was determined to be here when his brother woke up, I don't understand!"

"The patient, should we let him know his brother visited him?"

"I don't think so. I'd be pretty upset if somebody left just before I was about to wake up. Also, maybe something came up and his brother plans to visit him later. This one's out of our hands, that I do know!"

Tapping on the door of Eden's office half an hour later elicited no response. Michael turned the handle and found it unlocked. Loaded up with research papers and takeout he decided to take a seat and wait inside. Minutes continued to ebb around the clock as he sat with his patience dwindling. As he helped himself to a book on the desk that Eden had written, he found himself so engrossed in it that Eden's arrival went almost unnoticed. Eden went to a cupboard and pulled one of the books out of its box of twelve. "There you go," he said as he placed the book in front of Michael "you look so interested there that I think I'd better give you a copy."

"Gee, thanks. That's decent of you." he responded, still feeling startled out of his reading.

"Not really, it's one of the benefits of writing a book, you get heaps of copies. Now, what about this research? Hang on a minute, what's that smell?"

"Oh, I heard you're pretty partial to Japanese food so I thought I'd buy you dinner as a thanks for tonight. I don't know about you but I can't eat Japanese without saki so I got some of that too."

"Same here," Eden nodded as he picked up the phone to ring Sarah.

Michael opened the bottle and filled two disposable cups while Eden talked to Sarah to let her know that he would have a meal in his office and that he shouldn't be too late in getting home. "Ok let's enjoy this meal and then we'll go through your research data. What do you think?" he said as he hung up the phone.

152

"Great."

Eden's love of Japanese food was clearly apparent, he hardly paused to sip any saki and consumption seemed more predominant than conversation. Within ten minutes the takeout was history and Eden appeared outstandingly content. Michael, on the other hand, was starting to panic. He had fingered the tiny pill in his pocket for an unbearable amount of time and the simple task of transferring it to Eden's cup was proving to be more difficult than he had anticipated. "Shit!" he said as he surveyed the mess that he had intentionally made on his tie. "Have you got a damp cloth or facewasher I could use?"

"Sure." Eden responded as he dived towards the ensuite.

With Eden's presence withdrawn for a few seconds Michael was quick to grasp his opportunity. Dropping the tablet into the destined cup, he grabbed a pencil out of its holder and swiftly stirred the contents. As Eden returned with a towel, Michael laughed as he pulled the pencil from the cup "Would you believe I dropped my pencil in your saki? Gee, maybe I've had a bit much of the stuff. Sorry, I'm not usually so clumsy!"

"Well, if it is the saki, how about I relieve you of the rest of it?"

"Probably a good idea," he nodded, feeling quietly pleased with his theatrics as he mopped his tie.

The ensuing hour was spent sifting through realms of computer generated data, their work only interrupted by Michael's apparent distraction with the heating system and its setting and Eden's consumption of saki. At the end of the hour, Eden succumbed to almost instantaneous sleep. Michael stood up to quietly take his jacket off, noticing, as he did, that his shirt was soaked with perspiration. Perspiring was a usual reaction for Michael if he was unnerved, which usually wasn't often. He sat down in the comfort of the leather chair for ten minutes to ensure Eden was completely unconscious. Once sure of this he took the flask from the inner pocket of his jacket, opened it and gently grasped the syringe.

The contents of the syringe, he knew, was the passage to his greatest desire. The desire to hold Eden's position in the small world of cardiovascular excellence. The esteem of such a position was too high to miss and after all he hadn't worked this hard to have to wait in line for another decade or two. Having nothing as a child had made him determined to have what he wanted as an adult and the knowledge that his pursuits should cause harm to another was completely irrelevant to him. Life was for the taking, his taking. Anyone who stood in the way served only as a minor annoyance to be dealt with.

Michael inserted the needle into an accommodating vein in Eden's arm and slowly injected its bright crimson content. This done, he withdrew the needle with precision, for an obvious needle mark was not something that he wished Eden to see. Eden had made no movements during this and continued his unconscious slumber while Michael returned the syringe to its flask, putting it and the surgical gloves into his jacket pocket. He cleared the empty takeaway boxes and poured the leftover saki into the toilet bowel, then rinsed the disposable cups before putting all into a bag to dispose of in his office. Once his paperwork was gathered, in order and in a neat pile with the book Eden had given him he dialled Sarah's number using the phone on her husband's desk. "Hi, Sarah, sorry to ring you so late, it's Michael Berther here, we met at your daughter's party."

"Of course, how are you?" Sarah asked.

"Well, I'm a bit worried. I seem to have put your husband to sleep. He might have mentioned, he was going over some data with me. It's not particularly riveting research and to be honest I think it might have sent him to sleep."

"No," she paused "Eden's been working very hard. I'm quiet sure it's not your research, he's just been working a tad too hard lately. I'll come over and pick him up."

"I was actually going to mention that he looks so comfortable, maybe it's better if he enjoys his sleep. I can find a blanket and pop it over him."

"You're right, that would be more sensible. I'll ring him at seven to make sure he's awake.

Thanks for your concern Michael, I'm sure Eden will appreciate it too."

"I think he'll have a good nights sleep. I'll let you do the same and go and rustle up a blanket for Eden. See you Sarah."

Minutes later he turned the lights off and pulled the door behind him as he left Eden's office and went to lock his own. Walking through the hectic atmosphere of the hospital in night mode, he smiled at the thought of enjoying a glass of red at home as he congratulated himself on his accomplishment.

CHAPTER
NINE

While the wintry daylight made its way into the plush office, Eden's arm half-heartedly extended itself to quell the beep of the phone. With the receiver finally to his mouth he croaked "Hello, thank you..." and returned the receiver to its home "Gee, they could have spoken up a bit," he thought to himself "hang on, you hung up on them," he muttered. As he looked at his watch the phone rang again. "Eden Parks speaking..." he answered, this time with appropriate alertness.

"Hi darling, I thought I'd better give you a wake-up call. You must have been so tired, you poor thing, you fell asleep in your office!"

"I'm sorry darling, I don't know how I managed to do that."

"Michael Bertha rang last night. He said he was worried that he might have driven you to sleep with his research!" she laughed.

"Um..., pigs. He's researching pig-to-human transplants,

which is really quite a fascinating subject but he's right, his work on the subject was less than fascinating? Anyway, I'm sorry I wasn't home, I'll make a point to be home early tonight and whip up a couple of fillet-mignons. What do you think?"

"I think you're tempting me out of the cataloguing that I have to do. Ok you have a shower and I'll throw myself into my schedule, that way with luck, we'll have a nice dinner tonight."

As Eden showered he was surprised at how refreshed he felt. "Somehow, I think that's the best night's sleep I've had in a long time," he mused. An hour later as he was hurriedly typing some information into his pc his secretary brought him his usual black coffee and the charts for the day. "You're early this morning!" she said in her ever cheerful manner.

"It's a busy day ahead!" he responded as he warmed his hands on the coffee cup "Talking about being early, when are you going to believe me that you're working too hard? You should be starting later and finishing earlier. Just promise me you'll think about it?"

"Promise," she said jokingly with her hand over her heart.

"Good. Now James Weir and his wife are coming in today, could you see if you can get an approximate time and let me know before I grab a bit of breakfast."

"Give me two minutes," she confirmed as she left the room.

Back, well before two minutes, she continued "I've just spoken to Mr Weir's secretary and she thinks they should be just about in the lift by now and on their way up."

"Right. The file is?"

"Here," she said placing it in front of him.

James Weir was a well-known film director, who, at seventy-seven was still madly directing. He had married recently, for the first time, to a film producer, thirty years his junior. It was his wife, Rachel, who had sent her husband's medical history and details to Eden, anxious that he might offer a more optimistic approach to her husband's health than had already been given by numerous specialists. Eden, after a great deal of thought, suspected that James might be a candidate for a new type of laser surgery and if so, he would be the first such candidate in the world.

With introductions over, the couple and James's personal physician took their seats in Eden's office. "Well, Mr Weir," Eden began.

"James, call me James and the same for Rachel and Max." he responded with an amiable smile, checking his watch as he did.

"Ok, good. Now I've read and re-read your charts and everything your wife sent me. I am happy to say I believe I can help you."

"There you go James, here's a start, wonderful!" Rachel said, so excitedly that she almost tripped over her words.

"To start from the top you need to know that this surgery has never been done before; however, I believe you will be very interested in what I'm about to explain." he paused, sipped a mouthful of water, after noticing how their jaws had dropped in unison.

"We're listening," James said reassuringly.

"Well, we're talking about laser surgery. The technique is called percutaneous myocardial revascularization, the shorter version, PMR. The procedure is far less invasive and less risky than traditional open heart surgery," at this point, Eden noticed the softening of their expressions and went on "Basically, you will be sedated but fully conscious. I will insert a microscopic laser into a small incision in the groin and manouver it into the left ventricle of your heart. This creates a trauma which, within minutes, will trigger angiogenesis.

Angiogenesis is the heart's process of generating new blood vessels around the site of the injury to the existing vessel. The procedure itself, would take about thirty to forty-five minutes, under a local anesthetic. In conclusion, your stay in hospital should be no longer than forty-eight hours."

"Wow!" James said looking stunned, as did the others "so have I got this right? The only incision will be into my groin and not my chest."

"That's right."

"Wow! Ok," James paused to look for Rachel's and Max's confirmation, both responded with an instant nod "It seems that I'm all yours!" he confirmed.

"I must say Eden, your idea is brilliant. You've managed to turn the cards for James when the rest of us were scratching our heads," Max said.

"I had a degree of head scratching myself but then it just fell into place. I mean, this surgery was designed, in the first place, for people needing heart surgery, but unable to have it, for reasons like James. I must say though James, you couldn't have a better practitioner. I rarely see the standard of obvious attention and exactitude that I saw in Max's records. In fact," he said turning back to Max "without your records the puzzle would have been harder to solve."

"That's good to hear, thank you," Max responded.

"And Rachel, thanks for asking for my opinion. I'm really pleased that I can help."

"A pleasure I share entirely." she responded.

"I'm a lucky man, aren't I?" James said to Eden.

"You certainly are."

"The chances of this surgery being successful, are they high?" Rachel asked.

"Very, I'd say about ninety-five per cent."

"And after the operation, will he feel much pain or discomfort?" she continued.

"The five or so stitches in his groin might be a bit tender for a few days but essentially within a week or so, he will feel much better than he does right now. Now, if we admit you on Thursday?"

"Ideal." James confirmed "It's just that our first day of shooting my next film is in two weeks, so by the time you've finished with me I'll be really hopping around the set won't I!"

"You'll feel a lot better. It's been a pleasure meeting you all, I'm afraid now though, I'm due in theater in twenty minutes. I'll have my secretary contact you this afternoon to go over admission times, etc. Look after yourselves and I'll see you on Thursday."

As Eden made his way home through the traffic jammed streets of D.C., listening to Bach's Passacaglia on the radio, his mind kept wandering back to his and Sarah's childhood. He thought of the first time that he had set eyes on her, standing there, in the corner of the huge sandstone building clutching her doll and suitcase. He was the only one she would trust and this trust had allowed a friendship to begin. Both cherished the strength they brought each other and the strength that still lived with them each day, a strength, each still needed for the other. As the image of her standing in the corner remained in his mind, he knew that image was the image of his life beginning. On that day she had opened up a world of love and security that he had never known existed.

Beyond the warmth of his own car, people traveled up and down the sidewalks briskly, laden with thick coats, under umbrellas as they tried to keep the falling snow at bay. Snow was unusual for November, but Eden was glad of it. Washington, Eden thought, was stunning when pure white snow enveloped its city. Also, it reminded him that Christmas wasn't far away. When it came to Christmas, Eden was like a child. His first favorite activity was to collect a tree, which never ceased to worry Sarah. He seemed to be jinxed when it came to this annual tree collection. Right from the time he collected their first tree, managing to get himself entrapped with it, in a lift for the best part of half an hour, this accidental tradition went on. Dinner guests over the years had been entertained with the best of the stories, so much so, that they began looking forward to hearing all about the up-and-coming traditional accident.

Sarah and Eden had enjoyed a perfect meal that Eden had cooked, despite the staff they had, to do such things. Whenever they could, they would let the staff off and do their own thing, whether it be to cook a meal or wash some dishes, this gave them a blissful seclusion from their hectic lives. As they sat on the cushions in front of the open fire, they shared a tub of ice-cream while they talked. "You know, I was thinking about Christmas on my way home," Eden said.

"That's funny, so was I."

"Remember the first Christmas with Jane? She was so tiny, just seven weeks old and we put her in the Christmas stocking with her little head popping out, that's always been one of my favorite photo's," he said proudly.

"That was gorgeous," Sarah agreed. "I was thinking this year we could ask the staff to do the tree? You've done it every year and really you should take a break."

"You're worrying again, you've got that worried look," he laughed as he ran his fingers through her hair.

"Alright, I am worried, but considering what happened last year, I think there's a bit of cause for that."

"I still don't understand how that snake got in the tree, we wouldn't have known if I hadn't taken that photo. I think the flash scared it or maybe it just wanted to be in the photo." he recalled as Sarah shuddered "I'm sorry, no more creepies. I promise!" he said, feigning a serious expression.

"And what about the year before?" Sarah laughed "What were you doing? That's right, you sprayed the tree with something to make it a more vibrant green and ended up with a green face and hands for two weeks. Apart from that, anyway, a tree is green, how much greener can it get?"

"Quiet true," he conceded rubbing his chin in contemplation.

"Then there was the time you tied the tree to the roof of the wrong car and someone else drove home with it."

"That tree was too small anyway. I managed to get a better one the second time around, so I always thought that worked out quite well anyway!"

"At least let me come with you then," she insisted.

"You can't go out in the cold, you know that. Look, if it makes you feel better, I'll ask Jane to come along and supervise me," Eden suggested with a wink.

"It would make me feel better. It's just that I'm worried you might hurt yourself one day," she said as she scooped the last remnant from the ice-cream punnet "Now, you've done me a favor so you can have the last scoop" she concluded as she fed him the ice-cream.

"We've got a problem now. Here we are in front of an open fire, on a beautiful rug, all by ourselves with all this ice-cream to burn off!" he said with his eyes softly gazing into hers.

"Well, we'd better burn it off then." she responded as she slid close to him "and I'm going to make a point to buy some more ice-cream tomorrow!"

"What a good idea," he said as he began undressing his

wife, his eyes savoring her beauty and his hands passionately desperate to touch her. Within minutes, both were naked and feeling the sensations of their erotic foreplay. Half an hour later, as Sarah sat on top of Eden, pulling her long fair hair to the back of her neck, he ran his hands up her slim body to her supple breasts. Sarah drew his body into hers and both hardly breathed as the sensual eroticism prevailed over their bodies and minds. Later, with their lovemaking over they put the fire out and went to bed where they made love again and again, eventually falling asleep in their usual embrace.

The next morning they parted early, she to her studio to oversee last minute preparations for her next exhibition, then to take a Japanese contingent of corporate investors for a tour of the national museum of Women in the Arts, and he to do one bypass, give a luncheon speech to the American Heart Foundation and take his surgical staff through the coming procedure on James Weir the following day. The days proceeded quickly, one after the other with the same busy schedule for both.

Thanksgiving had arrived as quickly as the days had departed and for the first time ever Sarah, Eden and Jane enjoyed a meal, on the day without company. Thanksgiving in the past had always involved a gathering of at least a dozen or so guests, but this particular year the three were choked up with heavy colds. Thinking it best not to inflict their viruses on their friends they chose to celebrate alone. Jane was hosting the dinner in her newly completed studio, where her choice in designing it had proved to be amazing, both to the eye and in its practical use. Like her parents, she had a flair for cooking, and as the three sat down to the superbly decorated table, complete with silver cutlery and dishes and golden stemmed glasses, the meal brought to them was so sensational in appearance and taste that despite their lack of appetites, was almost consumed in its entirety. The highlight of the meal was wicker baskets, with handles, constructed from marzipan, filled with seasonal berries and topped with chocolate flecked cream.

"That was superb darling," Sarah said.

"Magical," Eden agreed as he swirled the last berry on his silver plate around its rim.

"I had good teachers," she grinned "and I managed to douse the main course with a huge quantity of fresh garlic so that should help us sickies a bit."

"You know after a bypass, we tell the patients to eat fresh ginger, a bulb of garlic and drink two glasses of red a day and I really believe a daily diet of that for everyone would probably stem heart disease by fifty per cent."

"I'd be interested in doing that although I must say, I'd prefer if they invented odorless garlic first." Sarah said.

"Actually, I picked up a book on preventative medicine the other day, just out of interest and I've found it really fascinating. I'll drop it by when I've finished with it if you want to read it." Jane volunteered.

"I'd like to but I can't see it happening," Eden paused to sneeze "I'm absolutely backlogged with my reading at the moment."

"Then I'll read it and fill you in on the interesting bits. How about that?" Sarah smiled.

"Ok, thanks, I'd be interested."

An hour later with full stomachs, watery faces and tired achy bodies, they all agreed on two points, the first, that it had been a lovely evening, the second, that any remaining energy each had would be spent getting themselves to the warmth and comfort of their beds.

The ensuing weeks saw their colds disappear and the foundation of their city become embedded in thick snow. Anything not covered in snow was, in most cases, covered in lights. As the sound of carols traveled through the streets, so too, did the people who sung them. Department stores were as full of procrastinators as children's wish lists, were of toys. Indeed, with Christmas forty-eight hours away, the city was full of activity. Ian Grant, his co-workers and his employers were equally active, determined to see their charities guide their recipients through the season warmly, happily and contentedly. Extra staff had been taken on, and Eden, Sarah and Jane had occupied many of their evenings helping with the massive workload. A constant stream of thank yous and smiles flooded back, proving their successes and for the hundreds of staff employed throughout the year in the charitable empire, their employers too, thanked them with hefty bonuses. Eden and Sarah's personal staff were far from forgotten. Sarah always gave them one extra duty in the weeks prior to Christmas, that was, to decide where they would prefer to take their vacation for the year, and when. Armed with this information she would mastermind their preferences to a tee, then conclude her efforts by placing an envelope into their hand, enclosing pre-paid travel and accommodation details; together, with some spending money. Over the years, the odd staff member would embarrassingly request that instead of a holiday, might they use the money for a medical expense or another special need. Sarah's answer was always the same when she informed them that both the particular need and the holiday would be catered for.

Sarah, Eden and Jane spent Christmas Eve as they always did, together. The only exception being when Eden headed off for his supervised Christmas tree collection. Forty-five minutes later he returned proudly carrying the tree through the front door, and across the marble floor of the foyer to its destined place in the sitting room, much like a man might carry his catch of the day to the kitchen for all to see. As Sarah entered the room she tiptoed up behind her husband, who was entirely engrossed with the sight of the tree and whispered in his ear "It's perfect darling."

"You think so?" he said looking pleased with himself "and no hiccups this time you'll be pleased to know!"

"That's wonderful!" she responded with relief. "Where's Jane?"

"Jane. Oh no!"

"What?"

"I left her there!"

"Oh Eden, how could you? You both left together, you only had to come back together!"

"I'm so used to going by myself, it must have thrown me." he said as he grabbed the phone from his pocket to ring her at which point his pager beeped. He scanned the message and re-read it to Sarah "Remember me? Don't worry, I'm heading back in a taxi."

With their exasperation having subsided, to a degree, they spent the following minutes laughing uncontrollably at what had transpired. "I've got an idea Sarah," he laughed "why don't we get the staff to find a tree next year?"

"They had better, because you certainly won't be. You even get into trouble when you're supervised!" she laughed.

Christmas day was perfect. Jane had slept over in her room, which was still as it was before she had moved into the apartment, she was the first one to rise. Her first port of call was to the kitchen where the staff were already hard at work as they juggled the cooking and preparation of food together with numerous other duties. "Happy Christmas Jane." they all said at once as she entered the room.

"Thanks," she said "and a Happy Christmas to you guys." she continued as her soft blue eyes made a point of focusing on each of the ten of them. For a second she paused and her face was vibrant as she continued "You know I miss waking up to you guys. It's a really nice way to start Christmas Day. Now, my coffee can wait while I make you guy's coffee and tea and of course Bonox for you Isabelle," she winked "and" she went on after stressing the word "when they are ready you're all going to sit down and take a break, ok?"

"I'll bet when I'm in my rocking chair, you'll still be looking after people." Isabelle laughed.

"No I won't, I'll be coming to visit you!" Jane laughed back.

"Gee, we all miss you. You're just going to have to move back home." another staff member volunteered.

"Well that would be nice but I am a bit in love with my apartment and a lot of the day I'm in the studio for fourteen hours straight doing what I do. In fact, in a couple of weeks I'm going to have a party there to christen it and you guys are already on the list."

"Wouldn't miss it for the world!"

"How many new pieces have you done?" Mary asked.

"Two, actually two and a half" Jane answered.

Mary, like most, was fascinated with Jane's work and years earlier had photographed her first piece to put it in her own album at home. Since then her album had more than a hundred photos of Jane's sculpture and as she had told Jane, every visitor to her home was given the album to peruse. As Jane made the drinks they all continued their chat. Jane had known for years exactly how they liked their particular drinks and as they sat down to them, to take their first sip, they knew, too well that it would be just the way they liked it. "Now," Jane said as she rose from the table to put her mug in the dishwasher, "Christmas or no Christmas, I'd better be a good girl and have that grueling swim for the day. Has anyone seen Junior? He'll hate me if I don't take him with me."

"The last I saw he was still in bed." Isabelle volunteered.

"So much for the early bird theory," Jane laughed "I'll see you guys after I've thoroughly exhausted myself in the pool." she finished with a wave as she left the room.

With the mansion complete with an indoor pool, gymnasium, spa, sauna and squash court, it was only minutes later, that Jane and Junior were having their morning exercise.

Later, the family had a quiet time around the Christmas tree, opening their presents. This was followed by an equally quiet Christmas lunch. The staff in the kitchen couldn't help giggling at the roars of laughter that were coming from the dining table in the adjoining room. Another favorite activity of Eden's at Christmas was to make his own Christmas crackers, complete with hilarious jokes. They, however, were not the highlight of his crackers; the odd things placed in them had that honor. On this occasion Sarah shrieked as she unlodged a lump of fake dog business that looked decidedly like the real thing. After her energetic shriek she burst into peels of laughter. Having pulled her cracker, Jane found she was the proud owner of a plastic eagle in flight which, when she put the tip of its beak on the tip of her finger, managed to balance the rest of its weight. In Eden's cracker was a small canister of what was eloquently called "Fart Gas" of which he insisted he would save for Camp David, after, of course, he had ensured Sarah and Jane had had a sample of it. Eden's childlike approach to Christmas every year had always had the effect of making Christmas just that little bit more special than it already was, both for the family and staff. That evening, however, as they hosted their annual Christmas dinner with their friends, Eden knew too well, to control himself, somewhat more. To the credit of the staff the dinner was superb and the company at the table proved to be equally so.

The following morning was the beginning of one week's holiday for Sarah and Eden, a break they had been looking forward to immensely. "I wish you'd change your mind and come with us," Sarah said to Jane, who was helping her pack.

"I wish I'd change my mind too, but you know me, I hate leaving my work half done. I'll tell you what, if I finish them earlier I'll come down for the last day or two."

"No you won't. You'll just start another piece. I know, I was the same."

"Mum, you still are."

"Well then, it's time I stop. I'm setting a bad example for you."

"You know Mum," Jane said, changing the subject "on Christmas Eve when I was laying in bed, trying to go to sleep, I kept thinking how much I love you and Dad and how lucky I am. You know, it's like, I love you both so much that it really overwhelms me. Anyway, I'm babbling but I wanted to tell you just how much I love you and Dad."

"What you've just said darling, will stay in my heart forever and you, my sweet, are everything to us. Everything." she finished as she lay down the sweater she was holding to hug her daughter.

Later that day as their black Mercedes turned into the security entrance of the White House, Eden and Sarah were given their usual spirited greeting from the staff. Bill strode towards them as they parked and hopped out of the car, spinning a frisbee as he did. "See, he's still playing with toys!" Eden jibbed.

"Not quite. It's ah, more professional playing," he responded "watch."

They watched as he took careful aim and spun the frisbee towards them. Eden put out his hand to catch it, but before he could it landed on the tip of the aerial of their car, then proceeded to spin around it for the best part of two minutes. "What do you think? Not bad ha. One of my agents taught me that."

"Oh come off it, you were practicing years ago when you threw that omelette at Sarah!"

"Alright smarty, I'll make a bet with you. If you can't do what I just did within forty-eight hours then you have to make an omelette, of my choice, for me, for every other morning that we're at Camp David!"

"That's not fair. What about if I win? I don't want you to make me an omelette, I'd be too nervous to eat it. You might have flung it somewhere and anyway, who said I'm going to Camp David, I still haven't decided. I mean the thought of spending seven days with Hillary is delightful but with you, that's a tough one!"

"I know. I had the same problem this morning when I was trying to decide, but unfortunately, Hillary decided for me, so it seems I'm stuck with you!" Bill said, purposely shrugging his shoulders.

"You two get worse with age," Sarah laughed as she picked up the frisbee, took a few steps back and mimicked Bill's trick to a tee "that will be a ham and cheese omelette with a sprig of coriander, placed nicely on the side, first thing in the morning." she laughed as she instructed Bill, before walking off to find his wife.

"How did you learn that?" Eden called after her.

"I didn't. I just did it!"

"Not bad…" the pair muttered to themselves.

Shortly after, all four and the frisbee were on their way to Camp David. The four had had many holidays together at the retreat. Marine one, the presidential helicopter, would complete the seventy-mile distance from the White House in just under half an hour. Once there, Hillary and Bill would take the Aspen lodge, while Eden and Sarah would choose between the Dogwood, Maple, Holly, Birch or Rosebud lodge. The most difficult task over the following days would be to choose whether to enjoy the pool or the putting green, or maybe the driving range, tennis courts or gymnasium and how much of their favorite food they could eat.

For the numerous military aids, it was work as usual, ensuring that the president, his wife and their guests had complete comfort and security. Their work was exacted quietly and in most cases, as much in the background as possible. For Eden, Sarah, Bill and Hillary, it was lunch by the pool. In the past Bill had horrified many guests by suggesting they dine by the pool in the middle of winter. Not having the gumption to point out that he must be quite mad, they would dutifully arrive for the meal in their warmest of coats, only to find that their host pushed a button that served to activate an instant cover from the outside elements and supply instant heating. Such tricks were fruitless when it came to Eden and Sarah they had been to the retreat on too many occasions to fall for them. "How was the omelette?" Bill asked Sarah.

"Well, it didn't bowl me over," Sarah laughed "no, I'm sorry. On a scale of one to ten, I'd rate it an eight."

"An eight! Gee the chef's slipping," Bill responded as he raised his eyebrows.

"You cheat, you were supposed to make it!" Eden said.

"That's right. I forgot." he said feigning guilt.

"And you forgot that I reminded you five minutes before you ordered it?" Hillary laughed as she gave her husband away. "Ok, I'll make amends in the morning. I promise!"

Having been previously confided in, Sarah and Hillary kept the conversation moving as Eden surruptitiously found a reason to pick something up behind Bill, letting some of his treasured fart gas off as he did. Bill shifted in his chair, unaware of what the others knew and waved his hand across his face. "Bit hot Bill?" Eden inquired, trying not to laugh.

"No," he paused "just exercising my hand." he continued waving his hand again for credibility.

By the time lunch was over, Bill was rubbing his aching wrist. "Too much exercise?" Eden inquired.

"I know that look. What's he been up to?" he asked, looking at Sarah and Hillary.

"Come on Eden, you've had your fun." Sarah prompted him.

Eden answered by handing the can to Bill. "You see Hillary, seven days with him is not easy!" he laughed.

"Now, now, who's your best friend?" Hillary asked her husband. Bill responded by pointing his finger at Eden.

"Now Eden, who's your best friend?' she continued.

"You and Sarah." he laughed.

"Eden!" Sarah said.

"Ok, Mr Smelly over there" he finally answered.

At that point the conversation collapsed as laughter dominated. Their theatrics, always played an endearing part of their friendship; as the years went by these theatrics had become more sophisticated and frequent.

With each of the four having both hectic and complex jobs they had established a rule many years earlier, that being, their careers would always remain backstage whenever they spent time together. Their adherence to this rule repaid them with relaxation and this relaxation rendered them refreshment they each needed. It was with this philosophy, that they spent the remainder of their holiday and by its conclusion each felt ready to step back into their respective jobs.

As Eden stood in his office examining some x-rays, his secretary entered with her daily narration of his schedule, together with his much awaited coffee. Now, four weeks since his return from Camp David, Eden was entirely back into his serious mode. This particular morning, however, there was one distraction, a distraction he simply didn't need, given the four operations that awaited him. He had woken with a headache which now, had gained momentum to such a point that staring at the light filled x-ray, had become impossible. "Damn!" he said as he flicked the light off "Any ideas on getting rid of a bad headache?" he groaned.

"I find a couple of paracetamol quite helpful." she answered "I'll get some from the bathroom. Don't drink your coffee, it will make you worse, wait and I'll get a glass of water instead."

Eden sat waiting as directed, staring at his coffee. "Great," he thought to himself "here I am with four operations to do today and I'm asking for advice on a headache." As the ironic thought came to him, he stopped himself from laughing, knowing too well, his head would not appreciate it. "My next appointment with Dr Coster, can you check when it is?" he asked, as his secretary returned.

"As soon as you swallow the paracetamol I will," she responded, standing her ground.

Having obliged her, she obliged him, then returned to say, "Your next appointment is on the third of March but I also checked if there was any openings this morning. There is one at ten a.m., so I asked them to hold it for you and I'd get back to them."

"No good. I'm in theater then."

"Do you know, you've never passed one of your ops over to anyone. Maybe this morning you should! With your headache you'll find it hard to concentrate anyway," she insisted.

"As usual, you're right. If you could get Michael Berther on the line for me and confirm that appointment, I'd appreciate it."

As Eden tried to enter the lift an hour later, to keep his appointment with Doctor Coster, the sister of a patient caught him as she exited "Doctor Parks!" she said, looking stunned "I thought you were operating on my brother?"

"I was operating on him but unfortunately I managed to come down with a splitting headache this morning, so I've arranged the best surgeon at my disposal. Your brother couldn't be in better hands, I can entirely assure you of that."

"Well?" she responded "if he's as good as you say, I suppose that's the main thing."

"Look, he's been in theater for nearly an hour now, why don't you head over to my office and tell my secretary that I want her to check how it's gone so far and fill you in."

"I'd really appreciate that. Thanks Doctor Parks. Oh, and I hope your headache gets better."

Doctor Coster, or Alvin as he preferred most people to call him, had been friends of Eden's and Sarah's for years. Eden and Alvin had worked together for many long hours into the night, over a period of five years, when both had enlisted in the, so-called, backyard clinics. On many of these occasions, Sarah had insisted on accompanying them. To help as much as she could. The necessity to keep quiet about their work at the time had remained a priority through their careers, for then and now, it was not legally permissible to provide someone with medical attention out of the realms of the hospital paying parameters. This quietness had never extended to the dining table of their own homes however, where, on countless occasions, Eden, Sarah, Alvin and his dog had relived their profound experiences over many meals.

Alvin now ran a private clinic of his own within Washington Heart but was also employed by the hospital to monitor their staff's health. For every staff member, regardless of position or age, their terms of employment included a six monthly physical to satisfy hospital records and patient health. "I heard you were coming," Alvin said as Eden walked in.

"So did I." Eden grinned "Ouch!"

"And I heard you've got a headache!"

"I heard that too."

"And I heard that I'm going to jump on your foot." Alvin said, determined to win the game.

"Oh, I didn't hear that." Eden gave in.

"Seriously, what are you doing with a headache? You're too fit for that."

"Alvin, you're supposed to tell me that."

"You're right. Ok, lets put you through the wringer and then conclude with a nice cup of tea!"

"Coffee."

"No, bad for a headache."

At that point Alvin threw himself into the job at hand and his lively chatter succumbed to concentration. This gave Eden an opportunity to just sit quietly. Despite all of Alvin's poking, prodding, listening and sample taking, Eden's headache had lessened by the end of the examination. "You must have done something for me, my headaches half gone," he said to Alvin, as they both lounged back in their chairs while they drank their tea.

"It's probably just my aura. So, how are the artists?"

"They're both busy, but good. How's Dodge?"

"He's great, but lately he's decided that chewing on mobile phones is entertaining," he shrugged.

"You don't think you spoil him a bit? I mean that doghouse you bought him looked better than Jane's cubby house when she was a kid."

"And this is coming from a man who lets his goose have a shower every day and buys him flowers to eat!" he grinned "incidentally, you'll be pleased to know that I took your advice. In a couple of weeks I'll be devoting all my time to my clinic and no more on staff work!"

"Good on you. You're too good to be doing the hospital work that's for someone else. Your place is one hundred per cent in that clinic. I think that's great!"

"Between you and me, I'm thrilled. I've always found the hospital work completely boring. I mean, the money's good but who needs it if you're bored? My clinic, it's the opposite, and it keeps me focused."

Both paused as someone's pager went off "It's me," Eden said grabbing it off his belt and reading the message "Oh! got to move!"

"Wait," Alvin took a box from a cupboard "any more headaches, take one of them when you feel it coming on, I'll ring you at home in a couple of days when I get your results back."

"Yes, Doctor Coster!" Eden joked as he left the room.

As Alvin busied himself marking the samples he had taken, his secretary alerted him to his overcrowded reception "Ok, you finish these and get them off to pathology and I'll get on with the other."

By mid afternoon Eden's headache had disappeared. Despite feeling washed out he insisted on doing the two remaining procedures and checking on the two patients who had been operated on by Michael. When all was well, he headed home, looking forward to a quiet evening with Sarah but such was not to prevail. Sarah had been in New York supervising another exhibition over the past two days; minutes after Eden walked through the front door she rang to tell him that they had closed the airport because of dangerous blizzards, that she would be yet another night in New York. With this news Eden poured a brandy, checked on Junior and went straight to bed.

The one extra night in New York turned into three, for no sooner had the airport reopened, it had frustrated its clients by closing again. When Sarah finally did fly into D.C. and rang Eden to say she would be home in twenty minutes, he was thrilled. An hour earlier he had given the staff a night off and prepared a lobster bouillabaisse; twenty minutes, he thought, would allow him just enough time to finish setting the table, open some wine and light the candles.

When Sarah got out of her car, twenty minutes later, looking a bit worn, she was met with a typical scene. There was her husband sitting on the steps of their home, in a raincoat, with two glasses of champagne which were starting to overflow as the rain fell into them. "I love coming home," she said as she put her briefcase down and wrapped her arms around him.

"Well, let's get you in, out of the rain and I'll tell you all the things I love about you."

"You can't, we'll be up all night."

"Sounds good to me" he said before kissing her.

Just as they were finishing their dinner the phone rang "It's all right," Eden said to Sarah as she started to get up "the answering machine's on." But as she sat back down the phone kept ringing. "Oh, it's the private line," he said, jumping up as he realised "That's strange," he said to Sarah as he returned to the room minutes later.

"What?"

"That was Alvin. He wants to come over."

"What, now?" she said, looking at her watch "It's ten o'clock."

"That's what I told him, but he insisted. He said it's important."

"Is he alright?"

"I don't know, he sounded a bit odd on the phone. Oh, I know, it's probably something about work. It's his last two weeks of working for the hospital and strictly his clinic after that."

"That's great," Sarah said "I'll bet he's excited." she concluded as she smiled at the thought.

Ten minutes later, Alvin stood in the foyer, dripping wet. "Gee, you look awful," Eden said as he took his friend's coat.

"Eden I need to talk to you alone."

"Why, what about?"

"Your medical check. I got the results back a couple of hours ago."

"Whatever it is Alvin, you can tell the both of us. Come on, Sarah's waiting and so is your Scotch."

"Alvin! What's wrong?" Sarah asked as he entered the room with Eden having noticed an expression on his face that she had never seen before.

Alvin sat down and took a sip of his Scotch as Sarah and Eden stared at him anxiously. "Well, I don't know how to tell you this...damn!" He paused taking another sip of his drink "I've been sitting in my office for three hours trying to work it out."

"Alvin," Eden said, "What is it?"

"As I said, I got your test results back."

"What results?" Sarah asked.

"I had a bad headache while you were away so I asked Alvin to check me over."

"One of the tests the hospital gets me to do but keep low key about, is an HIV test because of any exposure to patients who may or may not be carrying the virus." Alvin continued in a shaky voice.

"And?" Sarah and Eden asked in unison.

"Yours came back positive."

"Positive. That can't be. I'm too careful when I work," Eden said as he noticed Sarah trembling. "It's ok Sarah," he said putting his arm around her "it's got to be a mistake."

"It's not a mistake Eden," Alvin said quietly "I went over and over it hoping the same thing, but it's not a mistake."

"Well what about Sarah, are you going to tell us she's got it too?"

"We won't know until she's tested."

The room was silent as shock seeped in. As Eden and Sarah held each other, neither spoke nor cried but struggled to breathe. As Alvin stared at them, tears welled up in his eyes. In all his life he had never felt such anguish as he did now. "I'll be just outside if you need anything," he said as he filled their glasses and left the room to give them a minute to themselves. When he returned they were as he had left them. He could sense their fear it was monumental. A fear of a partition suddenly between them. A partition that encompassed a force that could and probably would, take away one or both of the two things they had, each other and their always desperate desire to be there for their daughter. How could they let this happen? How could it be? If it was, it was wrong and surely there was some way out. If not, their life was shattered. Without each other, they knew, too well, they couldn't survive. Not surviving, meant leaving Jane, this was beyond comprehension. Both knew, without saying it, Sarah's condition would not permit such a virus living in her body for too long. What would be the length? What should they do? They couldn't leave Jane, nor could they leave each other. They had always been dangerously close, was this their punishment for taking that risk? If it was, they could accept that for the love that they had had but did it need to hurt their daughter? Was this real or was it a dream? Their strength had always conquered everything, but conquering this, frightened them. It was as if some strange force had said "No" to everything they had lived for and to everything they needed to do. How would they respond? They didn't know, but the world was now different, it housed fear. A fear that neither could eradicate for the other, this was new, this gave life a different meaning. Their need to have this time to themselves, Alvin knew, was essential, so he quietly left them with the intention of phoning in the morning. They were as oblivious to his departure as they were to everything else. Every ounce of reality had drained from them as if it had been swept out from under their feet. The air, the ground, the room were different. It was as if turmoil was the only reality and this reality would engulf them without their consent.

The following seventy-two hours were like seventy-two days as they waited for Sarah's result. Once again Alvin came to their home to give them the answer though his face was to give it away first. This news, was the worst? Having lived through the condition of hypertensive pneumonia for the major part of her life it had already taken its toll on her lungs and immune system. Available drugs would provide numerous advantages to Eden but their ability to provide Sarah with such advantages would be remote.

Over the following months Sarah and Eden took an extended break from their work, a break that made many wonder why they hadn't done this before. Both, they believed had worked incredibly hard over the years, a break like this gave some sense to it. During this time they focused on Jane, spending all and any available time with her. By mid July, their time ran out when Sarah developed Pneumocystis carinii pneumonia, and was subsequently diagnosed with AIDS. Two weeks later, on the 30th July, their black Mercedes left the winding road, as they had intended it to, hurtled down the five hundred meter cliff face and smashed into the sea.

Their death was to look accidental, this was a privilege they had and chose, but Jane, they knew, was owed the privilege of knowing the truth. Alvin was the only one who knew of their health, it had been agreed that there was no need for him to alert the hospital until Eden returned from his break. To tell Jane, they had decided, would only serve to include her in their anguish and this they did not want. The anguish she would suffer after their death was enough. They had written her a letter explaining the truth and left it on the dresser in her bedroom of their home.

CHAPTER

TEN

Three months later Jane was in the same place that she had predominantly inhabited since her parent's funeral. The solace of her bedroom in the mansion with Junior was the only comfort to her. The only deviation to this was a daily swim in the pool, after which, both retired back to her room. Though some of the staff were permitted in, for one way conversations with themselves, their worry for her was beyond reproach. She had refused to take many of the phone calls from concerned friends and had treated visits from them in the same manner. Her apartment and studio had been devoid of her presence over the months and as her sculptures awaited completion, friends waited for her grief to subside.

Before the funeral she had not permitted herself to feel grief or her need for solitude, this being partly due to her immediate response of shock and the fact that giving her parents a fitting funeral had become her sole concern. The congregation that had gathered at Washington Cathedral had been only just short of one thousand people, the majority of whom had stood through the entirety of the service, which had commenced with an interrupted speech from Jane, who had to stop and pause on several occasions to regain her composure. This was proceeded with a speech from Bill and continued with many more speeches from people who loved the couple. After the service, half of the congregation continued to the cemetery where Eden and Sarah were put to rest beside Esme and Samuel's grave. It was at her parent's home, after the last person had left their wake that Jane's shock had dissipated and reality had sunk in. It was at that point that she sensed a need for solitude in which to process this reality. The letter her parent's had written had remained unopened and its presence unknown, for the day that had seen Eden's and Sarah's life end had been a stifling thirty-two degrees and for the well meaning staff member who had opened the windows in Jane's room to let in the early evening breeze she remained unaware that the letter had been blown off the dresser and under the bed.

On this particular day Jane had a reason that insisted she leave her room and in many ways she was glad of the prompt. Today, she was to unveil a bronze statue of her father, which had been commissioned by the hospital as a tribute to him. As she climbed the marble steps that led to the hospital she felt a calm strength within her. The past three months had introduced her to feelings and emotions she had never known. With this came a new knowledge and understanding and though this had scared her at first, she knew her wisdom had grown because of it. As she took the last step she stopped to stare at her silhouette that lay in front of her in the gleaming white marble, "You guys put too much into me for me to let you down and I promise you I won't," she thought to herself and then startled as she heard someone call her name.

"I'm sorry, I startled you."

"Don't be," Jane responded with a smile.

"I don't know if you remember me. We danced at your twenty-first birthday party?" he continued.

Jane remembered him too well. For months after that party she had hoped that he might call her but when this didn't eventuate she had resigned herself to believing that he was either preoccupied with someone else or his work, or simply not interested in her. She had, on occasions, considered calling him but considering was as far as her thoughts had reached. "I remember it well, we danced to three pieces and as I recall we had ninety-seven dances to go," she said as she glanced at her watch "Oh look, sorry! I'm afraid I have to go, it seems I'm running late."

"I know. I thought I'd better warn you, they're all in there waiting. There's a back door you can use and it'll look like you've come down from upstairs. Come on, I'll show you," Michael said beckoning her with a wave of his hand.

Within a minute he had her in a lift on the way to the down-stairs foyer where, when she appeared, she was met with hundreds of smiling faces and clapping hands. The cream of the medical profession had gathered together with a large group of Eden's personal patients, the hospital board and staff, Eden's secretary and a bevy of media people. Minutes later, the audience was transfixed as they listened to Jane's passionate speech about her father and his second home, the hospital. "When I was a little girl," she continued "I remember thinking that only people with a very kind heart could fix other people's hearts. As I grew older and came to a more appropriate understanding of the necessary qualifications, my father pointed out that my initial thoughts were far from wrong. The heart, he said is an organ that requires knowledge to fix, encompassing the heart is a human being and human beings need people with kind hearts. My father, your colleague or your doctor, gave to all of us that kind heart, coupled with his amazing knowledge and skill that made him the mastermind that he was in the world of cardiovascular medicine. This statue is an honor to my father, though, we know, a greatly deserved one and for me, it has been an honor to be here amongst you as you have paid him such a tribute. Thank you," she concluded. Over the proceeding hour Jane circled the foyer, speaking to as many people as she could. In the midst of this, a journalist, who was thankful to have her approval, aimed his camera to catch her through his lens but as he took the shot his picture changed as Michael stepped in aside his subject.

"You do have a way of appearing," Jane laughed.

"So it seems," he responded stepping away from her for a moment to allow the journalist another shot.

"That was my last shot," he said shrugging his shoulder "would it be ok to use it?" he asked Jane.

"That's fine," she answered with her mother's gentle smile "and, as for you" she continued as she turned back to Michael "I'm not up to any more startles today."

"Not even over dinner?" he asked looking into her blue eyes with an air of extreme certainty.

"Not even over dinner but I don't have a problem with a startle free dinner," she smiled.

"Great. Can I pick you up or would you prefer to meet? Let's say about eight!"

"Tonight, sorry, pre-arranged plans," she answered, thinking of the promise she'd made to the staff that she would have dinner with them. "I'm free tomorrow night if you are?"

"Already looking forward to it. Tell you what, how about I pick you up, make a booking and make it a surprise?"

"Ok," she nodded "I'd better keep mingling though, I'll see you tomorrow."

An hour later the foyer was empty of the gathering; its only inhabitants were busy clearing away tables and glasses in their swift attempt to return the hospital's foyer to its usual environment. Jane paused for a few minutes in front of the statue, winked a goodbye and walked out into the fresh air.

From the hospital Jane headed to her apartment to collect her mail and possibly work on her sculptures for a couple of hours. Once there, however, no such work was to eventuate. It seemed that her mobile phone had a mind of its own as it incessantly rang with one call after another. The news that she was out and about had traveled promptly and her mobile had become their first port of call. As she walked around the studio with phone in one hand and coffee in the other, the fragrance of the fresh flowers wafted through the air. Her housemaid had kept both the apartment and studio as impeccable as she always did. Having nearly lost her voice from hours of talking Jane diverted her phone to its message-bank service and drove home. She hadn't checked any of the seventy-three messages awaiting her on the answering machine, nor had she done any work. The paperwork that had been left over the past three months worried her and the unopened mail was overwhelming in quantity. With her head spinning she decided to give herself the remainder of the evening and the following day before she threw herself into the complexity of sorting it all out.

The following evening, true to his word, Michael managed to surprise Jane by arriving by helicopter. Neither Jane nor the staff were unused to helicopters landing on the property, since over the years Bill and Hillary had many times arrived and departed in the same fashion. They were, however, surprised to find it was Michael who had disembarked from it. As he strode up the steps of the mansion he found the huge door open and a staff member waiting to greet him. Striding into the foyer with his blonde hair blown back from his forehead he stopped and looked stunned as he stared at Jane "Beautiful is not the word," he said finally and paused again "in my entire life I have never seen anyone as beautiful as I see before me now. You are going to put that which I have to show you now to shame."

"And can I ask what you've got to show me?'

"Lights. Lots of lights," he grinned "are you ready?"

"Let's go," she answered.

"Have a lovely time," Isabel called after them as they walked hand in hand out of the door.

"We will Isabel. Love you. Goodnight," Jane called back.

Outside, despite the bitter cold, the night air was without its usual snow, rain or fog and when they took their seats in the helicopter, the heating disassociated them from the cold. "Good evening Ma'am," the pilot said with cheerful conviction "now, when you're comfortable let me know and we'll take off."

"I'm so comfortable that if I were any more so I'd be inclined to stay here all night." Jane laughed.

"We're off then," he nodded.

Within sixty seconds the mansion directly beneath them was as big as an open hand. As they headed towards the city Michael exhibited his knowledge of landmarks as he gave a verbal rendition of the names and history of many buildings that Jane didn't even know existed in their city "Your knowledge of what's down there is amazing."

"On the contrary, being up here with you is amazing, anyway don't pay my knowledge any attention, I've been coming up here at least once a month for years, so I should know what's down there anyway."

"Why so often?"

"I suppose it's because for me it's sort of meditative. It clears my head."

"Well it's certainly stunning."

"The best bit's about thirty seconds away and for that I brought some champagne to accompany it."

As they drank their champagne Jane was entranced by the beauty below. There was the heart of Washington lit up by a mass of bright lights. In some areas, where fog hovered, the lights defied their blanket and shone softly through. In other areas that were strikingly clear, the lights were so bright, they gleamed. The millions of lights culminated in a shimmering sea of beauty. Jane now understood why Michael described it as meditative, she herself, had for many minutes, forgotten her worries as she silently savored what lay below. "I can see you like it," Michael volunteered.

"How do you know."

He paused, staring into her eyes "Because you're speech-less!"

"Thank you for bringing me up here it's beautiful."

"Well, for me I've found something more beautiful, for you, I'll bring you back as often as you like. Now, are you hungry?"

"Starving."

"Good! James?"

"Aye-aye, sir," James responded from the front of the chopper.

"Well, they always say a big meal is good for jet lag," Michael said to Jane as he surveyed the menu.

"Jet lag!" she laughed.

"Ok, it's more like chopper lag but it's a good excuse to eat as much as you want," he grinned "Um, squid in its own ink, that's tempting, then again there's the quail or duck confit. What do you think you'll have?"

"I've had the salmon here before and it was absolutely divine, so, salmon it is for me."

"Then it's salmon for me... and entree?"

"Why don't you choose for both of us."

"A spirited gambler!"

"Not really, it's just that I like everything on the menu so I can't lose."

As the waiter left minutes later with their orders Michael picked up his glass and said "To your twenty-second birthday tomorrow!"

"You've got a good memory."

"I remember the first time I saw you and you've been floating in my head ever since."

"You should have called me then."

"I know. Stupid isn't it? Too obsessed with my work. Luckily, that's changed and I've come to my senses."

"I'm glad to hear it!"

"Jane..." he paused "I just wanted you to know that I was really sorry when I heard about your parents. I had a huge amount of respect and admiration for Eden, I'm just so sorry, sorry for you that it happened, I mean the accident. I don't know how you've been going, I mean, I tried to call a few times over the last couple of months, but you were understandably out of contact. If you'll let me, I'd really like to be there for you."

"Thanks Michael, that's really kind of you. I'm sorry you called for nothing. I don't know, I haven't really talked about it to anyone. I just sort of took some time by myself to grasp some things and I think that helped me a lot, but yes, there was a point when I just felt a bit crazy, but I know now, that it's just a part of processing the grief; when two people mean everything to you the grief just seems so much more intense," she paused "actually I don't believe I'm telling you all this. Suffice to say it's been hard but I'm improving. Coming out tonight has been great and I've really enjoyed your company."

"Well that's great because I was sort of hoping we could do this again."

"I'd love to do this again, oh! except for the next week. I'm absolutely inundated with paperwork and a thousand other things."

"Your salmon Madam… Sir." the waiter interrupted with an air of gentleness in his voice and with the same air extending in the way he placed the plates in front of them before purposely slipping away quietly so they could resume their conversation.

"Anyway, enough about me, what about you, does your family live in Washington?"

"No, I'm it. I had a younger brother, but he died."

"Oh Michael, I'm sorry."

"It's ok, he died when he was two hours old and my mother died during the birth."

"Oh Michael, that's terrible for you. What about your father, it must have been terrible for him too."

"It was. Enough for him to kill himself a month later."

"Oh, you poor thing. How old were you then?"

"Five or going on ten. I went to live with my aunt after that and she always thought that because of the whole thing I always seemed to act double my age, more mature or wiser or something. Anyway, when I was sixteen I moved in with some students and put myself through med school. I suppose, in a way it made me a bit tougher than the other students but all these years later I'm sort of used to it, I'm pretty self reliant."

"What about your aunt, do you spend much time with her?"

"Not really, we never really got on very well. We sort of drifted apart and then last year I heard she died of a heart attack."

"Well I think that's all pretty tough to have to handle and not having the chance to see or hold your brother couldn't have helped. Being self reliant is good, in fact I wish I could say the same, but I really think that a huge dose of daily tender loving care would do you the world of good, when you think about it, you don't miss what you haven't had and everybody, whether they know it or not, should have a bit of TLC around them."

"You're right, I never thought about it that way."

"Well, you've got to and if I have to make it my business to make sure you do, I will. Your childhood is similar to Mum's and Dad's. They both lost their parents when they were very young and were put into orphanages. In fact, that's where they met. When Mum was six and Dad was seven, she was moved from one orphanage to another, the one he was in. That was it, they were inseparable after that. The orphanages were pretty lacking when it came to treating the children like children. If they had the basics, like food, clothes, a bath once a week and a roof over their heads, they had done their job well or so they thought. Luckily for my parents they had each other, so they had that love and warmth there and a lot of tender loving care."

"I had no idea Eden had been through all that and your mother of course," Michael said as he put his hand down on hers.

"It's funny isn't it, people's lives are never as simple and straight forward as we often think and often the people who have had a harder life seem to go out and achieve more in their life. It's like you said, you were sort of made to feel self reliant, and self reliant you became, really, that's an attribute. What happened to you probably made you a stronger person and more mature. I mean, putting yourself through med school is no mean feat. Then again, mum and dad did the same thing too. Mum sold her paintings and that money was used to put Dad through med school and pay for general living expenses, oh, and Dad worked in the evenings in a jazz band and apparently that helped a lot."

Later that night Jane put all of her energy into trying to fall asleep but by three a.m. she was still far from it. She knew already that she loved this man. Whether it was his mesmerising good looks, his intelligent mind or his vibrant personality she didn't know, but her mind was captivated with him. Already she wished she would see him tomorrow and not in a week as she had requested. She now felt uncomfortable to be by herself, as if nothing was normal without his presence. She could neither sleep nor concentrate, he had changed her into somebody she didn't know, but that somebody she preferred, for its identity included an excitement and passion she couldn't resist. As her thoughts spun around in her mind she heard a soft knock at the door. "Yes." she responded.

"I was just getting some warm milk and I saw your light on. Would you like me to bring you some back?" Isabelle asked quietly.

"Better than that I'll come with you," Jane said as she came out of her room, feeling glad to have some company for a few minutes.

"How did your evening go?" Isabelle asked minutes later as she handed Jane a steaming mug of milk.

"Well we ate…"

"Jane!"

"Sorry but I adore that face you pull when you're trying to be patient," she paused "the evening, the evening was too good."

"What do you mean?"

"Our first night out; I've come home and realised I'm in love with him, I'm not sure what to do about it."

"Honey there's not much you can do, you can't change love."

"But that's just the point, I've had so many changes lately that I just don't know if I'm up to any more right now."

"You know what your mother would say."

"I know, let my heart direct me. She's right too. Thanks Isabelle, you just really helped me and I mean it's not as if being in love with somebody is a plague or something."

"I wish it was," Isabelle laughed "then I might catch it too!"

"Listen to you, you know Mark has been trying to get a ring on your finger for years."

"He is rather sweet, but I just need a little more time."

"Isabelle, you said the same thing five years ago. Anyway, thanks for the chat and helping me sort out my mind, I think I might just be able to go to sleep now."

"Jane, one last thing. Of all the people in the world that deserve to be happy, it's you and if you're in love with him then he'd better be the best part of perfect."

"Well my impression so far is that he's better than that," Jane assured her as she bent over and hugged her.

Jane's birthday came and went as quickly as Christmas and the New Year did. During this hectic three months Jane had been kept more than occupied. Commitments to the charities, the mansion and the staff had demanded a great deal of hard work. She loaned her apartment and studio to a collection of potential young artists who otherwise would have no such place to live or work. This done, she moved back into the house, neither wishing to render the staff there jobless, nor sell the stunning home that her parents had loved. She turned one of the rooms into a studio in which she could work. She directed the collaboration of her mother's work and sent it together with the gallery's staff on a worldwide exhibition. She worked with the publishers to ensure that the last book her father had written was published and circulated, this amongst attending more presentations and awards on her parents behalf.

Amid the realms of all of these responsibilities Jane had insisted on making time for Michael. When she was with him she was at her happiest. He had quickly become the focus in her life, she adored him. Though she still grieved for her parents she lived every day with an intense appreciation of this new love. Michael had been attentive to nothing but her with the exception of his work. His love and respect for Jane was as obvious as hers for him. If he wasn't working there was only one other place he would be, by her side. If she was sad he made her happy, if she was happy he made her happier. On social occasions the two were never seen apart and had become a favorite subject in the social columns. The first such occasion dating back to the shot that Michael had inadvertently stepped into and its accompanying article. The phone had gone mad at that time with friends wanting to know who was the man standing next to Jane. No one was surprised, when just, seven weeks after their first evening together, Michael's Christmas present to Jane was the most compact parcel under the tree, which, when opened displayed a sparkling engagement ring.

The wedding date had been set for the first Saturday in January, when Jane opened her eyes that morning she knew that day had come. What she didn't know but was made acutely aware of when her eyes met the alarm clock, was that she had slept in. She threw on her dressing gown and tore down the staircase only to be met by dozens of people tearing around in the same hectic fashion. Isabelle, who was busy with one of the florists, turned and noticed Jane standing there looking bewildered. Hurriedly she walked over "it's all right everything is running beautifully" she assured her.

"But I slept in, I can't believe it."

"I know. First I thought I'd wake you up, then I thought you could probably use the sleep.

It's such a rarity for you to sleep in anyway. So, I've made sure everything's under control and it is, so don't worry, anyway, you're not allowed to worry on your wedding day."

"Ok, well I'll go and make a quick call to Michael and have a shower. I'll see you in half an hour."

As morning turned into afternoon and afternoon into evening all were in their places at the church. "Jane, you look absolutely exquisite," Bill said as he kissed her on the cheek.

"Oh Bill, I'm so nervous. I would give anything to have mum and dad here today."

"Sweetheart they're here I promise you that and to see you now, I know how proud they must feel, I can just see their faces. You know you look exactly like your mother did on the day she married. I remember feeling quite a tad jealous of Eden, there he was marrying an angel and to look at you now I see a lucky young man again marrying an angel."

"Thanks," she said with a calmer expression on her face.

"Also I want you to know something very important and very important to me," he said taking her hands into his "No matter whatever happens to you in your life I will be there for you and if you ever need anything, anything at all, I will make sure you have it. Beyond being your godfather and your friend, it is paramount to me that you are safe and well and very happy. If any of those things are ever compromised I want you to know, now, that I need for you to tell me. Can you do that?"

"Yes. I promise," she smiled.

"Good. Now I'd better let you get married. I believe we have an aisle to walk down!"

As Bill walked down the aisle, taking the bride to her groom his partner took a second to look up from the smiling faces to the stained glass windows of the church. This was the church her parents were married in and as she walked, her mother's words floated back to her "Jane... it was beautiful," she had told her "the sun poured through the stained glass windows and flickered around the room and more sunlight streamed down the aisle, which lit up and made it almost shimmer."

"There was no sun today," Jane thought. The stained glass was dark, no sun was dancing around the room, and the aisle she was walking down was not shimmering, instead a dull red stared back at her.

"I wish there was some sun coming in the windows," she whispered to Bill.

"Bum," he whispered back.

"What?"

"Your first wish and I can't help you, it's the middle of winter."

Having reached their destination, Bill stepped back to take his seat and watched as the priest began the ceremony. "Do you, Jane Esme, take Michael David to be your lawful wedded husband, to love and to cherish, as long as you shall live, so help you God?" With her confirmation he continued with Michael. Minutes later, with vows exchanged, the guests cheered as Michael lifted Jane's veil from her face and they kissed each other for the first time as husband and wife. Twenty minutes later Michael scooped his wife up and insisted on carrying her, in his arms, out of the church to the waiting guests. Before leaving the church, Jane had again looked at the windows and the red carpet hoping for a skerrick of sun. "This worried her," she thought, but she didn't know why. Outside, the confetti-filled air distracted her from her thoughts.

Once the newly weds were suitably attired with confetti the guests watched as they made their way to the presidential helicopter then up into the air with Bill and Hillary and a newly wed banner dangling below, then they left to follow by car. All reunited in the meticulously decorated dining room where they experienced an evening that none wanted to end, but end it did, and as the guests went home, Jane and Michael boarded a flight to Switzerland. Upon their return, two weeks later, the change in their visible appearance was obvious to all. It was as if they had been to a health farm instead.

The following morning as Jane completed her tenth lap of the pool, Michael came in and called to her from the other end. Acknowledging him with a wave of her hand she turned and swam towards him. As she ascended from the pool he ran his fingers over her breasts and kissed her "You're so beautiful," he whispered in her ear. Jane savored his touch more than anything about him and she was still wondering whether the intense flutter in her body, when he did so, would ever subside. "You'll need to get a dressing gown darling, Ian Grant's waiting," he said.

"Waiting. Where?"

"In the sitting room," he paused "you've forgotten?"

"Forgotten what?"

"That we asked him to come over this morning."

"Did we, I'm sorry Michael, I don't know what's got into me lately. You go and talk to him and I'll throw some clothes on."

"Hi Ian, how have you been?" Jane asked minutes later as she entered the room wearing a knee length sweater and sneakers.

"I've been good. Gee, you look well. It's good to see you, I haven't seen you since the wedding. Michael tells me you had a great time in Switzerland."

"We sure did," she said smiling at Michael "and I brought everybody a little something back, except I've still got to unpack."

"I'll look forward to it. Now…" he said as he opened his briefcase "I've got the two wills here as you requested. I need you to read them and check that you're happy before you sign them."

"No," Jane said minutes later, after having read the main of her will while her husband perused his. "I know in my original will I left everything to charity but here you've got half going to charity and half going to Michael."

"That's right," Ian nodded "the fax you sent last week stipulated that."

"The fax I sent you last week," she repeated looking totally confused.

"Yeah, you dictated it and asked me to write it out and fax it from the lobby, which I did,"

Michael reminded her.

"Of course," Jane mumbled as she half remembered some dialogue about it late one night on their honeymoon. It still needs changing though. I want it all to go to Michael."

"But if you do that he would have to run the charities," Ian reminded her.

"Yes," she paused "as long as that's ok with you Michael?" she continued, realising that she had taken that for granted.

"Of course," he answered with determination.

"But how would he manage both, working at the hospital and running the charities?" Ian asked, feeling equally determined to persuade Jane not to bequeath all of it to him, simply because, as an attorney, he, unlike his clients, always saw the potential pitfalls of such decisions, not that he didn't trust Michael any less than others, but he was an attorney and part of his job was to be concerned about such things.

"Mum and dad worked and ran them," she answered.

"But in this situation he would be by himself."

"I've been by myself for six months and it's been ok. Look it's just not an option to give it to the charities in a lump sum if somebody is there to keep it going. Mum and dad could have done that twenty three years ago and so there would have been no corporation set up and the money wouldn't have been regenerating as it has over the last twenty-three years. If I was to give it, in a lump sum then that regeneration would stop and that's not what the charities need or have needed over the last two decades. I think you're forgetting how good you are too, I mean you're the one who does the brunt of the work," she reminded him "Don't worry about Michael he'll be ok, and anyway, I certainly don't plan to be going anywhere!" she laughed.

"Good. Now that's sorted out you'll be pleased to know my will is perfect," Michael interrupted as he took a pen from his pocket to sign and date it before handing it back to Ian.

"All right, well I'll redraft this one and get back to you," Ian said, even starting to doubt his own nervousness and feeling all to aware that Jane was right, regeneration was crucial to the many needy people who benifitted from the money.

"Great," Jane said, "I'll give you your present then."

"It is ok with you, all of that?" she asked Michael again as they walked arm in arm, back inside after having seen Ian off "I mean if something were to happen to me, would you want that responsibility?"

"Jane, I'm sure, the only thing that is going to happen to you is that you are going to grow old with me."

"I'll second that," she laughed.

"You know, I could spend all day staring at you in that sweater amongst other things but, unfortunately I've got three ops waiting for me."

"Fortunately would be the operative word for the patients," she reminded him.

"Quite right. Better go."

It was ten days later before they could share a meal, other than breakfast together and as they sat down to a beautiful dinner that Jane had cooked, she was feeling uncomfortably tired. "I'm glad it's Saturday tomorrow," she said to Michael "I never normally sleep in, but tomorrow I'm going to go out of my way to do so. I don't know, I just feel abnormally tired!"

"Sorry darling, you can't," he informed her.

"What?...Why?"

"I promised Peter we'd play tennis with them in the morning. They were going to play doubles but their partners pulled out so I volunteered."

"Well, we'll have to give them a ring and explain."

"We can't do that."

"Why not?"

"It's not a very good excuse. I can't play tennis because I'm too tired."

"You're right. Ok, I'll sleep in on Sunday instead."

Over the next hour they traded stories about the past week. By which time Jane's tiredness got the better of her and though she didn't want to, she knew she had to go to bed. "I've got to go up. I'm sorry, I'm just so tired. I'll be better company tomorrow I promise," she concluded as she bent over to kiss him goodnight. "What Michael?" she asked noticing a strange look on his face.

"Oh nothing, it's just something that's been worrying me. We can talk about it tomorrow. You get some sleep."

"If it's something worrying you I'd rather talk about it now. What is it?" she asked as she sat back down.

"It's just that you've had staff all around you, in your home, all your life and you're used to that but I'm not, I'm just finding it really hard, living like this. You know, if there's one thing that I've always cherished, it's privacy. At work, there are people around me all the time so, when I come home, I want to see you and only you, not a whole household of staff. I just can't relax like this."

"Ok, I can see what you're saying but don't you think over some time, you might get used to it?"

"Jane, I've had thirty years to experience privacy and I actually like it and miss it. I'm sorry, this is why I am talking to you, I just can't see myself getting used to it."

"Well, I don't know what to say. Most of the staff have been with us for years. I mean I want you to be happy, obviously, but how do I tell them we don't want them around anymore? This is their home and their positions here are their jobs. I just can't imagine how to do that. They'd be mortified.

Apart from all that, I'd miss them, because yes, I am used to them being around and I regard each one of them as a friend."

"As far as their jobs, couldn't we find them work within the charities?"

"Sure, we always need new people but they are used to and like their jobs here."

"Well, where does that put me? I mean, you're not married to them, you're married to me."

"But Michael, it's just not that simple, aside from all of that, this house is huge, you know that, and it needs a lot of work, inside and out to keep it this way. Then there's the cooking, the laundry and mounds of work every time we entertain. Who would do all of that?"

"Caterer's, gardener's, cleaner's etc. That's how everyone else does it. They come in, they do their stuff and they're out. All is done and we have, what a home should have, privacy."

"It's not that easy for me though. I've known these people for most of my life. Just the thought of telling them this horrifies me. In fact, I'm glad we gave them the night off. Look, actually, I can't do this anymore. Can you let me give what you've said some thought and in the meantime can we not discuss this in front of the staff?"

Feeling completely drained now, Jane went looking for Junior, which had become a habit when she was worried and finally went to sleep with Junior at the bottom of their bed.

When the alarm went off at its set time the next morning Junior trotted up the bed and brushed his soft head on Jane's cheek. "Hi Junior," she said patting him with one hand and reaching for the source of noise with the other. Downstairs, she found Michael showered, dressed and completely engross-ed in complementing his breakfast with the newspaper to the point he hadn't even noticed her enter the room. Jane stood for a minute staring at him, their discussion of last night worried her profusely. She couldn't bear to let the staff down and equally she couldn't bear to let him down, she loved him too much to ever do that. "Don't think about it for the rest of the day," she thought to herself.

Two hours later, while Michael and Peter chatted about work, Jane was helping Peter's wife in the kitchen who was determined to have a large jug of orange juice chilled and ready to drink after their game. "You know in five years it will be the year 2000 and still nobody has invented a better orange juicer," she laughed "talking about dates, it's the first of February so that means the two of you have been married for exactly twenty six days. Is it agreeing with you, married life?"

"Out of a score of ten I'd give it an eleven. It's been wonderful."

"Oh that's great. You certainly look as if it agrees with you, except you do look a dash tired."

"A bit more than a dash," Jane laughed.

"Well you make sure you look after yourself! You know, sometimes I spend so much time looking after Peter and the children that I just go by the wayside and lately, I've been actively trying to rectify that. Don't you get into the same habit? Anyway I suppose we'd better get on with this tennis match," she concluded with a heavy sigh.

"I suppose," Jane agreed "but I get the impression that neither of us like tennis."

"Can't stand it."

"Why are we playing it then?" Jane laughed.

"I don't know. Tell you what, you think of some things that interest you, I'll do the same and the next time we'll do that and leave them to their racquets. What do you think?"

"A very good idea."

Minutes later all four had assumed their places in the indoor tennis court and were waiting for Peter to give the first serve but as the ball went up into the air Jane crumbled to the ground. Michael threw his racket down and ran to her "She's ok, she's just fainted," he called to the others, who were now already at his side.

"Gee, that's a bit rough," Peter said looking worried.

"I'll get some water," Laura said.

By the time Laura had returned two minutes later, Jane was alert and relatively ok. "You poor thing," she said soothingly "and it's a shame, you won't be able to play tennis now," she winked. "Michael can you carry Jane inside, she'll have to rest for a while. You might be a bit weak still," she concluded to Jane. An hour later Jane was being checked over by a doctor, while Michael took a lengthy call on his phone out in the reception. Laura had insisted on making an appointment with her own doctor for Jane, who was around the corner. Jane had been reluctant at first but Laura had swayed her by reminding her of her tiredness on top of the fainting.

"Well," the doctor said happily as he put all of his ninety or so kilos down into his chair behind his desk "I'd say that given what we've talked about and the test that I've done, you should be due in twenty eight weeks, which will be..." he paused to consult his calender "mid August," he concluded with an enormous smile.

"Due," Jane responded blankly.

"Yes, your baby."

"My baby," she repeated with equal blankness.

"Yes, your baby."

"I'm pregnant?"

"Very much so," he beamed "congratulations!"

"Are you sure, I mean I often miss that time of the month for two to three months on end and the pill, I never miss it?"

"That's why we say it's only ninety nine per cent effective. It's not a hundred per cent guarantee. Are you comfortable with this news?" he asked kindly.

"Yes," she smiled "just a bit shocked. Other than that, I think I'm actually thrilled."

"Well, I'm thrilled for you," he said, again with his enormous smile "Would you like me to call your husband in and let him know the good news?"

"Ah, no, I think I'll do that over some dinner and a bottle of champagne."

"Sounds like a lovely evening."

"Could you just drop me at the entrance please?" Jane requested later that evening from the driver of the taxi, these words being the entirety of the conversation other than to give him her address.

"Are you sure? It looks like a long walk up that driveway," he asked.

Jane was sure, sure that she didn't want the staff to see her returning by herself from dinner in a taxi and not as they expected, in her own car with Michael. She had no desire to tell any of the staff, including Isabelle, what had happened, as she was still trying to comprehend it herself. "Irresponsible and stupid," were the words he had chosen when she had told him she was pregnant, thinking as she did, that he too, would be happy. She had felt dumbstruck then and still did now as she watched the taxi pull away and travel back down the road. Relieved to be alone, she burst into tears and as the cold of the night brushed against her face, tears ran down it. "What had happened, what had she done wrong to cause such a reaction?" she asked herself. "But how could this happen?" was a question that he had asked her. Being furnished with an answer to this did not quench his anger. "This can happen," she had told him "It's not as though I had any more choice than you." "Well it shouldn't have happened and it's not good enough!" he had responded. "The other thing he had said, what was it?" she thought, to herself, as she stood, still unmoved in the cold "it interrupts my plans." she remembered. "What did he mean, it interrupts his plans? What plans?" she had asked, but to no avail, as he stood up at that point and walked out. The embarrassment she had felt was insurmountable but now was worse. Here she stood in semi shock as the hurt magnified itself, his rudeness having become even more clear to her. The expression on his face, during this, had reminded her of the same expression he had exhibited for the first time, the previous night. In all the time she had spent with him she had never known his handsome face could have such an expression. "Maybe," she thought "it was all happening too fast for him, maybe this had unnerved him and if this was so, it might explain his reaction tonight. "Maybe, just as she couldn't help getting pregnant, he couldn't help being unnerved by too many events and changes." Suddenly, her chilled body and worried thoughts were interrupted by the familiar noise of her red porche screaming towards her. Turning into the driveway, Michael saw her dark figure and jumped out of the car.

"Jane, I'm so sorry, I don't know what's got into me. I should never have said those things. I suppose I always counted on us having at least a year to ourselves. I sort of had my own little plans of savoring you first and then thinking about adding to us. What can I say, I'm so sorry. Can you forgive me?"

"You really hurt me Michael."

"I know I did, I'm so sorry," he said as he wrapped his coat around her.

"Maybe it's not your fault. Maybe things have been happening too fast for both of us, I know they have for me. Let's look after each other and if one of us has a problem, then let's discuss it, not fight about it."

"I love you."

"And the baby?"

"And the baby," he answered.

CHAPTER
ELEVEN

T hree months had gone by when Hillary woke in the early hours of the morning to find her husband sitting up in bed. "Bill, what is it?"

"Sorry, I didn't mean to wake you. I couldn't sleep, I can't get Eden and Sarah out of my mind."

"I know, I'm the same, I miss them terribly."

"I wasn't thinking about that. Of course I miss them, sometimes it drives me nuts. No, it's just that yesterday I asked Jim to drive me up that stretch of the road, you know, where it happened. It hadn't occurred to me to do that before but something never quite clicked with me and that is that Eden was always an excellent driver. You could never feel safer with anyone more than Eden. When we got there, I got out of the car and walked around and it was as I expected, bloody difficult to have an accident on. It was the opposite of a dangerous stretch. To top that, I remember the day well, the weather was perfect. I mean, maybe it was an accident, but I have a feeling it wasn't and I have a feeling I'm right."

"But lot's of people have accidents in safe places and ideal weather conditions."

"Hillary, I've been in a car hundreds of times with Eden dating back to our Georgetown days and I'm telling you, you can't get a better driver."

"Well maybe they were talking or something and he was distracted for a minute. Hang on, being a good driver, he wouldn't let something distract him and come to think of it, you're right, he was a particularly good driver. I'd forgotten that. It does seem strange, when you look at it in that way. If it is strange, I mean something wrong has happened, then we have to do something."

"My thoughts exactly, that's what I've been sitting here thinking about. You see, it's not that easy with everything we do so damn public. Also, I can't ask any of our men to do it. It's too private for that and I wouldn't want Jane to know about it, she's been through enough," he paused, to pour some water from a jug, into the glass beside him. "There is one person we could get to look into it."

"Who?"

"You don't know him, I knew him before I met you and I haven't actually seen him since but I have heard about him on the odd occasion. He was an attorney for years but apparently he dropped that to become a private detective. We were quite good friends years ago and the one thing I remember most about him is you can trust him with your life."

"He sounds perfect."

"He does, doesn't he," he paused. "I'll arrange for a meeting with him tomorrow."

"If he's an old friend, I think over dinner would be better."

"Dinner then. You know, in a way I hope I'm wrong about this feeling. The thought of anyone wanting to do something wrong to them, of all people, just seems inconceivable."

"I hope you're wrong too but that's what an investigation is for, if it turns out that you're right then someone is going to pay."

There were now only fourteen weeks separating Jane from meeting her child but this meeting was often far from her mind as her husband commanded her complete attention and as much as she gave it, it was never enough. With the exclusion of his work, nothing at all seemed to please him anymore, least of all her. The only time he seemed pleased with her was when they had company. Jane had come to know that such occasions were the only times she could let her guard down. When they were alone the disquiet was constant. The unhappier he was the harder she tried to please him, believing that she was at the crux of their problems. She had been very emotional over the past twenty-six weeks and was still grieving over her parents. All in all, she felt she was letting him down and that she was the reason for his unhappiness.

In her efforts to please him, she had, unwillingly at first but more lately without any fuss, given in to numerous requests he had made of her. Initially, in the first three months of their marriage, she had felt strong, able to both love him and know that her sanctions should be respected and excepted. Over the past month this strength had ebbed and been replaced with a more focused determination to just love him and make him happy, no matter what the cost. The costs, however, were great, for on top of her already raw and vulnerable emotions, they had introduced loneliness and endless days of nothing to do. These things were far from compatible with Jane's personality and unbeknownst to Michael or indeed anyone else, they were impacting on her in a frightening way. For the first time in her life she was experiencing nerves in their numerous manifestations. She constantly felt faint and if she was sitting in a chair or lying on a bed she had frequent sensations that the piece of furniture would move abruptly with her in it or the bottom would simply fall from under her. Often when she walked she felt as if her legs had turned to jelly then they would become even more awkward, to the point, she thought, they would cease to function, right in the middle of getting from a to b, "What would she do then?" she had thought to herself. It was not as if she could tell anyone, for fear they might think she had gone mad. This was precisely what she feared herself. "Had she gone mad?" she asked herself many times. "Why was her body doing this to her. Was it just nerves or the other?" Even her voice seemed to be threatening her, often in mid speech, she felt as if she wouldn't be able to finish her words. At night she became accustomed to lying awake, dreading the occurrence of these problems the next day and whether or not someone might notice them. Her only comfort was knowing that until some-body did notice, she could keep these problems to herself.

Michael had had his way with the staff and they were long gone, so too, was the chatter around the huge house and as Michael worked fourteen-hour days, Jane, her unborn child and Junior were usually the only inhabitants. Caterers, gardeners and the like came in several times a week and were quickly out, there was no warmth or bond for the home they attended to nor for its inhabitants as had existed before. Aside from that, her contact with her friends had become less than minimal, as she had constantly postponed engagements, due either to her nervous problems, or to Michael's moody behavior. Similarly her nerves had reduced her outings away from the house and where she could she made arrangements for her appointments to come to her. If this wasn't happening and she was game enough to get ready to go, she would be on her way out and stop to say goodbye to her husband when he would insist she rang and cancelled with a headache, that way, as he told her, she could keep him company, but on such occasions, his company more often came in the form of a medical journal or one of her father's books.

The day after the staff had said their goodbys, ready to confront their new jobs and new apartments that Jane had arranged and purchased for each of them, Michael aired his next request. That Jane shouldn't be working whilst she was carrying their child nor for the first six months of their child's life. The latter she had agreed with but the former, she had found impossible to condone. The distraction of her beautiful child once he or she was born, she knew, would make giving up her work happily bearable, but giving it up for no reason and with no distraction would only serve as the reverse. For a week, she had protested, but despite presenting the obvious logical reasons that were at her disposal, Michael had refused to be swayed. Ever since, she had been constantly at a loss as to how to fill her time and as a great deal of time went by unfilled she found it an enemy to challenge.

Today was different, Michael had left that morning to attend a two-day conference in New York and she had been looking forward to the break from the inevitable tensions that usually came home with him. Added to this, a huge array of items that she had ordered, to decorate the baby's room, had arrived and the task of arranging it, she had been greatly looking forward to. As the day progressed she realised, luckily, that she had underestimated the amount of time required to complete the job, and so, by the end of the day, when her back was burning and she was forced to stop, she knew the next two days would be as equally busy and enjoyable. "It's bed for me after this. You can come too if you want" she said to Junior, as she sat down to a dinner that had been prepared for her. Picking the fork up to take the first mouthful of risotto, she found that just the sight of it made her feel more nauseous than she already was. "Here you go Junior, risotto's on the menu tonight," she said placing it in front of him. Minutes later as she took her first bite of the sandwich she had prepared, both instantly stopped eating as Michael walked in, flinging his briefcase onto the table as he did, sending the bowl of risotto across the table and onto the floor, where it shattered. "Michael, I thought you'd be in New York by now?" Jane volunteered as Junior scurried off in fright.

"I don't believe it," Michael paused "I come home to my wife and a bird sitting at the table. Jane, can't you see how stupid it is, not to mention you promised you'd stop doing that?"

"I know, I'm sorry. He was just a bit of company. It won't happen again," she paused nervously "What happened to the conference?"

"Postponed," he answered dully as he poured a glass of wine "aren't you going to clean that mess up?" he finished.

"Could I show you what I did today first?"

"You did something today? You're not supposed to be doing anything."

"Just come and have a look," she insisted, ignoring the condescending tone in his voice. "Well I wouldn't go to too much trouble," he said minutes later as they stood in the nursery.

"Why not?"

"Well it's only a bedroom. I mean, how much time is the kid

going to spend in it and in the bit of time he is here, he'll be asleep anyway."

"You're right, but I want it to be nice anyway," she paused, rubbing her back "I've got to take this back to bed, it's absolutely breaking. Is that ok?"

"It will have to be, I suppose."

"Oh Michael, I'm sorry. I tell you what, I'll start taking a nap in the afternoon. That might help my back and then I won't need to go up early, on the odd night."

"That would be something. Half the time I feel like I'm married to nobody. I mean, you spend more time with that bird than me. If you can't look after me, how are you going to look after a baby? And yes, I've noticed your nervous problems, everyone has. It's been the talk of the town. You know, I wonder that you can do anything. The nerves just seem to be controlling you."

For Jane the ensuing twelve weeks were only to get worse. Michael was doing exceedingly well at manipulating her into what he wanted. He had systematically attacked her mind as a cult leader might his follower. She had obliged all along. His mistakes, she was convinced, were hers. His inanimate love of her, she had remained unaware of and her intense love had become, if anything, stronger. He had made sure she was well versed on her vast array of shortcomings, the majority of which, he knew, didn't even exist but she believed them, and that was all that mattered. She now believed in his thoughts and words more than her own and, as such, had become reliant on him. Between her nerves and her many inadequacies she no longer trusted herself, instead, she trusted him.

He had ensured that their friends were as equally blissful to this as was his wife. Yes, they had noticed that they hadn't seen as much of Jane as they used to, but then, they knew marriage and pregnancy were more than capable of doing that. When they did visit, Michael made sure to talk of her highly. Any gifts he had given her, he made sure they were aware of them, including the racehorse he had bought, only to inform her she was not to ride it in her condition. All had been made aware of the new hospital wing that was named after her as, 'The Jane Esme Wing', which he had arranged after a great deal of wrangling and a greater degree of bribery. None of them doubted Michael, as Eden had, instead they saw him as an adoring husband and a wonderful person.

Jane had believed him when he had told her that Junior had died in his sleep, not knowing that he had been helped along by her husband, who, with one quick injection, had put him to sleep. Catching him, however, had not been quick but the process had proved to be fruitful. Junior had never taken to Michael, whose foot had often sent him flying when Jane wasn't present. On this particular day Michael had chased him all over the huge home, while Jane had her afternoon nap. For Junior, Jane's old bed had looked like a good refuge from his predator but as Michael got down on his hands and knees and reached in under the bed he grabbed Junior by his wing as it flapped in fright against his hand. During this, Michael's sleeve unearthed the envelope that had lain there for the past nine months. From there, it was folded and put into his wallet, to be read after he had finished with the bird.

Their son was born two weeks early and as Michael walked into the hospital to pick his wife and son up, having insisted they only stay twenty four hours, his request being met with her usual compliance, he was met by an enormous number of their friends, two of whom had supported her through the birth of which had ended in a caesarean, since Michael couldn't. He had told Jane at the very last minute that he couldn't bear to see her in pain. With perfect charm Michael thanked each of them for their congratulatory words and spirits before he walked over to kiss his wife and son. Taking the tiny infant from his mother's arms with its fair skin and thick white hair that stood straight, he looked at the tiny little face that his hand supported "Now I'm doubly proud, my beautiful wife and my beautiful son!" he said to everyone. "I never knew a person could be this happy as I am right at this moment." For the next half an hour he continued in this vein with most of the guests left unsure as to whether to be more impressed by him or by the baby. Jane was sure of one thing only as she smiled repeatedly from her baby to her husband, that she was not happy, she was ecstatic. Finally, Michael concluded his thirty minutes of charm by quietly seeing the guests out of the hospital room while telling them that he was anxious to get his family home to rest. When all had left, however, he locked the door, pulled down the blinds, took his son from his mother to place him in the hospital crib and climbed into the bed beside his wife "I'm not used to making love to a slim woman, it's been a while," he whispered in her ear.

That night Jane insisted on having their son, in his crib, by her side of the bed. She felt totally exhausted and physically as if she had been hit by a truck. Sitting was near impossible and going from sitting to standing wasn't much better. It was not the exhaustion or the soreness that kept her awake it was the exhilaration. She felt as if she were in utopia. This tiny creature whom they had called Jonathon, melted her heart. She couldn't believe how lucky she was to be able to be this child's mother. She felt both honored and proud. Already she idolised him, he was precious. Slowly and awkwardly she pulled herself to sitting and manoeuvered her legs down the side of the bed. For the past thirty minutes she had lain on the bed wanting to go to sleep but also wanting to listen to her son breathe. Finally, she had decided if she was going to listen to him breathe then it would be even more preferable to watch him breathe. As she stared into the crib, again she was stunned, she could not believe his beauty, but it was a fact, she reminded herself again, he was beautiful, he was precious, and she had the honor of sitting beside him now, an honor, she knew, that would make every day as precious as he was. Hours later, at five a.m. she lay down and somehow went straight to sleep only to be happily woken at five thirty by her hungry son. That day, with Michael's orders, she stayed in bed with her son at her side and though he had ordered a week of this, somehow she had her way.

On the third day she carried Jonathon to his room. There she introduced him to everything, every teddy, every toy and every picture on the wall. From there she took him to meet his grandparents or at least the enlarged photo of them, in its silver frame, in the sitting room. It was in the sitting room minutes later that she took her child to one of the many large windows and gave him his first words of the world. "That's the world Jonathon," she said to him "or at least part of it. The world is a beautiful and special place. There is some bad in it but the best thing is that most of it is good. You are going to be a very special person in the world and the world will think of you as very special. I will always protect you and I will always make sure your life is good and happy, to the best of my ability, every day that I live," she finished as she kissed his tiny head and felt his soft hair against her skin.

As the proceeding weeks ascended on top of each other, little Jonathon spent most of his time in his mother's arms throughout the days, while his father worked; the same proportion of time was spent in his crib during the evenings, when his father was at home. Michael had not yet bonded with his son and had shown little interest in him. This worried Jane but she had decided that time would naturally rectify this. Michael was unhappier than he had ever been which served to make Jane feel more guilty. Guilty that she was spending too much time with the baby and not enough time with her husband. As such, she began putting Jonathon in his crib the moment she heard the huge front door open, only to pick him up if he insisted on it. She had taken to placing the crib, which was portable, relatively close to where her husband would usually sit but had ceased this practice after Michael had constantly complained that it was a distraction to his reading.

During the initial four weeks there had been a constant stream of visitors, with more gifts for Jonathon. Throughout this Michael had exhibited his usual charm, coupled with an unusual tolerance at the home being so constantly open to them. Jonathon had had a semi-calming effect on his mother and as the intensity of her nerves had subsequently eased; she had enjoyed these visits enormously. The following four weeks, however, was starkly lacking in visitors, not a single person had shared Jane or Jonathon's company. Finding this odd Jane had put it down to a belief that maybe they were giving her a break intentionally to allow her some more rest time. In many ways she was grateful for this. She quietly relished focusing all of her attention on Jonathon. With Michael at work and a lack of visitors she was able to do just that. Also, over the past eight weeks she had hardly slept. Jonathon was born much smaller than his counterparts in the hospital and had been dubbed the smallest baby in the ward, weighing in at just six pounds. "He will need hourly feeds at first and two hourly feeds by six weeks," the staff had instructed her at the hospital. Jonathon, however, had instructed differently and his mother had happily met his instructions with hourly feeds from the beginning, he had yet to deviate from this busy schedule. After her husband and her son, Jane had come to view sleep as the third most precious thing in life. Never before had she know exhaustion like this. Before Jonathon was born she had assumed they would have the services of a nanny as she had had as a child but Michael had disagreed. "It's more natural for a child to have his mother not a nanny," he had told her. Jane was unsure of this but had decided that since she wasn't working for the first six months of her son's life then after that they could reconsider the subject. The first weeks she had spent with her child had, in fact, made her grateful that they had not called in a nanny. She had enjoyed being with him and attending to him too much to share that time with anyone.

As Michael pulled up at the lights, on his way home, his phone started ringing. "That better not be the hospital," he thought to himself before he took the call "Hello…"

"Hi Michael, it's Sandra. How are you stranger?"

"Top of the world. How are you and Rick?"

"We're good. Now you said wait a few weeks before we come over. It's been four weeks now, so we're heading over there tomorrow ok?"

"As much as I'd love to see you guys, can't do. Jane hasn't improved, if anything, she's worse."

"Really?"

"I don't know. It's just all the classic symptoms of postnatal depression."

"Oh, the poor sweetheart. Look, I really think it would be good if I talked to her, you know, just on a one to one."

"Sandra I can't even talk to her. She's making no sense of anything, least of all Jonathon.

Tomorrow I've got a dozen or so nannies lined up to interview. You know she never wanted a nanny in the beginning and in retrospect I should have insisted."

"Well it's good you're getting one now. Is she getting much sleep?"

"No. She's not sleeping or eating. Oh, except when I can give her the odd sleeping tablet, but usually she won't have a bar to do with them. I'm really worried. She's in a daze most of the time, if not crying. She barely looks at Jonathon, even when she's feeding him. She just looks utterly depressed. She won't even get out of her dressing gown. I don't know Sandra, I just feel like I'm losing her, and our son is too. Anyway, I'm going to try and talk to her tonight about getting some help for this. I don't think she's going to be too happy about it. I've tried to be so gentle with her but she just gets so angry so easily, it's amazing, but visitor's right now is just out of the question."

"Of course. I didn't realise it was that bad. She must see a doctor. You know of all the people I know, Jane's the last one I would have thought to go through something like this."

"I know."

"And she looked so happy at the hospital and when I last saw her."

"Yes, but Jonathon's eight weeks now, maybe it was just building up. I don't really know, but what I do know is that I'm going to do everything to fix it. I hate seeing her like this," he paused "I'm about to pull in the driveway so I've got to go. Don't worry, she'll be better soon and when she is everyone can come over."

"Ok, give her my love and give Jonathon a kiss for me. Oh, and Michael, look after yourself too."

"I will," he said, smiling to himself as he ended the call.

Later that night, as Jane and Michael lay in bed trying to go to sleep, Jonathon began to cry. "That's strange, it's not that long since his last feed," Jane said as she sat up to get out of bed.

"I'll go and check, you get some sleep," Michael volunteered.

"Are you sure?" she paused "Thanks," she said cheerfully but surprised that he had offered.

Five minutes later, he returned, looking worried "Jane you'd better get up," he said as he handed her her dressing gown.

"What's wrong?" she asked, looking more than worried.

"It's ok, he just seems to have a bit of a temp. I thought you might want to give him some paracetamol and sit with him for an hour."

Having collected the paracetamol, Jane was staring at her sleeping baby minutes later. "That's' strange," she thought to herself as she put her hand on his forehead "you seem fine," she whispered to him as he slept "but I'll sit here with you for a while just to double check." she finished, as she sat down in the armchair next to his crib.

In the dimly lit room, an hour later, the doorway of the baby's room framed his father as his tall figure stood, stationary in it, staring at his wife. It was exactly as he had anticipated. He knew she was exhausted and that she would more than likely fall asleep in the chair, beside her son and here, as expected, she was fast asleep. Quietly he walked into the room and had a closer look at her and his son, both were sound asleep. Gently he picked up the baby pillow that had been perched on the arm of the chair, his wife was sitting in, for weeks. "You are beautiful," he thought as he stared at his son "but that's all you are." he finished. As he covered his son's face with the pillow and held it securely down for many minutes. The child made no noise as his tiny body went into the instinctive spasms that accompany a loss of oxygen and when he finally lay perfectly still the pillow was taken from his face. Michael was as unperturbed by his son's death as he was by the spasm's that he had just watched and felt. At first, when Jane had told him she was pregnant he was irate, for this had confused his plans. Two weeks after that he had realized that it was to his advantage and thus found himself with a better set of plans. Now, tonight, was just another step in the plan achieved. He didn't look back at his dead son but focused on the pillow. Slowly he lifted Jane's hand off her lap and placed the pillow on it and then placed her hand back upon the pillow. This done, he stood back to evaluate his work "Perfect," he thought to himself as he took his gloves off and left the room. "Jane! Jane!" he yelled as he tried to wake her minutes later.

"Um..." she responded with a startle "Michael, what's wrong?" she asked, noticing the tears in his eyes.

"You killed our son!" he sobbed.

"Had she been dreaming? Was she dreaming now?" she thought to herself as she stared back at him. As her eyes diverted to the crib she jumped up. Putting her arms out instinctively to pick her child up, she was stopped by Michael "Don't touch him, you can't touch him." he told her gently. Her eyes then moved to Jonathon's chest and she waited with no doubt that it would rise then fall, then rise again. Somewhere in the background, as she continued to wait she could hear Michael telling her what she had done. She had deprived him of air. He could not move or smile or breath again. She had robbed him of that and of his life. She had robbed herself of him. There was not even a memory of what she had done. She knew then, she had gone mad and any spirit within her was broken.

CHAPTER
TWELVE

Over the following week and months, Jane slept through the nightmare she was living. During this time she spoke not a word, with her muteness accompanied by a vacant stare. She had been interviewed by countless psychologists and psychiatrists during the trial and after. All had agreed that she had and was suffering from post partum psychosis. The jury had been told the illness only affected zero point two to zero point four per cent of new mothers, that it was serious but fortunately rare. "I believe she would have been suffering the illness within the first three weeks of delivery," the doctor had replied to the defence lawyer "possibly even during the pregnancy itself. She is a first time mother and had a caesarean birth both of those factors contribute heavily to this condition occurring."

"And with your medical knowledge, is it your belief that the defendant was fully aware of what she was doing on the night of the thirtieth of September?"

"No. She would have been completely unaware."

"Why?" The defence lawyer had continued.

"With this illness, actions, feelings thoughts, become disorganized. At the time she took her son's life, she would have been delusional, in other words, unaware of reality but fully aware of a delusion."

"Could she have snapped out of this delusion if she had wanted to?"

"A person in this condition does not know that they are delusional and as such it is not possible for someone to snap out of something that they don't know they're in."

"One last question doctor. Is it your belief that the defendant did not know that what she was doing was wrong when she took her son's life."

"Yes, that is my belief," he had answered.

The insanity charge had been fought and won within the courtroom and beyond it. The trial had been prolific in the media's arena. Some of the citizens of Washington believed she was a murderer. The majority, however, had supported her and understood the illness and had hoped the sentence would be light. It was a majority, too, that had cheered in the courtroom as the judge had handed down his sentence. "I am sentencing you to a minimum of twelve months in an appropriate departmental psychiatric hospital, to be determined by the prosecution, within three days from now, of which I will be notified of. If, after twelve months they are satisfied that you are well and past the illness, you will be eligible for release. If, however, they are not satisfied by such time, I order that you remain there until this can be reached."

None of this had meant anything to Jane. On the night of the thirtieth of September she had gone into shock and there she had stayed. It was now six months since she had arrived at the hospital and she had related to nobody within its walls. Her many visitors were greeted with the same response. Michael had never come to the hospital. Though the most significant player in the trial, having to give his account of what had transpired, on the night of the murder and before, due to his wife's muteness, he had rendered himself always in the witness box. Since he had made it known that, though he still loved her deeply, he was too upset at the loss of his son and by his wife's incarceration, to visit her. All along, his agenda had remained his secret, now all he had to do was wait. Wait for her to be deemed legally insane at the end of the twelve months, at which point, with the appropriately diplomatic period of time having elapsed, he could then have her will revoked and thus singularly own the entirety of the estate.

On this particular day as Jane sat listlessly in the garden of the institution, the private investigator that Bill and Hillary had hired sat together with two senior detectives from the D.C. Police, with a grossly frail man who had an equal degree of listlessness. They waited, silently by his bedside as the nurse refilled his drip. "I want the nurse to stay and I want what I am going to tell you to be recorded. I want a copy of the tape to be given to the nurse, the other is yours," he stopped to breathe in some oxygen from a mask in his hand. Each of the men had microcassette recorders in their pockets and by the time he had taken enough oxygen, two sat on the bed in front of him and the other was turned on in its pocket.

"When you're ready we'll start. Take as much time as you need."

"Time is what I don't have. I was supposed to be dead six months ago."

"I'll turn them on then shall I?" the detective asked.

"I'm ready," he paused. "I am David Bertha, the only

brother to Michael Bertha. The information I want to tell you concerns my brother," he paused to take some more oxygen "Last Winter, the fourth of November, ninety-three, to be more precise, I was heavily sedated from an operation. As you know I have the AIDS virus and had it in November ninety-three as my brother well new. About an hour after my operation, the nurse let my brother into my room, at his request, to supposedly visit me. At the time Michael took some blood from my left arm using a syringe," he stopped, to put the mask to his face. "I couldn't move or speak, I was too heavily sedated, but I could hear. Before he put the needle in my arm he said, that I could do him a favor. Then he filled the syringe with my blood. When that was done he told me that I had increased his career prospects one hundred per cent. Then he said someone by the name of Eden would have the pleasure of sampling my blood and that he, my brother, would have the pleasure of assuming this man's job," he stopped, as he struggled to breathe, this time the nurse placing the mask over his nose and mouth.

Minutes later, he continued "That is all my brother did and said and at the time I believe he assumed that I couldn't hear him."

"Why didn't you tell anyone this at the time?" the private investigator asked.

"By the time I was out of sedation I figured he would have used the blood already. I mean he is a doctor and I'm sure he knows the importance of its freshness."

"Since then, why have you waited until now to say this?"

"Because despite the lack of a bond he's my brother. I thought I could take it with me, to my grave but as time has passed I realized I can't"

For the rest of the day and throughout the night the three

men analysed the information they had and searched for more. Early the following morning, they had obtained the necessary paperwork to have both Eden's and Sarah's body exhumed. Two days later as the pathologist confirmed the virus was present in both bodies and had progressed in Sarah's, they had a phone call informing them that David Bertha had passed away the previous night.

The days that followed were equally as busy. They talked to Alvin Coster, who had given Eden his physical. They established Sarah's previous medical condition, the fact that it was common knowledge around the staff at the hospital and that Michael would have easily known about it. They talked to the previous staff from the house and discovered that Michael had lied to Jane about his first family. In their meeting with Ian Grant, he was quick to point out that Michael had made enquiries of him as to who would have control and ownership of the estate if his wife was still legally insane beyond twelve months. Armed with all of this they went to a judge and secured a warrant to have the house searched without Michael's knowledge. It was this search that produced the letter that Michael had inadvertently found under the bed, this they took a photo of and left the original where they had found it. "What a character," the detective said to his partner as they sat with the private investigator, surrounded by masses of paperwork and evidence, in one of the rooms of the busy precinct.

"The point is, he has no character. He's slime. I've seen a few creeps in my time but this one's the worst," the private investigator said as he fidgeted with his pen.

"I'll agree with you there John," the detective nodded.

"Anyway, we know he caused the death of her parents. We know if she just happens to get better before the end of twelve months he'll probably kill her and we know that since he's into getting rid of people he was most likely the one who got rid of the child. Now, I've got an answer on the second one but not the third."

"Well then you'll be interested to know, we found out this morning that nobody thought to hypnotise her. Can you believe it?"

"At this stage, I'll believe anything," John paused "but that's on our side now. I'm sure the post natal depression is rubbish, I'm sure of it," he repeated.

"More like PMM I reckon. Post Michael Manipulation," the detective laughed wryly.

"Right, we arrange to put Jane under hypnosis tomorrow, the results of which, we all agree, will be interesting! Getting back to her legal insanity, firstly we could set him up by having someone tell him she's suddenly better, then sit back behind the scenes and wait for him to act on it. For that option we need her consent, which considering she hasn't spoken a word for eight months will be hard to get. On that point, I think I know why she hasn't spoken, she's in shock and has been since she lost her child," John paused, to hold his coffee mug up as a hint to someone walking past with their own.

"Of course…" the detectives mumbled in unison.

"Sorry," he resumed "now secondly, I know you don't know who I'm working for and that has to remain, it's his privilege, but if I can set up a meeting with Jane, my client and myself, then I can put all the evidence in front of her, her parents, the lot. That, in itself, might bring her out of it. If that doesn't work my client could point out to her that we desperately need her to snap out of it, if we're going to get the person who killed her parents and probably killed her son.

What do you think?"

"I think you'd better ask your client for a pay rise."

"Good. Well let's get to it!" John responded.

It was now two weeks since David Bertha had told them his story and throughout this time John, and the other two detectives had worked night and day, taking only an hour, here and there, for a quick nap. They were exhausted but utterly determined to rectify the remnants of Michael's destruction and to make him pay for what they couldn't rectify. John had kept Bill and Hillary constantly informed on even the smallest of things over the past many months. Over the last two weeks however, the expressions on their faces had been beyond reproach. "I know it's hard," John had told them on one of these daily reports "but we'll make sure he suffers in the end."

"Suffers," Hillary had responded "he doesn't even deserve to suffer!"

Two days later, as John sat flicking his pen repeatedly on the table, Bill paced up and down the compact room, they had been shown to, in the hospital, where they could talk to Jane without interruption. The previous day Jane had sat in another room with a psychologist and doctor from the hospital, together, with her lawyer; the two detectives and John, while they all observed her under hypnosis. During the session Jane calmly supplied all of the information of what really happened that night including Michael's story to her of how she had killed her son. The palms of everyone's hands had sweated profusely as the truth came out and unbeknownst to Jane, the gravity of what she was saying, rendered them stunned throughout the session. As Jane entered the room, twenty minutes later, their pacing and flicking stopped abruptly. When the staff member, who had accompanied her, left the room, seconds later, John locked the door while Bill took Jane's hands into his and kissed her forehead, only to be issued with her vacant gaze. "You've met John," Bill said to her "he's come here with me because we both need to talk to you about some very important things, the most important of which is you. Many months ago I asked John to look into your mother and father's death and to check any other information he came across. I asked him because I trust him and I need you to trust him now. Can you do that?" he finished. Jane's gaze remained unchanged as John commenced to explain the story.

"Your parents, I'm sorry to say, were killed by your husband. He didn't drive the car over the cliff but he did inject your father with the HIV virus, knowing that, during intercourse, your mother would also become infected, which she did. Michael knew your mother suffered from hypertensive pneumonia, he also knew, according to the staff at the hospital, who knew your father, that your father often said that if anything ever happened to Sarah it would have to happen to him. Your parents wrote you a letter explaining their death and amongst the many things they said in it, they confirmed that if one was to go first then the other would go with them." John paused, realising the impact his words would probably be having on her but then continuing through necessity. "Whether you've read this letter or not, we don't know, but we do know that as we found it in your husbands possession in your house, which we obtained a warrant to search, without his knowledge, that he has read it. Michael gave your parents a virus that would eventually take their lives, and in your parent's case, he knew that it would take their lives sooner than later. The law will see this as the murder of two people."

He paused, to wait as Bill offered Jane a glass of water, which she didn't except. "Michael lied to you about his previous family. His parents are both dead, as he said. His mother was beaten to death by his drunken father and a month later, when Michael was sixteen, his father drank himself to death. Your husband had one brother, who died of AIDS a couple of weeks ago. It was his blood that Michael obtained and injected into your father. It was your husband's brother who helped us in our investigations, two days before he died. I'm sorry to give you all of this at once but it is for your concern that we do. What I am going to tell you now is one of the most important things. You did not take your child's life, your husband did, not you!" he paused, noticing for the first time, her eyes move for a second from their gaze. "that is a fact that we have proved. Michael caused your child's death while you slept. Which now gives him three counts of murder," he stopped suddenly as both men saw Jane's mouth open.

"I didn't?" she whispered, at which point Bill leaned over to her and said with sheer conviction in his voice "No you didn't!"

"I waited for his chest to rise and fall but it didn't," she said as tears ran down her face.

"I know," Bill said putting his arms around her "I wish I could bring him back for you but as much as it breaks my heart, I can't. I can look after you though, I will always do that."

For a moment the room was quiet until Jane, wiping the tears from her eyes, turned to John and asked, "Why did he do all of this?"

"He wanted your father's position as the top cardiologist in the world and the only way to get that was to wait a good few years or to get rid of your father."

"And my son?"

"Sadly, he was in the way at first but then Michael realized he could utillize him, which gets to the next point I need to tell you. Michael had one interest only when he married you, your money. To get that money he either had to marry you and kill you or systematically get you to the point where you believed and others believed, for want of a better word, you were mad. Mad enough to stay mad for at least one day over twelve months. That way he, as your spouse, could solely own and control the entirety of your estate and assets which is only possible to do if you are still deemed to be legally insane beyond twelve months. For him, your son came in handy, he could tell friends you had post natal depression, which he did convince them of, behind your back and he convinced you that you killed your child. Thus he would have achieved having your father's job and a great deal of wealth. Would you like a few minutes before I go on?" he asked, worried that he was telling her too much too fast.

"No, it's ok."

"Michael is completely unaware of our investigations into any of these things. We could have arrested him weeks ago but if we had, he would have got away with the final grab at the money. In prison, he can't do what we know he intends to do. He's taken your son's life and got you here. He's two thirds home already, or so he thinks. We need to make it known to him, now, that you are fully recovered, then sit back and wait for him to do what we know he's going to do, and that is attempt to kill you. To do this, we need to set you up ready and waiting for him, with us only feet away ready to pounce on him. That way he'll be rightfully charged with three counts of murder, one of attempted murder and one of intended theft by deception. Do you think you're up to helping us?" he asked.

Jane looked at Bill and then at John and answered in a

tone, that neither man would ever forget "I am more than up to it!"

One month later, Michael was imprisoned for the rest of his life, never to be released. He had illustrated complete shock, when, ready to put the pillow over his wife's face, in the darkened room, two days later, he was stopped, arrested and taken away. The only other thing he was to illustrate was a complete lack of remorse during the trial and after the verdict. Jane was driven away from the hospital an hour after the attempt on her life and had gone directly to the White House where she would stay with Bill and Hillary for the following month, while she bought a new apartment and made arrangements for her family home to become an orphanage. An orphanage where love and attention would be as important as food and water. As Jane walked along the Potomac on this particular day, holding the letter from her parents in the palm of one hand and a photo of her son in the other, she knew she had lost the three people she loved the most, but it was this love for them, that made her determined to be strong and to retain that strength, ready for when she was with them again.